新聞英文
年度關鍵字

2020 News Words

International

國際　　#UK　#Megxit　#Middle East　#Russia　#Turkey

Politics

政治

#2020 US Presidential Election
#monarchy #pro-democracy

Entertainment

娛樂

#Blackpink #BTS #Oscars #BadGuy #LGBTQ #Netflix

Sports

運動 #World Cup #NBA #MLB

Society

社會

#Taiwan #NCC #BLM #Super Bowl
#bullying #metoo

Health & Medicine

健康醫療   #Covid-19 #vaccine

Science & Technology

科技新知　　　　　#space travel #green energy #escooter

Environment

環境　　　　　#typhoon #wildfire #invasive species

Business & Economy

財經

Consumer

民生消費

音檔使用說明

STEP ①

先掃描本 QR Code

STEP ②

快速註冊或登入 EZCourse

STEP ③

回答問題按送出

答案就在書中（需注意空格與大小寫）。

STEP ④

完成訂閱

該書右側會顯示「**已訂閱**」，
表示已成功訂閱，
即可點選播放本書音檔。

STEP ⑤

點選個人檔案

查看「**我的訂閱紀錄**」
會顯示已訂閱本書，
點選封面可到本書線上聆聽。

EZ TALK 編輯台

　　距離總編嚴選出版前一本關於新聞英文的主題，已經是三年前的事，這三年來發生的事情遠比想像中要多，世界前進的速度比想像中要快，三年前任誰會想到，如今串流平台上看劇、作直播會成為主流。再加上 2020 年對全球而言，是不平靜的一年，因此便催生了本期的新聞英文，集結了 2020 這一年來各類知識與時事的結晶。

　　本期主題為新聞英文，在學習單元的規劃上，我們除了挑出每篇新聞的重點文法「Grammar Master」外，也精心挑選了讀懂國際新聞必備的「News Words」，除了說明新聞較常見的用字之外，也疏理了理解該新聞所需要的背景知識，希望各位讀者在閱讀國際新聞時能更為順暢。

　　此外，在頁面的呈現上，我們結合時下流行的 hashtag（不曉得各位讀者是否有發現，我們在封面也藏了一個大大的 # hashtag ！），搭配每類新聞獨有的關鍵字，更貼近現代人的數位閱讀習慣，字級等等也調整到能舒適閱讀的狀態，希望能帶給各位讀者更好的閱讀體驗。

　　即使 2020 年發生了許多令人難過、不愉快的事件，如疫情爆發、商家倒閉、名人如 Kobe Bryant 逝世等，但是在蒐集新聞主題的過程中，我們也發現，2020 年也有許多令人期待的事情，如永續能源正透過電動車輛逐步實現，越來越多不同的聲音受到重視，NASA 第二波登月計畫於 2020 年推動，其中尤以病毒疫苗已經研發出來的新聞最令人歡欣鼓舞……希望各位讀者在閱讀本書時，除了能收穫滿滿的英文之外，也能獲得往前邁進的能量。

EZ TALK
本期責任編輯

Libby

'Hit the Jackpot'

全文朗讀 ♪ 001　　單字 ♪ 002

Vocabulary

1. **lottery** [ˋlɑtərɪ] (n.)
   抽籤，摸彩，樂透

2. **persistence** [pəˋzɪstəns] (n.)
   堅持不懈，動詞 **persist** [pəˋsɪst]

3. **pay off** (phr.)
   清償；得到好結果，取得成功

4. **odds** [ɑdz] (n.)（固定用複數）
   機率，可能性

5. **option** [ˋɑpʃən] (n.)
   選項，可選擇的東西

6. **a couple of** (phr.)
   幾個（不一定是兩個），
   亦作 **a couple**

7. **shift** [ʃɪft] (n.) 輪班

8. **bonus** [ˋbonəs] (n.)
   額外給予的東西、好處

Persistence Pays Off
for Maine Lottery Winner
緬因州男子用同一組數字終於中彩券頭獎

A Maine man won a $3.2 million [1]**lottery *jackpot** using the same numbers he's been using in the **Tri-State Megabucks** lottery for 35 years. Gregory McAllister of Windsor told Maine Lottery officials that he adopted his Tri-State Megabucks numbers on his 27th birthday and has been using them ever since.

一名緬因州男子 35 年來一直使用同一組號碼簽三州百萬樂透彩券，這次贏得 320 萬美元樂透頭獎。溫莎鎮的葛列格里麥卡利斯特告訴緬因州彩券官員，這組中了三州百萬樂透頭獎的號碼是他在 27 歲生日那天開始使用，此後便一直使用這組號碼。

McAllister's [2]**persistence** finally [3]**paid off** in the Oct. 28 ***drawing**, when the numbers came up 02-09-16-27-30 with the **MegaBall** 5. The [4]**odds** of ℗ **hitting the jackpot** are about one in 4.5 million. "I just can't believe I finally won," said McAllister. "I feel great!" He chose to take $2,546,249 in cash rather than the ***annuity** [5]**option**.

After tax **withholding**, he'll take home $1,807,837.

麥卡利斯特的堅持終於在 10 月 28 日開獎這天獲得回報，中獎號碼是 2、9、16、27、30，大彩球號碼是 5。中頭獎機率約為 450 萬之一。麥卡利斯特表示：「真不敢相信我終於中獎，感覺棒極了！」他選擇一次領取 254 萬 6249 元現金，而非每年領取，扣稅後他能把 180 萬 7837 美元抱回家（相當於台幣 5130 萬元）。

JJava Designs©shutterstock

McAllister, who's worked as bar manager at Sarah's Café & Twin **Schooner**'s Pub in Wiscasset for the past 20 years, won't be quitting his job. "I'm planning to stay there for now as the people and the place are like home to me, but I may drop ⁶⁾**a couple of** ⁷⁾**shifts**," he said. McAllister bought his ticket at the Wiscasset Quik Stop, which received a $30,000 ⁸⁾**bonus** for selling the winning ticket.

過去 20 年來，麥卡利斯特一直在威斯卡西特鎮的莎拉咖啡廳與雙子杯酒吧擔任酒吧經理，他表示不會辭職。他說：「我打算一直待下去，那裡的人和地方對我來說就像家一樣，但我可能會少兼幾個排班。」麥卡利斯特是在威斯卡西特便利店購買彩券，該商店因售出中獎彩券而分得三萬元獎金。

"We're all very happy for Gregory," said Maine Lottery official Michael Boardman. "It's always nice to meet our winners and see how excited they are."

緬因州彩券官員麥可博德曼說：「我們都為葛列格里感到開心，很高興能見到中獎人並看到他們有多興奮。」

News Word

1. Tri-State Megabucks & Megaball 三州百萬大樂彩與特別號
美國簽樂透風氣豐盛，各州都有許多彩券，此彩券是由美國的緬因州、新罕布什爾州 New Hampshire 跟佛蒙特州 Vermont 三州聯合發行的跨州樂透彩，每週三、六開獎，共有 6 組號碼，玩家可以自選 5 個號碼跟 1 個 Megaball 特別號。頭獎得主可以選擇 cash 現金一次領完或是 annuity 逐年領取（分 30 年領，似領年金概念）。中獎人需繳聯邦稅與州稅，州稅各州不同。

2. Phrase hit the jackpot 中大獎，挖到寶
jackpot 出自撲克牌的梭哈遊戲，jack 是撲克牌的 J，如果玩家手中有一對 J 或是更大的牌，就可以叫牌並開始賭局，每局的賭注稱做 pot。經過幾輪叫牌累積賭注會越來越多，最後贏得所有賭金就叫做 hit the jackpot，後引申為「中大獎，挖到寶」。

A: Did you hear about Fiona marrying a millionaire? 你有聽說費歐娜要嫁給一個百萬富翁嗎？
B: Yeah. She really hit the jackpot! 有，她真是挖到寶了！

Singing Bad Language

全文朗讀 ♫ 003　　單字 ♫ 004

Vocabulary

1. **wildlife** [ˋwaɪldˌlaɪf] *(n.)*
   野生動物

2. **patron** [ˋpetrən] *(n.)*
   老主顧，常客

3. **colony** [ˋkɑlənɪ] *(n.)*
   （動植物的）群落

4. **delicate** [ˋdɛlɪkət] *(a.)*
   細膩的，精細的

5. **executive** [ɪgˋzɛkjətɪv] *(n.)*
   高階主管，經理人

6. **trigger** [ˋtrɪɡɚ] *(v.)*
   引起，觸發

7. **carry on** *(phr.)* 持續下去

8. **curse** [kɝs] *(v./n.)* 詛咒

9. **rendition** [rɛnˋdɪʃən] *(n.)*
   （對歌曲、表演等）詮釋

Swearing Parrots Cause Stir
園區鸚鵡罵髒話引起騷動

Five African gray parrots at a [1)]**wildlife** park have been removed from public display after they started *cussing at [2)]**patrons**. The *potty-mouthed parrots were adopted by the Lincolnshire Wildlife Park in August and placed in quarantine together.
一座野生動物公園的五隻非洲灰鸚鵡朝遊客罵髒話後，被撤離展示區。這幾隻罵髒話的鸚鵡於八月由林肯郡野生動物公園收容，並一起接受隔離。

But after being moved into the main outdoor aviaries, the birds started *ruffling feathers with their *salty language. They've now been moved into different [3)]**colonies** away from [4)]**delicate** ears.
這些鸚鵡被移往主要戶外鳥舍後，卻開始說起令人不悅的污言穢語，牠們現在已經各自移往不同的生態區，以免擾人清聽。

Park staff originally hoped putting the parrots outdoors would improve their manners. Sadly, this didn't go according to plan, said park chief [5)]**executive** Steve Nichols. The parrots swear to [6)]**trigger** a reaction or response, so if people look shocked or laugh, it just encourages them to do it more. "When a parrot tells you to *f*ck off, it amuses people very highly," he said.

園區員工原本希望放這些鸚鵡在戶外能改善牠們的態度，園區執行長史帝夫尼可斯表示，可惜未能如願。鸚鵡罵髒話會引發遊客反應或回應，若有人表現出震驚或大笑，便使得鸚鵡變本加厲。他說：「當鸚鵡大叫『他Ｘ的滾開』，遊客反而被逗得相當開心。」

"With the five, one would swear and another would laugh and that would [7]**carry on**," Nichols said. "Some visitors found it funny, but with kids visiting on weekends, we decided to move them. I'm hoping they learn different words within colonies—but if they teach the others bad language and I end up with 250 swearing birds, I don't know what we'll do."

尼可斯說：「這五隻鸚鵡中若有一隻開始罵髒話，另一隻就會笑，於是接二連三地仿效。有些遊客覺得很有趣，但週末會有小孩來參觀，所以我們決定將牠們撤下。我本來是希望牠們在不同的生態區學說不同的話，但牠們若是教其他鸚鵡說髒話，園區最後會有250隻罵髒話的鸚鵡，到時可就無法挽回了。」

The [8]**cursing** birds aren't the first at the park to cause a *stir. Earlier in the year, Chico the Parrot *went viral with his [9]**rendition** of Beyoncé's "If I Were a Boy."

鸚鵡罵髒話並不是該園區第一次引起騷動。今年稍早，鸚鵡奇科才因為模仿碧昂絲唱〈如果我是男生〉而爆紅。

Tinseltown©Shutterstock

上為 Beyoncé，右為 yellow-crowned parrot 黃冠鸚鵡，模仿影片：https://www.youtube.com/watch?v=l2fGAKrweoY

進階字彙

* **cuss** [kʌs] (v.)（口）咒罵

* **potty-mouthed** [ˋpɑtɪ ˋmauθt] (a.)（口）滿口髒話的，**potty** 指嬰兒便盆

* **ruffle sb. feathers** (phr.) 使某人心煩意亂，惱怒某人

* **salty** [ˋsɔltɪ] (a.)（俚）粗俗的，**salty language**「粗話」

* **f*ck off** (phr.)（俚）滾開

* **stir** [stɜ] (n.) 騷動

* **go viral** 爆紅，**viral**「病毒般的」形容消息如病毒般快速傳開

News Word

1. quarantine 隔離
這個最近常出現在新聞頭條的字，除了指隔離人，也可以隔離動物。可當動詞，當名詞時指「隔離檢疫期間」。

2. aviary 鳥舍
有時也稱作 flying cage，比起一般的 birdcage，aviary [ˋevɪˏɛrɪ] 有更大的活動空間讓鳥類在裡頭飛翔，並且用樹木打造出自然環境，許多國外動物園都採用 aviary 讓鳥類棲息。

Zabotnova Inna©Shutterstock

Fired by *The New Yorker*

Rob Crandal©shutterstock

Jeffery Toobin 於 2009 年獲得美國律師協會獎項 ABA Silver Gavel Awards。

全文朗讀 ♪ 005　　單字 ♪ 006

Vocabulary

1. **investigation** [ɪn,vɛstə`geʃən] *(n.)* 調查，研究

2. **incident** [`ɪnsədənt] *(n.)* 事件，事變，衝突

3. **colleague** [`kɑlig] *(n.)* 同事，同僚

4. **allegedly** [ə`lɛdʒɪdli] *(adv.)* 據稱，即消息是未經證實的

5. **embarrassingly** [ɪm`bærəsɪŋli] *(adv.)* 尷尬地，窘迫地

6. **mute** [mjut] *(v.)* 按靜音，消音

7. **apologize** [ə`pɑlə,dʒaɪz] *(v.)* 道歉

8. **analyst** [`ænəlɪst] *(n.)* 分析師

Jeffrey Toobin Fired from Magazine after Exposing Himself
傑佛瑞圖賓因露下體遭雜誌社解雇

Jeffrey Toobin has been sacked by *The New Yorker* after the magazine's [1]**investigation** into an [2]**incident** last month in which he *exposed himself during a staff Zoom call. "As a result of our investigation, Jeffrey Toobin is no longer with the company," said *The New Yorker*.

傑佛瑞圖賓因上月一起意外事件遭《紐約客》調查後被解雇，他在一場員工視訊會議中露下體。《紐約客》表示：「根據調查結果，傑佛瑞圖賓不再隸屬本公司。」

Toobin confirmed he'd gotten the ax in a November 11 *tweet. "I was fired today by *New Yorker* after 27 years as a Staff Writer," he wrote. "I will always love the magazine, will miss my [3]**colleagues**, and will look forward to reading their work."

圖賓於 11 月 11 日在推特上證實遭到解雇。他寫道：「我在《紐約客》擔任了27 年的特約撰稿人，今天被解雇。我會永遠愛這家雜誌，會想念我的同事，也會期待繼續讀他們的文章。」

But 60-year-old Toobin didn't just expose himself—he was [4]**allegedly** caught *****masturbating** in the call with some of the magazine's biggest names. "I made an [5]**embarrassingly** stupid mistake, believing I was *****off-camera**," the Harvard Law graduate said in an interview. "I thought no one on the Zoom call could see me. I thought I had [6]**muted** the Zoom video," he added. "I [7]**apologize** to my wife, family, friends and *****co-workers**."

olesea vetrila©Shutterstock

但 60 歲的圖賓不僅露下體，據稱他在視訊會議中被抓到自慰，與會人士中還有幾個是雜誌社重要人物。畢業於哈佛法學院的圖賓在受訪時說：「我犯下難堪而愚蠢的錯誤，我當時以為我沒入鏡。我以為視訊會議中沒人看得到我。我以為我已經關掉視訊的聲音了。」他補充說道：「我要向我妻子、家人、朋友和同事道歉。」

According to two people who participated in the conference call, Toobin, who also works as a CNN legal [8]**analyst**, began *****pleasuring himself** during a break in the meeting. So far, Toobin hasn't been canned by the cable network. "Jeff Toobin has asked for some time off while he deals with a personal issue," CNN said.

根據當時參與視訊會議的其中兩人表示，圖賓在會議休息時間自慰。圖賓同時也是有 CNN 有線電視新聞網的法律分析師，目前為止他尚未被該電視網解雇。CNN 新聞網說：「傑夫圖賓已要求請假一段時間處理私事。」

進階字彙

* **expose oneself** (phr.)
  裸露下體，**expose** [ɪkˋspoz] 指「暴露，露出」

* **tweet** [twit] (n.)
  Twitter（推特）的推文

* **masturbate** [ˋmæstɚˏbet] (v.)
  手淫，自慰，也可說 **pleasure oneself**

* **off-camera** [ˋɔfˋkæmrə] (a.)
  非錄影中的，私生活的

* **co-worker** [ˋkoˏwɝkɚ] (n.) 同事，也可拼做 **coworker**

News Word 📖

1. sack 開除，解雇
get the ax, get canned 被炒魷魚

sack 發音為 [sæk]，指員工做了公司不認同的事或因表現不好，使公司主動開除員工。公司解雇員工的動詞還有：**fire**、**dismiss**。

本篇新聞也出現許多「被解雇」的口語說法。ax 是「斧頭」，英式英文拼做 axe，因此 get the ax 取「砍」的意思，引伸「被解雇」。而 can「罐頭」是容易得到也容易被丟棄的東西，因此 get canned 也用來描述「被解聘」。「被解聘」的口語說法還有很多：**get sacked**、**get the boot** 或 **get the pink slip**。

2. Zoom & conference call　Zoom 與視訊會議
Zoom 是多人視訊 app，電腦、手機與平板上都能安裝使用。Zoom 之所以爆紅，是因為它讓多人視訊會議像打電話一樣簡單，與會者不需註冊，只要輸入會議室號碼，就能加入會議室進行視訊討論。「視訊會議」的英文是 conference call，也可說 video conference 或 teleconference。不過國內常聽到的 con call 其實是不正確的說法，英文沒有這種說法。

No Free Lunch

Chick-fil-A 是美國知名的速食炸雞連鎖店。

全文朗讀 ♫ 007　　單字 ♫ 008

Vocabulary

1. **charge (with)** [tʃɑrdʒ] (v./n.)
   控訴、控告犯了…罪

2. **impersonate** [ɪmˋpɝsəˏnet]
   (v.) 冒充，假冒

3. **identify** [aɪˋdɛntəˏfaɪ] (v.)
   表示、證明身份，
   identification
   [aɪˏdɛntəfəˋkeʃən] (n.) 身分證明

4. **agent** [ˋedʒənt] (n.)
   探員，特工

5. **complimentary**
   [ˏkɑmpləˋmɛntəri] (a.)
   贈送的，免費的

6. **federal** [ˋfɛdərəl] (a.)
   聯邦政府的

7. **handcuff** [ˋhændˏkʌf] (v./n.)
   給…戴上手銬；（固定用複數）
   手銬

8. **suspect** [ˋsʌspɛkt] (n.) 嫌犯

Woman Arrested for Impersonating FBI Agent
女子假冒 FBI 探員被捕

A Dallas, Georgia woman has been arrested and [1]**charged** with [2]**impersonating** an officer after attempting to get a free fast food meal by [3]**identifying** herself as an **FBI** [4]**agent**. Kimberly Ragsdale of Dallas was arrested by Rockmart Police on Thursday afternoon in the parking lot of a Chick-fil-A restaurant in Rockmart after employees called 911 following her attempt at ***scoring** a [5]**complimentary** meal.

喬治亞州達拉斯市一名女子為了向速食店索取霸王餐，自稱是聯邦調查局探員後被逮捕，並被指控假冒執法人員罪名。達拉斯市的金柏莉拉絲黛爾，於週四下午於福來雞餐廳停車場遭到洛克馬特市警方逮捕，當時她企圖騙取餐點，餐廳員工便打 911 電話報警。

Ragsdale identified herself as a [6]**federal** agent to the arresting officers, and when asked to provide [3]**identification**, claimed that her ***credentials** were electronic only. After the officers removed her from her white ***minivan** and [7]**handcuffed** her, the [8]**suspect** began talking into her shirt like she was talking into a radio, saying she was being arrested and to send somebody to the Rockmart Police Department. She was ***booked** into the Polk County Jail and later released on 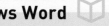 bail after posting a $3,000 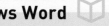 bond.

拉絲黛爾向逮捕她的警察自稱是聯邦探員，當她被要求提供身份證明時，她聲稱身上只有電子證件。警察要她從白色小休旅車下車並將她銬上手銬後，嫌犯開始朝襯衫內講話，一副對著無線電話說話的樣子，並說自己正遭到逮捕，要對方派人到洛克馬特警局。她被移送波爾克郡立監獄，後來以 3000 美元保釋金獲釋。

Rockmart Police Chief Randy Turner said Ragsdale had attempted to [9]**scam** free food from the Chick-fil-A several times that week, threatening to [10]**take** workers **into custody** if they didn't ***comply**. "You will not hear a real officer [11]**demand** a meal anywhere," said Turner. "If it is discounted, we appreciate it. We will not ask for it or make threats and demand it." There is, after all, no such thing as a free lunch.

洛克馬特警局長蘭迪杜納表示，拉絲黛爾在當週數次企圖從福來雞餐廳騙取免費餐點，並要脅若不聽從便要拘留員工。杜納說：「你不可能聽到真正的執法人員會去索要免費餐點。如果餐點有優惠，我們會很感激。我們不會要求或威脅提供餐點。」畢竟，天下沒有白吃的午餐。

9. **scam** [skæm] (v./n.)
   騙取，詐騙；騙局

10. **take into custody** 拘押，名詞 **custody** [ˈkʌstədɪ] 指「監禁，拘留」

11. **demand** [dɪˈmænd] (v./n.)
    要求，需求

進階字彙

* **score** [skor] (v.)（俚）非法取得

* **credentials** [krɪˈdɛnʃəls] (n.)（固定用複數）身份證明，證件

* **minivan** [ˈmɪnɪˌvæn] (n.) 廂型休旅車

* **book** [bʊk] (v.) 登記入冊以作指控之用

* **comply (with)** [kəmˈplaɪ] (v.) 遵守，順從

News Word

1. FBI (Federal Bureau of Investigation) 聯邦調查局
美國司法部 Department of Justice 主要調查機關，負責處理國家機密事件、跨州犯罪及情報蒐集，工作人員稱為 special agent 特別探員。FBI 調查的犯罪行為有 kidnapping 綁架、bank robbery 搶銀行、interstate transportation of stolen vehicles 跨州贓車運送、espionage 間諜事件等 180 多種。

2. Phrase bail 保釋、保釋金
bond 保釋保證書
bail 當名詞則指保釋這件事或「保釋金（不可數）」，當動詞 bail (out) 指「保釋某人」。bond 是 bail bond「保釋保證」的簡稱，是被告（defendant）與保釋擔保人（bail bondsman）所簽署的協議，也可指保釋金。

例：I hear the criminal is out on bail now. 我聽說那名罪犯現在已經保釋出獄。

例：My father hired a lawyer and bailed me out. 我父親雇用律師保我出去。

Child Takes Breath Test

示意圖。Tesla 特斯拉是目前電動汽車龍頭。

全文朗讀 ♫ 009　單字 ♫ 010

Vocabulary

1. **accidentally** [ˌæksəˋdɛntəli]
   (adv.) 意外地，不小心地

2. **come to light** (phr.)
   真相為人所知、被揭露

3. **criticize** [ˋkrɪtəˌsaɪz] (v.)
   批評，指責，名詞 **criticism**
   [ˋkrɪtəˌsɪzəm]

4. **defend** [dɪˋfɛnd] (v.)
   辯護，辯解，名詞 **defense**
   [dɪˋfɛns]

5. **intention** [ɪnˋtɛnʃən] (n.)
   意圖，目的

6. **insurance** [ɪnˋʃʊrəns] (n.)
   保險

7. **claim** [klem] (n.)
   （保險公司）索賠

8. **district** [ˋdɪstrɪkt] (n.)
   區，行政區

Police Give Breath Test to 5-year-old
警察替五歲男童做酒測

Police in Taichung **ᴾare on blast** for giving a five-year-old boy a **breathalyzer** test after he [1]**accidentally** crashed his bicycle into a parked car. The little boy's *scrape with the law [2]**came to light** when the vehicle's owner posted a picture of the young boy blowing into the breathalyzer on social media.

台中市警察因對一名五歲男童進行酒測遭受抨擊。該男童騎腳踏車時意外撞上一輛停在路邊的汽車。車主在社群媒體張貼一張幼童進行酒測的照片後，男童觸法的消息因此曝光。

While some *netizens [3]**criticized** the police for performing a **sobriety test** on a young child, others *chided the owner of the car—a white Tesla 3—for overreacting over a **fender bender** with a five-year-old. The general opinion seemed to be that he should have just settled the matter with the boy's parents instead of calling the police.

雖然部分網友批評警察對幼童進行酒測一事，但也有人指責白色特斯拉車主對五歲小孩輕微擦撞車身的反應是小題大做。普遍網友認為，他應該與男童的父母私下和解，而不是報警。

After *taking heat for the photo, the Tesla owner [4]defended himself by saying his [5]intention in posting it was to show how brave and responsible the boy was. He also explained that he called the police because he needed an official police report in order to *file an [6]insurance [7]claim.

因為照片遭到批評的特斯拉車主為自己辯護，他表示，張貼這張照片是為了展現男孩有多勇敢和負責。他並解釋說，報警是因為他需要警方正式筆錄才能申請保險理賠。

Meanwhile, police in the Taichung [8]district of Wufeng defended the actions of their officers, stating that all parties involved in a traffic accident must take a DUI test. Later, however, they said they would ask the National Police Agency if children could be *exempted from breathalyzer tests in the future.

同時，台中市霧峰區的警方也為警員的行為辯護，指出涉及交通事故的所有當事人都必須進行酒測。但後來他們表示會詢問警政署，未來兒童是否可以免除酒測。

進階字彙

* **scrape with the law**
（輕微）觸法，scrape 指「麻煩」

* **netizen** [ˋnɛtɪzən] (n.)
鄉民，網路使用者

* **chide** [tʃaɪd] (v.) 責罵，訓斥

* **take heat** (phr.)
（俚）承受批評或責罵

* **file** [faɪl] (v.)
備案，提出（申請、訴訟等）

* **exempt** [ɪgˋzɛmpt] (v.)
免除，豁免

News Word

1. `Phrase` **sb. be on blast** 某人被公審
blast 延伸出來的俚語很多，這次介紹 **put sb. on blast**「公開讓某人出醜」，尤指透過社群媒體斥責抵制某人，要某人「出來面對」。類似的表達還有 **dis sb.**。

A: Did you hear that Tom was cheating on his girlfriend? 你知道湯姆背著他女友偷吃嗎？
B: Yeah. Everybody put him on blast on Facebook. 知道啊，他的臉書被人肉搜。

2. sobriety test & DUI test 酒測；酒醉／嗑藥後駕駛
sobriety [səˋbraɪətɪ] 為 sober「清醒的，沒酒醉的」的名詞，因此 sobriety test 就是酒精濃度測試，常見的是用 **breathalyzer** [ˋbrɛθə͵laɪzə] 的酒測儀器讓駕駛人吹氣，測呼吸中的酒精濃度，這種方式叫 **breath test**。

ChameleonsEye©Shutterstock

DUI 則是 driving under the influence 縮寫，意思是在受影響的狀況下（如喝醉或嗑藥）開車，是美國法定 drunk driving 酒駕的一種。

3. fender bender 小車禍，擦撞
fender bender 字面是「把擋泥板弄彎者」，延伸為「輕微車禍，擦撞」，人通常沒有受傷。車子擦撞不見得是把 fender（擋泥板）撞壞，但因為 fender 跟 bender 押韻，念起來很順，久而久之就成習慣用法。

International 國際

#Europe #The British Royal Family
#Prince Harry #Meghan #Megxit

Lorna Roberts©Shutterstock

Prince Harry 跟 Meghan Markle 大喜當天。

全文朗讀 ♫ 011　單字 ♫ 012

Harry and Meghan to Step Back as Senior Royals
哈利王子夫婦退出英國皇室

🕐 **January 8, 2020**

The **Duke and Duchess of Sussex**, better known as Prince Harry and Meghan Markle, announced on Wednesday that they will step back from their duties as [1]**senior** members of the **British Royal Family**. The couple, who welcomed their son Archie in May 2019, say they [2]**intend** to become [3]**financially** independent. Harry is sixth in the **line of succession** to the British [4]**throne**, after his father Charles, his older brother William, and William's three children.

薩塞克斯公爵與公爵夫人，或稱哈利王子與梅根馬克爾更廣為人知，他們於週三宣布將退出英國皇室的高級成員職責。這對夫婦於 2019 年 5 月誕下一子亞契，他們表示打算財務獨立。哈利是英國王位第六順位繼承人，在他之前的繼承順位依次是他父親查爾斯、哥哥威廉和威廉的三名子女。

In a statement released Wednesday evening, Harry and Meghan explained their decision. "After many months of [5]**reflection** and internal discussions, we have chosen to make a [6]**transition** this

Vocabulary

1. **senior** [ˋsinjɚ] (a.)
   資深的，地位較高的

2. **intend** [ɪnˋtɛnd] (v.)
   打算，想要

3. **financially** [faɪˋnænʃəlɪ] (a.)
   財務上，金融上，形容詞
   financial

4. **throne** [θron] (n.) 寶座，王位

5. **reflection** [rɪˋflɛkʃən] (n.)
   反省，反映，反射

6. **transition** [trænˋzɪʃən] (n.)
   轉變，變革

Prince Harry 與 Meghan 長子 Archie 於 2019 年 5 月 6 日誕生。

7. **progressive** [prə`grɛsɪv] (a.)
進步的，開通的

8. **institution** [ˌɪnstɪ`tuʃən] (n.)
機構，機關

9. **geographic** [ˌdʒiə`græfɪk] (a.)
地理上的

10. **appreciation** [əˌpriʃɪ`eʃən] (n.) 體會，欣賞
   appreciate [ə`priʃɪˌet] (v.)

11. **launch** [lɔntʃ] (n./v.)
推出，發行

12. **charitable** [`tʃærɪtəbəl] (a.)
慈善的，樂善好施的

13. **complicated** [`kɑmpləˌketɪd] (a.) 複雜的，難懂的

14. **issue** [`ɪʃu] (n.)
問題，議題，爭議

15. **consult** [kən`sʌlt] (v.)
與…商量，請教

16. **anticipate** [æn`tɪsəˌpet] (v.)
期待，預料

17. **air** [ɛr] (v.) 播送，播放

---

year in starting to ℗**carve out** a [7]**progressive** new role within this [8]**institution**," they wrote. "We intend to step back as senior members of the Royal Family, and work to become financially independent, while continuing to fully support **Her Majesty The Queen**."

哈利與梅根在週三晚間發布的聲明中，解釋他們的決定：「經過多月的慎重考慮和內部討論，我們選擇以今年為轉型期，開始在這體制中開拓革新的角色。我們打算退出皇室高級成員，努力實現財務獨立，同時繼續全力支持女王陛下。」

The couple say they plan to divide their time between the U.K. and North America, "continuing to honor our duty to The Queen, **the Commonwealth**, and our **patronages**. This [9]**geographic** balance will enable us to raise our son with an [10]**appreciation** for the royal tradition into which he was born, while also providing our family with the space to focus on the next chapter, including the [11]**launch** of our new [12]**charitable *entity**."

這對夫婦表示，他們計畫在英國和北美輪流生活，「繼續履行我們對女王、大英國協和捐資工作的職責。當我們在養育出生於皇室的兒子時，這種地域平衡，讓他更加體會皇室傳統，同時也為我們家人提供一個專心發展下一個重要人生階段的空間，包括發起新的慈善組織。」

Buckingham Palace followed with its own short statement. "We understand their desire to take a different approach but these are [13]**complicated** [14]**issues** that will take time to work through," the statement read. "Discussions with the Duke and Duchess of Sussex are at an early stage." No other member of Buckingham Palace was [15]**consulted** before the couple released their statement, and other senior royals were ***reportedly** disappointed.

白金漢宮隨後發表自己的簡短聲明，表示：「我們瞭解他們渴望採取不同的方式，但這是複雜的問題，需要時間解決。目前仍在與薩塞克斯公爵和公爵夫人進行初步討論。」在這對夫婦發表聲明前，未與白金漢宮其他成員商討，據悉其他高級皇室成員也感到失望。

A step back from royal duties has been [16]**anticipated** since Harry, Meghan and Archie returned from a six-week stay in Canada on January 6. In an interview with the couple that [17]**aired** last October, Meghan said that [18]**adjusting** to royal life had been hard, and that she wasn't prepared for the [19]**intense *scrutiny** of Britain's **tabloid media**.

NeydtStock©Shutterstock

Meghan 無法適應被狗仔盯著的皇室生活，據說是她脫離皇室的主因。

18. **adjust (to)** [əˋdʒʌst] (v.) 調整

19. **intense** [ɪnˋtɛns] (a.) 激烈的，強烈的

進階字彙

* **entity** [ˋɛntəti] (n.) 實體，組織

* **reportedly** [rɪˋportɪdli] (adv.) 據說，據報導

* **scrutiny** [ˋskrutəni] (n.) 仔細檢視

自從哈利、梅根和亞契在加拿大待六星期並於 1 月 6 日回國以來，便傳出退出皇室職務的預測。這對夫婦在去年 10 月播出的節目中接受訪談時，梅根已表示難以適應皇室生活，而且她尚未準備好面對英國八卦媒體的嚴密監視。

Grammar Master

介系詞 + 關係代名詞

本文的「This geographic balance will enable us to raise our son with an appreciation for the royal tradition **into which** he was born...」，關係代名詞 which 前方出現介系詞 into，其實是從形容詞子句中的介系詞前挪而來：**which** he was born **into** (the royal tradition)，be born into 指「出身於⋯」。

換言之，「介系詞＋關代」中的介系詞，其實是從不及物動詞或固定用法而來，或是表達時間或地點介系詞的一部分：

● 介系詞是不及物動詞的一部分：
例：Linda is the girl **to whom** Larry was talking. 跟賴瑞講話的女生是琳達。
[介系詞 to 為動詞 talking to 前挪。]

● 介系詞是固定用法的一部分
例：The construction project **on which** the company spent years working needs extra time to complete. 公司花費數年改善的建築工程需要更多時間完工。
[介系詞 on 為動詞片語 work on「改善、修理」前挪。]

● 介系詞是地點、時間介系詞組：
例：London is the city **in which** I met Susan. 倫敦是我遇到蘇珊的城市。
[介系詞 in 是 I met Susan in (London) 前挪而來。註：此例句的 in which 由於是表達地點，可以用關係副詞 **where** 代替。]

Bart Lenoir©Shutterstock

1. Duke and Duchess of Sussex 薩塞克斯公爵與公爵夫人

Duke「公爵」次於 Prince「王子，親王」，為英國勳爵中最高級，Duke of Sussex 屬於英國皇室公爵爵位，2018 年 5 月 19 日哈利王子迎娶 Meghan 因而獲封此爵位，Meghan 也獲封 Duchess of Sussex（**duchess** [ˋdʌtʃɪs]，指「公爵夫人，女公爵」），不過他們已經於 2020 年 3 月 31 日正式脫離英國皇室。

2. British Royal Family 英國皇室

英國是目前少數保有君主制的國家，目前英國皇室已虛位化，但皇室仍是英國民眾生活的重要部分。君王在英國現行的君主立憲制中仍具有諮詢權、褒獎權與警告權，君王必須在政治上扮演超黨派角色，發揮穩定和平衡作用。擁有以下頭銜的通常都是皇室成員：

Lorna Roberts©Shutterstock

· 女王／國王（**Queen/King**）：尊稱 Your Majesty，間接尊稱 His/her Majesty（簡稱 HM）

· 王子／公主（**Prince/Princess**）：尊稱 Your Royal Highness，間接尊稱 His/Her Royal Highness（簡稱 HRH）

3. line of succession 王儲順位

英國王位的繼承順序依輩份跟出生順序而定，目前高齡 94 歲的維多利亞女王二世仍在位，未傳位給大兒子查爾斯王子，使得查爾斯王子成為全球目前在位最久的王儲。以下是目前英國王儲順位：

Featureflash Photo Agency©Shutterstock

▲ Prince Charles 和妻子 Camilla。

· 第一順位：Charles, Prince of Wales 查爾斯王子，伊莉莎白女王和菲利浦親王長子。

· 第二順位：Prince William, Duke of Cambridge 威廉王子，查爾斯王子與黛安娜王妃的長子。

· 第三順位：Prince George of Cambridge 喬治王子，威廉王子跟凱特王妃的長子。

· 第四順位：Princess Charlotte of Cambridge 夏洛特公主，威廉王子跟凱特王妃的長女。

· 第五順位：Prince Louis of Cambridge 路易斯王子，威廉王子跟凱特王妃的次子。

· 第六順位：Prince Harry, Duke of Sussex 哈利王子，查爾斯王子與黛安娜王妃的次子。

4. Phrase **carve out 靠自己努力開創出、謀得（職位）**

carve 指「雕刻」，將原石或圓木雕刻成美麗作品需要花上許多時間跟心力，因此 carve out 常延伸有「努力打拚、開創出…」，如打造聲譽（reputation）、開創市場等。

例 **Martin carved out a successful career in the antique business.** 馬丁在古董市場上開創出自己的王國。

5. Her Majesty The Queen 伊莉莎白二世女王

Queen Elizabeth II 是英國現任君主，Her Majesty「女王陛下」則是對於英國女王的尊稱。伊莉莎白二世於 1952 年 6 月 2 日登基，是英國與大英國協王國（the Commonwealth Realm）15 個會員國的國家元首，她是英國史上最長壽的君主，也是目前最年長的君主。

▶ 伊莉莎白女王二世喜愛穿著鮮亮色套裝，其中最愛粉色，帽子是她每次出場的搶眼焦點。

Shaun Jeffers©shutterstock

6. the Commonwealth 大英國協

二戰後，在去殖民化的風潮下，受戰爭重創的英國為了保持跟前殖民地的關係，並在外交上保持彈性與實力，而以英國為首所建立的組織。大英國協目前有 54 個會員國，現今目標是讓所有會員國能有平等且互助的合作。The Commonwealth 和 **The Commonwealth Realm**「大英國協王國」不同，後者是「共主邦聯」的政治體制，成員包含英國與 15 個國家，這些會員國都承認英國皇室是它們的國家元首，加拿大與澳洲就是成員之一。

7. patronage 資助，支持

在本新聞中，patronage [ˋpætrənɪdʒ] 一字指哈利王子夫婦對英國皇室的「贊助，援助」（charity work）。而 **political patronage** 則指「裙帶政治」，即讓那些在選舉上有幫助過自己的人任命政府官員。

8. Buckingham Palace 白金漢宮

白金漢宮位於倫敦西敏寺 Palace of Westminster，是英國議會所在地，也是英國君主居住與辦公的地方，延伸指英國皇室。

9. tabloid media 通俗小報，八卦小報

tabloid [ˋtæblɔɪd] 原本指比一般報紙（newspaper）小一半的報紙，多半報導庶民有興趣的八卦新聞，現延伸通稱這類報導風格的各種文字媒體。英國小報一直喜愛報導英國皇室的八卦，對從黛安娜王妃到現在的梅根造成許多困擾。

Lenscap Photography©Shutterstock

#Middle East #Lebanon
#explosion #nitrate #orangecloud

Alex Gakos©Shutterstock

當地時間 2020 年 8 月 4 日，黎巴嫩首都貝魯特港口發生大爆炸時的空拍圖（aerial view）。

全文朗讀 🎵 013　　單字 🎵 014

Beirut Blast Kills Over 70
貝魯特爆炸事件造成逾 70 人死亡

⏱ **August 4, 2020**

Vocabulary

1. **preliminary** [prɪˋlɪmɪˏnɛri] (a.)
   初步的，預備的

2. **minister** [ˋmɪnɪstə] (n.)
   （政府部門）部長，大臣

3. **warehouse** [ˋwɛrˏhaʊs] (n.)
   倉庫，倉儲

4. **nuclear** [ˋnuklɪə] (n.)
   核子的，原子彈的，
   nuclear plant「核能電廠」

5. **ambulance** [ˋæmbjələns] (n.)
   救護車

6. **cope (with)** [kop] (v.)
   處理，應付，意同 **handle**

A huge **explosion** hit Beirut on Tuesday, **leveling** much of the city's port, damaging buildings all over the capital and sending a giant orange cloud into the sky. The [1]**preliminary death toll** was 70, with over 3,000 injured and many bodies still buried in the **rubble**, Lebanon Health [2]**Minister** Hassan Hamad said.

貝魯特週二發生一場大爆炸，幾乎夷平該城市的港口，首都各處建築遭炸毀，並朝空中冒出一團巨大的橘色蕈狀雲。黎巴嫩衛生部長哈桑哈馬德表示，死亡人數初步估計為 70 人，逾 3000 人受傷，許多遺體仍被埋在瓦礫堆中。

The cause of the explosion, which struck with the force of a 3.3 **magnitude** earthquake, was not yet clear. The **blast** was strong enough to be felt in Turkey, Syria and Israel, and was heard over 200 kilometers across the Mediterranean in Cyprus. Interior Minister Mohammed Fahmi said it appeared that a large supply of **ammonium nitrate** stored in a port [3]**warehouse** had **detonated**.

這次爆炸引發相當於 3.3 級地震強度的力道，事發原因尚不清楚。爆炸力道強到土耳其、敘利亞和以色列皆能感受到其威力，遠在地中海外 200 多公里的賽

爆炸後街道幾乎成了廢墟。據說當時爆炸威力相當於廣島原子彈的 1/5。

普勒斯都能聽到爆炸聲。內政部長穆罕默德法米表示，可能是港口倉庫存放的大量硝酸銨觸發爆炸。

In the hours following the explosion, one of the most powerful non-[4]**nuclear** blasts in history, [5]**ambulances** rushed into Beirut from all over the country to transport the wounded. Three hospitals were completely destroyed in the blast, and the ones that remained struggled to [6]**cope** with the flood of new patients, quickly filling to [7]**capacity**. At Saint George Hospital, one of the city's largest medical [8]**facilities**, four nurses died in the explosion, and damage was so [9]**extensive** that doctors were forced to treat patients on the street.

這次爆炸是史上威力最強大的非核爆之一，在爆炸發生後數小時內，來自全國各地的救護車趕到貝魯特運送傷者。有三家醫院在爆炸中徹底炸毀，其餘醫院竭力應付大量湧進的新傷患，很快人滿為患。該市最大醫療機構之一的聖喬治醫院有四名護士在爆炸中喪生，由於損毀程度十分嚴重，醫生被迫在街頭治療傷患。

In the neighborhoods around the port, injured [10]**residents** [11]**staggered** along streets [12]**lined** with [13]**overturned** cars and littered with **debris** and broken glass. Homes as far as 10 kilometers away were damaged by the explosion, and up to 300,000 people were left homeless. At the port itself, Army [14]**helicopters** helped battle ***raging** fires.

截至 9 日，貝魯特爆炸事件在當地已經造成 150 名死亡，數千人受傷。當地民眾聚集抗議，要政府為這次事件負責。

在港口周圍的社區，受傷的居民在街上蹣跚而行，街旁都是翻覆的汽車，到處都是破瓦殘礫和碎玻璃。方圓 10 公里的房屋遭到破壞，多達 30 萬人無家可歸。軍方直升機已在港口協助撲滅熊熊火勢。

15. **cargo** [`kɑrgo] (n.)
貨船、貨機所裝載的貨物

16. **abandon** [ə`bændən] (v.)
拋棄，丟棄

17. **witness** [`wɪtnəs] (v./n.)
目擊，證明；目擊者，證人

18. **involve** [ɪn`vɑlv] (v.)
牽涉，連累

進階字彙

* **raging** [`redʒɪŋ] (a.) 劇烈的，狂
暴的，動詞 **rage** 指「（怒火、火
勢、戰爭等）肆虐，席捲」

* **confiscate** [`kɑnfɪ.sket] (v.) 充公

爆炸隔日民眾主動上街整理家園。

In a local news interview, Interior Minister Fahmi said the blast was likely caused by the **detonation** of over 2,700 tons of **ammonium nitrate** that had been stored in a warehouse at the dock since 2014. The substance was ***confiscated** from a [15]**cargo** ship that had been [16]**abandoned** at the port in late 2013. [17]**Witnesses** reported seeing a large orange cloud similar to the kind that appears when **nitrogen dioxide** gas is released after an explosion [18]**involving nitrates**.

內政部長法米在當地新聞採訪中表示，這起爆炸可能是自 2014 年以來囤放在碼頭倉庫的 2700 噸硝酸銨引爆而起。該物質是從一艘在 2013 年底廢棄的貨船上沒收而來。根據目擊者報告，他們看到一團巨大的橘色蕈狀雲，類似硝酸鹽爆炸後釋放出二氧化氮氣體時會出現的那種煙霧。

Grammar Master

關係代名詞的省略

第一段第二句「The preliminary death toll was 70, with over 3,000 **injured** and many bodies still **buried** in the rubble.」介系詞 with 後面接了 over 3,000 (people) 和 many bodies 兩個名詞，附加說明爆炸的傷亡狀況。3,000 people 與 many bodies 後方接上省略關係代名詞 who 與 be 動詞 are（分別是 be injured 以及 be buried）的形容詞子句，進一步說明前面的名詞。還原本句：…with over 3,000 (people) **(who are) injured** and many bodies **(that are)** still **buried** in the rubble. 以下整理可以省略關係代名詞的狀況：

● be 動詞跟關代放一起可一併省略，如本句。
● 關係代名詞當受詞時：

例：This is the cat (that) I saw last night. 這是我昨晚看到的貓。

1. explosion「爆炸相關單字

「爆炸」名詞為 explosion [ɪkˋsploʒən]，動詞為 explode [ɪkˋsplod]，這組字不僅指炸彈爆炸，瓦斯氣爆也可以用這個字。另外，**detonate** 指「引爆、爆炸」，名詞是 **detonation** [ˌdɛtəˋneʃən]。文章後半出現的 **blast** [blæst] 則指「炸藥所引發的爆炸」，可當名詞與動詞。此外，「爆裂物，引爆裝置」可用名詞 **explosive** [ɪkˋsplosɪv] 表示。

炸彈轟炸過後，建築物通常會被「夷為平地」，**level** 當動詞有「使平整」的意思，可借指將房屋等「夷平，徹底摧毀」。

爆炸或地震後的碎磚瓦礫，就稱 **rubble** [ˋrʌbəl]，本指「碎石」，單數名詞，也可以用 **debris** [dəˋbri] 表示，指「瓦礫，殘骸，碎片」。

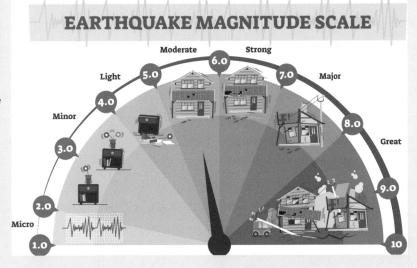

▶ 黎巴嫩居民上街清理爆炸後的殘骸（debris）。

Hiba Al Kallas©Shutterstock

2. death toll 死亡人數

這裡的 toll 指「傷亡，損失」，death toll「死亡總人數」，當集體名詞，與單數動詞連用：The death toll has risen to 250.（死亡人數上升到 250 人。）

3. magnitude 地震規模

地震 earthquake 常簡稱 quake，想知道地震本身的大小，就要測量地震規模，常用單位是 Richter magnitude 芮氏地震規模，簡稱 magnitude [ˋmægnəˌtud]。地震相關單字還有：

- foreshock [ˋforˌʃɑk] 前震
- aftershock [ˋæftəˌʃɑk] 餘震
- epicenter [ˋɛpɪˌsɛntə] 震央
- earthquake [ˋɝθˌkwek] 地震，也可簡寫為 quake
- temblor [ˋtɛmblə] 地震
- tremor [ˋtrɛmə] 微震
- meltdown 爐心熔毀

EARTHQUAKE MAGNITUDE SCALE

Micro 1.0
2.0
Minor 3.0
4.0
Light 5.0
Moderate 6.0
Strong 7.0
Major 8.0
Great 9.0
10

4. nitrogen dioxide & ammonium nitrate 二氧化氮與硝酸銨

nitrate 指「硝酸鹽」，而其化合物 ammonium nitrate [ə`moniəm `naɪtret]「硝酸銨」則是一種多用途化合物，可製成工業炸藥，曾引發美國史上最嚴重的工傷爆炸事故。即使不爆炸，也會對環境產生污染，遇熱會產生對人體有害的二氧化氮 nitrogen dioxide [`naɪtrədʒən daɪ`ɑksaɪd]，吸入之後對肺部會產生刺激並具腐蝕性。貝魯特港口爆炸時天空出現橘色氣霧，正是硝酸銨遇熱產生的顏色，之後確認這起爆炸與囤放在港口倉庫多年但不處置的 2750 噸炸山用炸藥有關，相關官員在事件發生後被拘捕。

Hussein saifi Tv©WikiCommons

▶ 目擊者拍到貝魯特港爆炸後的天空。

5. 補充 火山爆發相關單字

火山爆發（**eruption**，動詞 **erupt**）也會產生爆炸後的氣體雲，這裡一併介紹火山相關常見單字：

- active volcano 活火山

- dormant volcano 休火山

- extinct volcano 死火山

- volcanic crater 火山口
火山活動所造成的火山頂部環形凹陷區域，較大的火山口有可能成為盆地地形或積水成湖。

- vent 火山通道噴發口
是地下的熔岩或其它其他固體、氣體的噴發口。

- fumarole 火山噴氣孔
是通常出現於火山附近的地殼裂縫，會冒出蒸氣或其它其他氣體。

- cone 火山錐
指火山噴發物在通道口堆積而成的錐形山丘。

- lava 熔岩
因高溫而熔化成液體狀的岩石，溫度可達攝氏七百到一千兩百度之間。一般來說，當熔岩冒出地表後，被稱為岩漿 (magma)。

- volcanic ash 火山灰
火山噴發時造成的固體噴發物，是由岩石或其它其他礦物所組成。直徑不超過二釐米稱為火山灰，較大的稱為火山礫及火山彈。

- pyroclastic flow 火山碎屑流
火山噴發時，常伴有由極高溫的氣體及其它其他固體（如火山碎屑及岩石）所組成的火山碎屑流隨著山坡的坡度滾滾而下。由於噴發速度很快，破壞性極大且來得又快又急，使人無法躲避不及。

- pyroclastic rock 火山碎屑岩
火山碎屑岩主要由火山碎屑流的噴發物所形成，經過固結而成的岩石。

#Caucasus
#Armenia #Azerbaijan
#Russia #Turkey
#separatism

Lorna Roberts©Shutterstock

亞塞拜然的孩子高舉國旗，慶祝 11 月 8 日收回納卡地區的舒沙 Shusha。

全文朗讀 ♫ 015　單字 ♫ 016

Azerbaijan and Armenia Sign Peace Deal

🕐 **November. 10, 2020**

血戰六週，亞塞拜然與亞美尼亞達成停火協議

Armenia, Azerbaijan and Russia have signed a **ceasefire** agreement to end military conflict over the ¹⁾**disputed** region of **Nagorno-Karabakh**. The deal follows six weeks of fighting between Azerbaijani and Armenian forces for control of the **Caucasus** territory.

亞美尼亞、亞塞拜然和俄羅斯已簽署一項停火協議，結束爭議地區納戈爾諾-卡拉巴赫的軍事衝突。這項協議是在亞塞拜然與亞美尼亞軍隊為控制這塊高加索地區而作戰六週後簽署。

Nagorno-Karabakh lies within the borders of Azerbaijan, but has been under the control of ²⁾**ethnic** Armenians backed by Armenia since a **separatist war** there ended in 1994. That war left Nagorno-Karabakh and several ³⁾**surrounding** areas in Armenian hands. A Russian-***brokered** **truce** was signed at the time, but there was no peace deal.

Vocabulary

1. **disputed** [dɪˋspjutɪd] *(a.)*
   有主權爭議的，**dispute**
   [dɪˋspjut] *(v./n.)* 爭執；爭端，糾紛

2. **ethnic** [ˋɛθnɪk] *(a.)*
   民族的，異國的

3. **surrounding** [səˋraʊndɪŋ] *(a.)*
   周遭的，附近的

Mato Z©Shutterstock

戰爭的轉捩點，是 11 月 8 日亞塞拜然軍成功「敵後包抄」，攻陷納卡地區關鍵的補給要塞—Shusha，圖片為 Shusha 的堡壘。

4. **erupt** [ɪˋrʌpt] (v.)
   火山爆發，噴發，延伸指戰火、衝突等爆發

5. **neutral** [ˋnutrəl] (a.)
   中立的，中性的

6. **prime minister** (phr.)
   首相，總理

7. **take effect** (phr.) 生效，施行

8. **strategic** [strəˋtidʒɪk] (a.)
   策略的，戰略的，也寫作 **strategical**

9. **overlook** [͵ovəˋluk] (v.)
   眺望，俯瞰

10. **territorial** [͵tɛrəˋtorɪəl] (a.) 領土的

11. **withdraw** [wɪðˋdrɔ] (v.)
   撤退，過去式與過去分詞 **withdrew, withdrawn**

12. **guarantee** [͵gærənˋti] (v./n.)
   保證；保證（書）

13. **monitor** [ˋmɑnɪtə] (v.)
   監視，監控

14. **spark** [spɑrk] (v./n.)
   冒火花，引發，點燃；火花

納戈爾諾 - 卡拉巴赫位於亞塞拜然境內，但自 1994 年分離主義戰爭結束以來，一直受到亞美尼亞支持的亞美尼亞族裔之控制。那場戰爭使納戈爾諾 - 卡拉巴赫與部分周圍地區落入亞美尼亞手中。當時已簽署由俄羅斯調停的休戰書，但未曾達成和平協議。

The decades-long dispute between Armenia and Azerbaijan, both of which are former **Soviet republics**, [4]**erupted** into military conflict again in late September. During 44 days of intense fighting, thousands were killed and even more ***displaced**. Azerbaijan had strong support from Turkey, while Russia, the main power in the Caucasus, sought to remain [5]**neutral**.
亞美尼亞和亞塞拜然之間的爭端已持續數十年，雙方都是前蘇聯共和國，於九月下旬再度爆發軍事衝突。經過 44 天的激戰，有數千人喪生，更多人流離失所。亞塞拜然獲得土耳其的大力支持，而高加索地區的主要強權俄羅斯則試圖保持中立。

The peace deal, which was signed by Armenian [6]**Prime Minister** Nikol Pashinyan, Azerbaijani President Ilham Aliyev and Russian President Vladimir Putin, [7]**took effect** in the early hours of Tuesday morning. The deal follows weeks of advances by Azerbaijani troops, ending in the capture of the [8]**strategic** city of Shusha, which lies in the mountains [9]**overlooking** the Nagorno-Karabakh capital of Stepanakert.
這項和平協議是由亞美尼亞總理尼科爾帕辛揚、亞塞拜然總統伊利哈姆阿利耶夫和俄羅斯總統普丁簽署，已於週二清晨生效。這項協議是在亞塞拜然軍隊取得進展數週後簽署，亞塞拜然最終攻占了戰略城市舒沙，該城市位於山區，俯瞰著納戈爾諾 - 卡拉巴赫的首都斯捷潘奈克特。

Under the deal, Azerbaijan will maintain control of the [10]**territorial** gains it made in Nagorno-Karabakh during the conflict. Armenia has also agreed to [11]**withdraw** from several other nearby areas over the next few weeks. The deal also [12]**guarantees** a **land corridor** between Nagorno-Karabakh and Armenia, which will be [13]**monitored** by Russian **peacekeepers**.
根據該協議，亞塞拜然將繼續控制在納戈爾諾 - 卡拉巴赫衝突期間所取得的領土。亞美尼亞也同意於未來數週從周圍其他幾個地區撤軍。該協議也保證在納戈爾諾 - 卡拉巴赫和亞美尼亞之間設陸地走廊，並由俄羅斯維和部隊監控。

Hiba Al Kallas©Shutterstock

11月9日簽訂停火協議後，納卡居民相當於亡國，離去前許多人燒毀自己家園，也不願讓亞塞拜然討到便宜。

News of the settlement, which is seen by both sides as a major victory for Azerbaijan, [14]**sparked *unrest** in the Armenian capital of Yerevan, with [15]**protesters** damaging government buildings and demanding the [16]**resignation** of Prime Minster Pashinyan.
雙方都將和解的消息視為亞塞拜然的重大勝利，而此消息在亞美尼亞的首都葉里溫引起動亂，示威者破壞了政府建築物，並要求帕辛揚總理下台。

Videos posted on social media appeared to show protesters pulling Ararat Mirzoyan, the speaker of Armenia's [17]**parliament**, out of his car and beating him on the street.
在社群媒體上發布的影片，看得到示威者似乎將亞美尼亞國會議長阿拉烈米爾佐揚從汽車中拖出來，並在大街上毆打他。

Alex Gakos©Shutterstock

民眾攻佔政府，抗議政府簽下等同亡國的停火協定。

Grammar Master

lie 的用法整理

本文出現多次的 lie 當「位於」之意，以下整理 lie 的不同定義與用法以及易混淆字。注意，各自的動詞三態變化也不太一樣喔。

● **lie 當「說謊」，動詞三態為「規則變化」：lie-lied-lied**

例：The kid was punished for lying to the teacher. 那孩子因為說謊被老師處罰。

● **lie 當「位於，坐落在；平躺；（責任）落在」，動詞三態「不規則變化」：lie-lay-lain**

例：The river lies 10 km to the north. 那條河流位於往北十公里處。

例：A cat lay in front of the fire. 一支貓咪趴在爐火前。

例：Responsibility for the disaster will lie with the government. 這次災難的責任會落在政府身上。

● **lay 當動詞，可指「放置（物品）；（動物）下蛋」，動詞三態：lay-laid-laid**

例：She laid the baby on the bed. 她把嬰兒放在床上。

N ews Word

1. ceasefire & truce 停火協定與休戰

cease 指「停止」，fire 指戰火，ceasefire [ˋsis.faɪr] 便指「戰爭中兩軍之間協議的停火協定」，當名詞。truce [trus] 指「休戰」，可當動詞與名詞，用途較廣，不只用在戰爭當中。戰爭中用到 truce 一字，指的是雙方休戰，但這個休戰不見得有正式的協商過程。相比起來，**ceasefire** 更為正式，通常有經過協商（negotiation）並立下協定（agreement）。

▲ 褐色區就是 Nagorno-Karabakh，土黃色區是亞美尼亞駐軍範圍。

2. Nagorno-Karabakh 納戈爾諾 - 卡拉巴赫區

1920 年代，蘇俄為安撫土耳其，將納戈爾諾 - 卡拉巴赫（簡稱納卡）這塊以信仰基督教的亞美尼亞族為大宗的地區，劃歸給信仰伊斯蘭教的亞塞拜然管理，埋下日後兩國衝突的種子。1994 年發生納卡戰爭，亞美尼亞大獲全勝，納卡地區便建立獨立政體，自稱 Republic of Artsakh「阿爾沙赫共和國」。此次的停火協議，除了為此區戰火畫下休止符，也使此共和國「亡國」。失去家園的納卡居民透過僅僅一條細長的走廊逃往亞美尼亞，成為這次戰爭中的難民。

3. Caucasus 高加索地區

高加索地區（Caucasus [ˋkɔkəsəs]）指黑海（Black Sea）與裡海（Caspian Sea）之間的高加索山脈地區、西亞與東歐的交界處。此區被高加索山分成南北兩部分，亞美尼亞與亞塞拜然屬於 South Caucasus（亦稱 Transcaucasia 外高加索），以北 North Caucasus 則有俄羅斯與喬治亞等。蘇聯解體之後，由於當地種族構成複雜，加上地勢被群山阻隔，彼此語言文化宗教不同，難以同理，使得這裡有「世界火藥庫」之稱。

▲ 為 2008 年高加索地區與周遭國家的政治地圖。　©WikiCommons

4. separatist war 分離主義戰爭

分離主義（**separatism** [ˋsɛpərə͵tɪzm]），又稱分裂主義，指一個國家內，一部分族群因民族信仰等差異，想爭取獨立並建立自己的國家。許多國家境內都有分離主義，如文中處於伊斯蘭勢力內的前納卡地區、俄羅斯內的車臣、受到中國控制的新疆西藏等。因分離主義而產生的戰爭便稱 separatist [ˋsɛpərətɪst] war。

5. Soviet Republics 「蘇聯」與俄羅斯各時期名稱

首先要先知道 Soviet 意思，俄文 Soviet「蘇維埃」原本指「委員會，代表會議」，1917 年列寧推翻沙皇，控制蘇維埃會議，建立共產政權後，Soviet 就成為「蘇聯共產制度」的代稱。

我們常聽到的「蘇聯」，英文是 **the Soviet Union**，正式名稱為 Union of Soviet Socialist Republics「蘇維埃社會主義共和國聯邦」，簡稱 USSR，於 1922 年組成。「蘇俄」**Soviet Russia** 是蘇聯 15 個共和國中的主要共和國，其他 14 個共和國只是名義上的「國家」，實質上是由蘇聯完全控制的一黨制國家。我們所稱的「俄羅斯」或「俄國」（**Russia**）在蘇聯之前就一直稱之，在蘇聯期間稱 **Soviet Russia**「蘇俄」（其正式名稱為 Russian Soviet Republic「俄羅斯蘇維埃共和國」）。蘇聯解體之後，名稱就又回到 Russia「俄羅斯」（其正式名稱為 Russian Federation）。

Alex Gakos©Shutterstock

6. land corridor 陸地走廊

corridor [ˋkɔrɪdə] 一般指「長而窄的廊道」，尤其是兩側有許多房間的長廊。文中則指「一國通過他國境內的狹長地帶」，**land corridor** 就是「陸地走廊」，如古代的絲路便是。文中提及的停火協議中規定，亞塞拜然要給納卡區的亞美尼亞族一條陸上通道，讓他們能回到亞美尼亞。

◀ 由俄國居中協調簽下停戰協議後，納卡區居民打包行李撤退回亞美尼亞。

7. peacekeeper 維和士兵

是為了防止某些地區發生戰爭而被派往駐紮的士兵，尤其是駐紮在經常發生戰事的地區或種族。這些士兵的集合稱為 **peacekeeping force**「維和部隊」或 **peacekeeping troops**「維和部隊」。

例 UN peacekeepers were sent to enforce the ceasefire.
聯合國維和士兵被派往執行停火。

Richard Juilliart©Shutterstock

Politics

政治

4

#2020USElection #Trump
#Republican #Democratic
#RBG

The White House ©Shealah Craighead

全文朗讀 🎵 017　單字 🎵 018

Barrett Confirmed to U.S. Supreme Court
巴瑞特任命擔任美國最高法院大法官

🕐 **October 27, 2020**

The **Republican**-led **Senate** voted Monday to confirm Amy Coney Barrett to the **Supreme Court**, ending a bitter [1]**confirmation** process and giving President Donald Trump a political victory a week before the 2020 election. Her confirmation gives the Republicans a 6-3 majority likely to last for years.

共和黨佔多數的參議院於週一結束激烈的任命之爭，表決通過艾美康尼巴瑞特擔任最高法院大法官。此為川普總統在 2020 年大選前一週的政治勝利。此任命結果賦予共和黨 6 比 3 的多數席次，這個狀況可能會維持多年。

Barrett is the third **Supreme Court *justice** [2]**appointed** by the Republican president, after Neil Gorsuch in 2017 and Brett Kavanaugh in 2018. The 48-year-old **federal appeals court** judge from Indiana fills the vacancy left by Justice **Ruth Bader Ginsburg**, the **liberal *icon** who died on September 18.

巴瑞特是繼 2017 年尼爾戈蘇奇和 2018 年布雷特卡瓦諾任命通過後，由這位共和黨總統任命的第三位最高法院大法官。這位 48 歲、來自印第安納州的聯邦上

Vocabulary

1. **confirmation** [ˌkɑnfəˋmeʃən]
   (n.)（對人事任命、行政行為的）
   批准、認可，（對事件聲明的）
   證實、確認

2. **appoint** [əˋpɔɪnt] (v.)
   任命，任用，指定，名詞為
   appointment

Lucy.Sanders.999
©WikiCommons

美國民眾高舉「No Rushed Justice」（不要草草上任的大法官），抗議川普在選舉前亟欲補上保守派大法官缺的舉動。

3. **campaign** [kæm`pen] *(n.)*
   競選活動，宣傳活動

4. **finance** [`faɪˌnæns] *(n.)*
   資金；財務，財政，金融

5. **nomination** [ˌnɑmə`neʃən]
   (n.) 提名，動詞 **nominate**
   [`nɑməˌnet]，「被提名人」為
   nominee [ˌnɑmə`ni]

6. **enthusiasm** [ɪn`θuziˌæzəm]
   (n.) 熱忱，熱衷的事物

7. **priority** [praɪ`ɔrəti] *(n.)*
   優先，優先考量的事

8. **vacancy** [`vekənsi] *(n.)*
   空缺，空房

9. **in favor of** *(phr.)* 支持，贊成

10. **reelection** [ˌriə`lɛkʃən] *(n.)*
    競選連任，動詞為 **reelect**

11. **era** [`ɛrə / `ɪrə] *(n.)* 時代

訴法院法官，填補露絲貝德金斯伯格大法官所留下的空缺，這位自由派代表人物於 9 月 18 日過世。

The addition of Gorsuch, Kavanaugh and now Barrett mark a sharp turn to the **right** on the Supreme Court. Some legal experts are even calling it the most **conservative** court since the 1930s. This 6-3 majority will give conservatives an advantage on issues like gun rights and [3]**campaign** [4]**finance**, while ℗**posing a threat** to liberals on issues like **Roe v. Wade** and **Obamacare**.
繼戈蘇奇和卡瓦諾的加入，現在又多了巴瑞特，象徵最高法院向右派急轉彎。部分法律專家甚至稱之為 1930 年代以來最保守的法院。6 比 3 的多數席次將使保守派在持槍權利和競選資金等議題上佔有優勢，並在羅告韋德案與歐記健保等議題上對自由派構成威脅。

Barrett's [5]**nomination** was met with [6]**enthusiasm** from Republicans, who have made filling the courts with conservative judges their [7]**priority** in the Senate, and anger from Democrats, who warned against filling a [8]**vacancy** in an election year, particularly after **GOP** leaders blocked the confirmation of President Obama's [5]**nominee**, Judge Merrick Garland, in 2016.
巴瑞特的提名引起共和黨人熱烈迴響，他們在參議院的首要任務就是讓保守派法官填補法院空缺，而此舉激怒民主黨人，他們早就警告執政黨不要在選舉年填補空缺，尤其是共和黨領袖還在 2016 年阻止了當時總統歐巴馬提名梅瑞克賈蘭德法官一事。

The vote was 52-48, with only Republicans voting [9]**in favor of** Barrett and all **Democrats** voting against her. Only one Republican, Senator Susan Collins, who faces a tough [10]**reelection** race in Maine, joined the Democrats in voting no. Barrett, who was confirmed 30 days after her nomination by Trump, is the first nominee in the modern [11]**era** to be confirmed with no votes from the minority party.
在這場 52 比 48 的表決中，只有共和黨人投票支持巴瑞特，所有民主黨人皆投反對票。唯有一名共和黨參議員蘇珊柯林斯因為在緬因州面臨艱困的連任競選，所以加入民主黨人投下反對票。在川普提名後 30 天便任命通過的巴瑞特，是近代第一位未獲得任何少數黨投票支持而上任的大法官提名人。

Fred Schilling©WikiCommons

Barrett 就任大法官的司法宣示儀式。左為首席大法官 John Roberts。

12. **ceremony** [ˋsɛrəˌmoni] *(n.)*
儀式，典禮

13. **constitutional**
[ˌkɑnstəˋtuʃənəl] *(a.)*
憲法的，名詞為 **constitution**

14. **oath** [oθ] *(n.)*
誓言，**take an oath** 宣誓

15. **administer** [ədˋmɪnəstə] *(v.)*
主持（儀式），掌管，治理

進階字彙

* **justice** [ˋdʒʌstɪs] *(n.)*
專指美國聯邦最高法院的大法官，
其他下級法院的法官則稱 **judge**

* **icon** [ˋaɪkɑn] *(n.)*
偶像，代表性人物

* **swearing-in** [ˋswɛrɪŋˋɪn] *(n.)*
宣示就職

* **judicial** [dʒuˋdɪʃəl] *(a.)*
司法的，審判的

The White House held a ***swearing-in** [12] **ceremony** Monday night where Barrett's official [13] **constitutional** [14] **oath** was [15] **administered** by Justice Clarence Thomas, the most conservative member of the Supreme Court. On Tuesday, Chief Justice John Roberts will administer the ***judicial** oath in a private ceremony, officially making Barrett a justice.

週一晚上白宮舉行了宣誓就職典禮，巴瑞特的官方憲法宣誓儀式是由最高法院中最保守的大法官克拉倫斯托馬斯主持。首席大法官約翰羅勃茲將於週二的私人儀式中主持司法宣誓，巴瑞特將在此儀式中正式成為大法官。

Grammar Master

分詞片語

本新聞第一句「The Republican-led Senate voted Monday to confirm Amy Coney Barrett to the Supreme Court, **ending** a bitter confirmation process...」第二個子句省略了當主詞的關係代名詞 which，簡化成分詞片語，原本句子應該是：The Republican-led Senate voted Monday to confirm Amy Coney Barrett to the Supreme Court, **which ended** a bitter confirmation process. 將 ended 變成 was ending，關代 which 與 be 動詞 was 一起省略之後，就形成了現在的句子。

本文其他段落也有出現類似句型。找一找，是哪一句呢？（答案請見本新聞最後。）

1. Republicans & Democrats 共和黨人與民主黨人

共和黨 **Republican** [rɪˋpʌblɪkən] **Party** 與民主黨 **Democratic Party** 為美國兩大主要政黨，共和黨又稱 Grand Old Party 大老黨，縮寫為 **GOP**。共和黨代表顏色為紅色；民主黨代表顏色為藍色。其各自成員分別稱 Republican(s)「共和黨人」與 Democrat(s)「民主黨人」。

2. left & right 左派與右派
  liberal & conservative 自由派與保守派

「左派」**left wing**、「右派」**right wing** 的說法，起源於十八世紀的法國大革命，大革命期間的議會上，溫和的保王黨人都坐在議場的右邊，而激進的革命黨人則都坐在左邊，此後便產生這兩種稱呼。如今常用來區分兩種相對的政治立場。左派通常指自由派 **liberal** [ˋlɪbərəl]、社會自由主義、社會民主主義、共產主義或無政府主義等人士，而右派則指保守人士 **conservative** [kənˋsɝvətɪv]、反動派、資本主義者、擁護君主制度者、國家主義者、法西斯主義者等。拿美國兩大黨來說，民主黨與共和黨各自都有中間份子，但整體上而言共和黨偏保守、右派一些，民主黨偏自由、左派。

3. Senate 美國參議院

美國國會（Congress）採兩院制，由 **Senate** [ˋsɛnɪt] 參議院與 **House of Representatives** 眾議院組成，任何新法都需經兩院一致同意才能生效。參議院是較慎重的參謀議院，參議員稱 **Senator**；眾議院則是較貼近民意的人民議院，眾議員稱 **Representative**。

4. Congress vs. Parliament 都是國會，有什麼不同？

國會 congress 與議會 parliament 功能相似，都是國家最高立法機關，也是由兩院所組成。但最大不同之處，**congress** 的兩院皆由直接民選選出，一般見於新興民主制國家，如美國、台灣；但 **parliament** 的上院則是由政府選出，下院才是由民選選出，parliament 議會制度歷史較為悠久，常見於歷史悠久、（曾）施行君主立憲的歐洲國家，如英國。

5. Supreme Court & Justice 最高法院與大法官

美國最高法院 Supreme Court of the United States，俗稱 SCOTUS（首字母縮寫，念 [ˋskotəs]），目前由一位首席大法官跟八位大法官組成。大法官皆由總統提名，獲得參議院投票通過任命後，大法官就享有終身任期，可不受原本所屬政黨意志做審判。

6. appeals court 上訴法院

美國幾乎所有州與聯邦法院都設有三級司法系統：「初審－上訴－終審」。初審由 **trial court**「初審／一審法院」負責；接著是上訴法院，負責對一審不服的上訴案件，終審由 **Supreme Court**「最高法院」負責。

法律上 **appeal** [əˋpil] 一字指「上訴」，可當名詞與動詞。appeals court 是上訴法院 **appellate court** 的俗稱，也稱 **court of appeals** 或 **circuit court** 巡迴法院。appellate [əˋpɛlɪt] 是形容詞，指「有權審理上訴的」。

7. federal 聯邦政府制的

美國就是聯邦政府，擁有一個全國政府跟 50 個州政府。美國幅員廣大，為了提升效率，各州擁有各自州法，聯邦政府則負責外交、國土安全、並處理州際相關事件。

8. Ruth Bader Ginsburg 金斯伯格大法官

全名為 Ruth Bader Ginsburg 的金斯伯格，大家更愛叫她 RBG，是美國最高法院第一位猶太裔女性大法官，也是第二位女性大法官。她以堅定的自由派立場著稱，於 2020 年 9 月 18 日胰臟癌病逝，任期大法官長達 27 年，享年 87 歲。

▶ 在美國哥倫比亞特區（District of Columbia）的最高法院外，民眾持蠟燭悼念剛離世的大法官 Ruth Bader Ginsburg。「When there are nine.」（有九個女大法官才夠。）是 RBG 最為世人所知的名言。

Allison C Bailey@Shutterstock

9. Phrase pose a threat 構成威脅

動詞 pose 有「造成或引起問題或困難」之意，因此 **pose a threat** 就是「構成威脅」。片語 **pose a challenge** 則是「提出質疑、挑戰」。

例 Climate change poses a threat to our planet's natural resources.
氣候變遷對地球生態資源造成威脅。

例 A stronger currency could pose a challenge to exporters.
強勢貨幣會對出口商造成衝擊。

10. Roe v. Wade 羅氏告韋德案

1973 年，化名 Jane Roe 的懷孕婦女控告當時德州達拉斯的司法長官 Henry Wade，因為 Jane Roe 意外懷孕，但在德州不能合法墮胎，轉向地下診所求助，卻發現診所已被查封。她指控德州法律對墮胎的限制，侵犯了她的隱私權。這項訴訟最後打到聯邦最高法院，最後承認婦女的墮胎權受到美國憲法保障。該判決至今仍頗受爭議。從此 Roe v. Wade 便成為墮胎權的代名詞。

11. Obamacare 歐記健保

前美國總統歐巴馬於 2010 年簽署的「平價醫療法案」Affordable Care Act，俗稱 Obamacare「歐記健保，歐巴馬健保」。

Grammar Master 解答：本新聞中其他使用「分詞片語」共有 3 句：

第五段第一行：The vote was 52-48, with only Republicans **voting** in favor of Barrett and all Democrats voting against her.（使用到 voting 現在分詞片語）

第二段第一句：Barrett is the third Supreme Court justice **appointed** by the Republican president.（使用 appointed by 過去分詞片語）

第二段第三行：The 48-year-old federal appeals court judge from Indiana fills the vacancy **left** by Justice Ruth Bader Ginsburg.（使用 left by 過去分詞片語）

NOTORIOUS RBG – RUTH BADER GINSBURG

網紅級自由派代表人物——
美國大法官 Ruth Bader Ginsburg

©U.S. National Archives and Records Administration

▲1993 年美國總統柯林頓提名 Ginsburg 成為最高法院大法官。

除了是美國史上第二位女性大法官，Ruth Bader Ginsburg 也是美國女性平權先鋒，她數度挑戰敏感話題，為女權、墮胎權、同性婚姻發聲。她並不只為女性辯護，她也曾為一名單親爸爸爭取單親補助（當時單親補助只限女性申請）。大膽的言論作風，讓她一度有「notorious R.B.G」的稱號，這個來自饒舌歌手 notorious B.I.G 的負面詞彙，反因為她而成為勇敢的代名詞。

讓 RBG 一夕之間成為大家愛戴的原因，是因為她曾在公開場合批評川普，而事後她發布聲明公開道歉，承認自己言行不夠謹慎。身為大法官的 RBG 公開坦承自己的過失，此舉贏得了美國民眾的心。

◀金斯伯格獨特又搶眼的品味一直是媒體焦點，她總戴著顯眼耳飾與領片，配上一身黑的法官罩袍，為傳統男性法官形象注入女性象徵。而從她所配戴的領片，也能一窺她對當時判決的態度。

RBG 充滿人格魅力的人生故事，被陸續拍成劇情片《法律女王》（*On the Basis of Sex*）與紀錄片《RBG：不恐龍大法官》（*RBG*）。如果你有注意到的話，她也以縮小版樂高人物在《樂高玩電影 2》（*The Lego Movie 2: The Second Part*）軋上一角。　▶電影《RBG：不恐龍大法官》的海報。

- 關於平權

People ask me sometimes, "When will there be enough women on the court?" And my answer is, "When there are nine." People are shocked. But there'd been nine men, and nobody's ever raised a question about that.

有時候會有人問我，「在九位最高法院大法官中，要有幾名女性才夠？」我回答「九位」。有人對這個答案感到驚訝，但是以前九位大法官都是由男性擔任時，卻沒人對此提出質疑。

I ask no favor for my sex. All I ask of our brethren is that they take their feet off our necks.

我不要求給我的性別特權。我只要求男性同胞們可以把他們的腳從我們的脖子上挪開。

- 關於處事

Fight for the things that you care about, but do it in a way that will lead others to join you.

為你在乎的事而戰，但要用能引導其他人加入的方式進行。

I would like to be remembered as someone who used whatever talent she had to do her work to the very best of her ability.

我希望大家這樣記得我：一個竭盡全力以自己僅有的才能完成所交待任務的人。

▼2020 年三月，RBG 現身在 LBJ Foundation 所頒發的 Liberty & Justice for All Award 典禮上。

- 關於生活

I remember envying the boys long before I even knew the word feminism, because I liked shop better than cooking or sewing.

我從還不懂女性主義這詞的時候，就開始嫉妒男性了。因為比起烹飪或縫紉，我更喜歡木工課。

Of all the boys I had dated, he was the only one who really cared that I had a brain.

我丈夫是我約會過所有男性中，唯一在乎我有腦的男人。

©WikiCommons

The U.S. Presidential Election

關於美國總統大選，你要知道的幾件事

何謂選舉人團

美國總統大選並非由選民一人一票能決定，真正勝負關鍵是美國獨有的「選舉人團」Electoral College 制度。美國選民所投下的一票，其實是先選出由一組官員所組成的選舉人團，college 在這裡指有共同任務的一組人馬，而 Electoral College 的任務就是根據普選民意，選出美國總統與副總統。因此，美國選舉其實是間接選舉（indirect election）。

選舉人團的運作方式

美國一共有 538 個選舉人（elector），各州選舉人數量大致反應該州的人口規模，因此州人口越多，選舉人票（electoral vote）就越多，如 California 加州有 55 張選舉人票，而人口稀少的州如 Alaska 阿拉斯加就很少。一州的選舉人至少要有三個，也就是三票。

總統候選人需贏得選舉人票的多數才算當選——也就是 270 張。

除了 Maine 緬因州與 Nebraska 內布拉斯加州之外，其他州會把所有選舉人票都投給在該州普選中勝出的人，假設共和黨在德州得到 51% 的選民投票，共和黨總統候選人就能得到該州的全部 38 張選舉人票。

這種特殊的大選制度，造成過去五次大選有兩次贏得普選的候選人無法當選總統。如 2016 年川普的總票數就比 Hillary Clinton 希拉蕊少了三百萬張票，但川普贏得 304 張選舉人票因而當選。

V☆TE
ECTION 2020

藍州 紅州 搖擺州

紅州 red state 指習慣投給共和黨的州，如 Alaska、Indiana 印第安那州就是共和黨的鐵票倉；藍州 blue state 則是多數支持民主黨的州份。本次美國大選前出現的 blue shift「藍色移動」與 red mirage「紅色幻想」兩詞，就是指原本穩定的紅州開始跑票到民主黨的現象。

可想而知，搖擺州（swing state，也稱 battleground state 戰場州）就是指該州兩黨間的選票差距不大，其代表色就是紅色加上藍色的紫色。

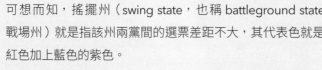

| DEMOCRATS | 306 | 232 | REPUBLICANS |

為什麼採用這種選舉制度

美國立國初期，當時選民多是農夫，加上國土遼闊資訊不流通，多數人不知道什麼是投票。此外，當時奴隸沒有投票權，造成有蓄奴制度的南方州份在選舉上佔弱勢。因此，為避免選舉受人操控以及公平起見，美國憲法便制定選舉人團制度，這樣的制度也讓小州有更多發聲的機會。

為什麼今年的美國選舉時間更長

美國選舉制度複雜，因此開票過程一直很長，這也是為什麼 11 月投票，要到隔年一月才舉行總統就職。今年加上疫情影響，郵寄選票（mail-in voting）數量高達 6500 萬張，加上等待郵票寄回選務中心的時間，勢必要投注更多人力與時間才能完成計票。

美國選舉必懂單字

- **Electoral College** 選舉人團
- **elector** 選舉人
- **voter** 一般選民
- **electoral vote** 選舉人票
- **popular vote** 普選，即一般選民投票
- **undecided voter**
  尚未決定投票意向的一般選民
- **faithless elector** 失信選舉人
- **blue state** 藍州
- **red state** 紅州

- **swing state, battleground state** 搖擺州
- **early voting**
  提早投票，因應疫情的投票方式，選民可以在投票日前投票
- **absentee ballot**
  不在席選票，35 州允許選民申請不在席投票，可申請郵寄投票
- **mail-in voting** 郵寄投票

選舉常見單字

- **candidate** 候選人
- **run for election/office** 競選
- **poll** 民調
- **debate** 辯論
- **cast a vote** 投票
- **polling station** 投票所
- **polling/voting booth** 投票亭
- **electoral fraud** 選舉舞弊
- **campaign rally** 造勢集會
- **canvass** 拜票

#2020 US Presidential Election
#Electoral College
#Joe Biden #Kamala Harris

Stratos Brilakis©Shutterstock

Joe Biden 拿到 306 張選舉人票,當選 2020 年美國總統。

全文朗讀 ♫ 019　　單字 ♫ 020

Electoral College Confirms Biden Victory
2020 美國總統大選,選舉人團確認拜登勝選

🕐 **December 14, 2020**

Vocabulary

1. **defeat** [dɪ`fit] (n./v.)
   擊敗;戰勝

2. **concede** [kən`sid] (v.)
   認輸,(勉強)承認

3. **threshold** [`θrɛʃ.hold] (n.)
   門檻

4. **milestone** [`maɪl.ston] (n.)
   里程碑

5. **significance** [sɪg`nɪfɪkəns] (n.)
   意義,重要性

6. **widespread** [`waɪd`sprɛd] (a.)
   普遍的,廣泛的

Joe Biden was formally elected next president of the United States by members of the **Electoral College** on Monday, despite Donald Trump refusing to accept [1]**defeat** and [2]**concede** the race. With California's 55 **electoral votes**, Biden crossed the 270-vote [3]**threshold** needed to win the White House, a [4]**milestone** that moves him one step closer to his **inauguration** on January 20.
儘管川普拒絕接受並承認敗選,但選舉人團成員仍於週一正式選出拜登為美國下一任總統。加上加州的 55 張選舉人票,拜登跨過了入主白宮所需的 270 票門檻,這一里程碑讓他距離 1 月 20 日就職典禮更進一步。

Usually a ***formality**, the Electoral College vote has taken on greater [5]**significance** due to Trump's efforts to ***subvert** the process with ***allegations** of [6]**widespread** voter [7]**fraud** and ***irregularities** in the Nov. 3 election. Hours after the vote, **President-elect** Biden made a speech to the nation from his hometown of Wilmington, Delaware.

通常只是走過場的選舉人團投票在這次選舉中更具意義，因為川普指控 11 月 3 日大選時有普遍作票和違規的情形，設法阻擾這次程序。選舉人團投票完數小時後，總統當選人拜登在家鄉德拉瓦州威明頓向全美發表演講。

"In this battle for the soul of America, democracy [8]**prevailed**," said Biden. "We the people voted. Faith in our institutions held. The [9]**integrity** of our elections remains [10]**intact**. And so, now it is time to turn the page. To unite. To heal. Together, **vice-president-elect** Harris and I earned 306 electoral votes," Biden [11]**remarked**, noting that has won by the same [12]**margin** as Donald Trump in 2016. "Trump called that a [13]**landslide**."

拜登說：「在這場爭取美國靈魂的戰役中，民主戰勝了。我們人民投了票。我們守住了對制度的信任。我們保全了選舉的公正性。所以現在該翻頁、該團結、該治癒。我和副總統當選人賀錦麗共同贏得 306 張選舉人票。」拜登並指出這與川普在 2016 年的勝選差距一樣。「川普當時稱那是大獲全勝。」

Following **Trump's unsuccessful legal campaign** to challenge the election results in state and federal court, the Electoral College vote went [14]**relatively** smoothly. **Electors** from all 50 states and the **District of Columbia *cast** their [15]**ballots**, ending with Hawaii casting the final votes at 7 p.m. **ET** to award Biden and his **running mate**, Kamala Harris, a total of 306 votes. Trump ended the day with a total of 232 votes.

川普在州立和聯邦法院訴諸司法戰，挑戰選舉結果不成功後，選舉人團的投票過程則相對順利。來自所有 50 州和華盛頓特區的選舉人皆完成投票，夏威夷州在美國東部時間晚上七點投下最後票數後，投票就此結束，確認拜登和其競選搭檔賀錦麗共獲得 306 票，川普最後共獲得 232 票。

Under a complex system dating back to the 1700s, a [16]**candidate** becomes U.S. president not by winning the **popular vote**, but through the Electoral College, which [17]**allots** votes to the 50 states and Washington D.C. based largely on population. Electoral votes are cast by paper ballots in **state capitols** and Washington by individual electors, typically elected officials, [18]**prominent** politicians or party officials.

此複雜的選舉體制可追溯到 1700 年代，總統候選人不是透過贏得普選成為美國總統，而是透過選舉人團按人口將票分配給 50 州和華盛頓特區。選舉人票是由選舉人個別在州議會大廈和華府以紙本選票的形式投出，選舉人通常是由民選官員、知名政治人物或政黨官員擔任。

Nuno21©Shutterstock

Kamala Harris 賀錦麗成為美國首位亞非裔女副總統當選人。

7. **fraud** [frɔd] (n.)
   欺騙，詐欺，騙局

8. **prevail** [prɪˋvel] (v.)
   獲勝，戰勝

9. **integrity** [ɪnˋtɛgrəti] (n.)
   正直，誠實；完整性

10. **intact** [ɪnˋtækt] (a.) 完整無損的

11. **remark** [rɪˋmɑrk] (v./n.)
    談到，談論；言辭，評論

12. **margin** [ˋmɑrdʒɪn] (n.)
    幅度，差距

13. **landslide** [ˋlænd͵slaɪd] (n.)
    （選舉）大勝；土石流

14. **relatively** [ˋrɛlətɪvli] (adv.)
    相對地，相較而言

15. **ballot** [ˋbælət] (n.)
    選票，候選人名單

16. **candidate** [ˋkændɪ͵det] (n.)
    候選人；求職應試者

17. **allot** [əˋlɑt] (v.) 分配

18. **prominent** [ˋprɑmənənt] (a.)
    卓越的，著名的

19. **vast** [væst] *(a.)* 龐大的，遼闊的

進階字彙

* **formality** [fɔˋmælətɪ] *(n.)*
  例行公事

* **subvert** [səbˋvɝt] *(v.)* 顛覆，推翻

* **allegation** [͵ælɪˋgeʃən] *(n.)*
  （無證據的）指控，動詞 **allege**
  [əˋlɛdʒ]

* **irregularity** [͵ɪrɛgjəˋlærətɪ] *(n.)*
  違規，舞弊

* **cast** [kæst] *(v.)*
  投票，動詞變化三態同型

Nicole Glass Photography©Shutterstock

美國人民高舉「拜登 2020」，慶祝拜登當選總統。

While there are sometimes **faithless electors** who vote for a candidate other than the winner of their state's popular vote, the [20]**vast** majority **rubber-stamp** the results. While there were seven faithless electors in 2016 (five went against Hillary Clinton, two against Trump), there were none this time around.

儘管有時會有失信選舉人投票給不是由該州普選選出的候選人，但絕大多數都照按普選結果投出選舉人票。雖然 2016 年有七名失信選舉人（五人投票反對希拉蕊，兩人反對川普），但這次並沒有出現失信選舉人。

Grammar Master

despite 用法

despite「儘管，雖然」是表達「轉折」的語氣詞，為介系詞，後面接名詞或動名詞。因此開頭句「..., **despite** Donald Trump refusing to accept defeat and concede the race.」的動詞 refuse 要改為動名詞形式。與 **in spite of** 同義：

● **despite + N/Ving = in spite of + N/Ving = regardless of N/Ving**

例：Despite the bad weather, we had fun on our vacation.
  =In spite of the bad weather, we had fun on our vacation.
  儘管天候不佳，我們還是開心度過了假期。

● 要表達轉折語氣，但需接「子句」時，可用 **although/though/while+ S+V**

例：Although the weather was bad, we still had fun on our trip.
  儘管天候不佳，我們還是開心度過了假期。

找找看，本新聞中哪裡也出現了接完整句子的轉折詞呢？

1. Electoral College & popular vote （美國）選舉人團與普選

美國大選制度為間接選舉，第一階段是普選（popular vote），也就是全民投票，等普選民意出來之後，再由代表各州民意的「選舉人」**elector** 所組成的「選舉人團」Electoral College 進行最後投票，**electoral vote** 即「選舉人票」，一位選舉人有一票，一共有 538 票，贏得半數選舉人票（270 票）就能當選。

2. inauguration 就職

inauguration [ɪnˌɔgjə`reʃən] 為名詞，指「就職」或「就職典禮」，動詞是 inaugurate [ɪn`ɔgjəˌret]，大寫 **Inauguration Day** 即「美國總統就職日」。

3. President-elect & vice-president-elect 總統與副總統當選人

也就是確定當選但尚未就職的總統與副總統，**elect** 在這裡當形容詞，指「等待上任的」。美國總統選舉在 11 月底舉行，隔年 1 月才舉行總統就職典禮。這兩個字常見於宣布勝選者的新聞中，在選舉當晚確認當選後就會開始使用。

4. Trump's unsuccessful legal campaign 川普訴諸司法選戰

2020 年美國大選開票之後，川普陣營見選情不妙，開始在拜登微幅領先的幾個州如密西根州、賓州、喬治亞州、德州等提出法律異議，質疑通訊選票與開票過程的真實性，試圖延後宣布大選結果，不過皆被該州法院或最高法院駁回。

NumenaStudios©Shutterstock

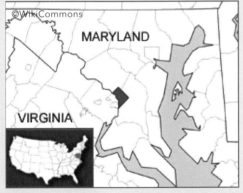
©WikiCommons

▲ 位於美國東岸 Maryland 馬里蘭州與 Virgina 維吉尼亞州交界，Potomac River 波多馬克河由西北向東南流貫此特區。

5. District of Columbia 華盛頓哥倫比亞特區

簡稱 Washington, D.C. 或 D.C.，有時翻成「華府」，是美國首都。此特區建於 1791 年，為了紀念美國開國元勳 George Washington 而命名之。包含 White House 白宮等多數聯邦政府機關都位在此處，Lincoln Memorial 等美國歷史建築也坐落於此。

©WikiCommons

▶ 林肯紀念堂 (Lincoln Memorial)。美國前總統林肯 (Abraham Lincoln) 於 1865 年遇刺，兩年後國會通過法案，於華盛頓特區國家廣場西側設立的紀念堂。紀念堂中央豎立林肯大理石坐像，高 5.8 公尺。林肯執政期間，美國經歷南北戰爭，廢除奴隸制，也維護聯邦完整性，因此視為美國歷史上最偉大的總統之一。

6. ET 美國東部時間

為 Eastern Time 的簡稱，可指東部標準時間 Eastern Standard Time（EST）與東部夏令時間 Eastern Daylight Time（EDT），應用於北美東海岸與南美西海岸，比世界協調時間（Coordinated Universal Time，簡稱 UTC）晚五小時（標示為 UTC-5），實施夏令時間（Daylight Saving Time）時則為 UTC-4。美國境內統一用 ET 稱之，如此無論冬夏都不用改變。台灣時間比世界協調時間快八小時（UTC+8），換言之，台灣時間比美國東岸快 13 小時。

7. running mate 副手

在美國，政治副手就稱 running mate，文中指美國副總統當選人 Kamala Harris 賀錦麗。

8. state capitols 州議會大廈

capitol [ˋkæpətəl] 指美國各州的州議會大廈，大寫 **Capitol** 則專指位於華盛頓特區的美國國會大廈。

▶ 位於華府的美國國會大廈。

9. faithless elector 失信選舉人

若該州選舉人所投出的票與該州選民投出的總統人選有衝突，就稱 faithless elector「失信選舉人」。

10. rubber-stamp 橡皮圖章

rubber stamp 本指橡皮圖章，公文常需要用到上司簽名，為方便行事，便刻成橡皮圖章給下級行政人員使用。延伸在政治中，就是比喻那些名義上握有很大權力，但其實只是拿橡皮圖章蓋下「准」印的人物或機構，在本新聞就是指 elector 選舉人看似可以決定美國總統人選，但實際上他們只是代替民意投票而已。

Grammar Master 解答：本新聞中出現能接完整句的轉折詞共有兩句，都出現在最後一段：

最後一段第一行：**While** there are sometimes faithless electors who vote for a candidate other than the winner of their state's popular vote, the vast majority rubber-stamp the results.

最後一段第三行：**While** there were seven faithless electors in 2016 (five went against Hillary Clinton, two against Trump), there were none this time around.

#International #Asia
#Thailand
#pro-democracy

kan Sangtong©Shutterstock

數千名支持民主（pro-democracy）的泰國示威民眾，呼籲軍政府改善多項社會問題。

全文朗讀 ♫ 021　　單字 ♫ 022

Thai Protesters March on Royal Guard Barracks
泰國人民上街示威，挑戰君主制與軍政府

🕐 **November 29, 2020**

Thousands of protesters marched to a Thai royal guard *barracks in Bangkok on Sunday, demanding that **King Maha Vajiralongkorn** give up control of two army *regiments that were placed under his command last year. The protest came after days of [1]**rallies** in the Thai capital, where a student-led [2]**pro-democracy** movement that began in July has placed increasing pressure on the country's government and *monarchy.

曼谷成千上萬示威群眾於週日遊行至泰國皇家衛隊兵營，要求國王瑪哈瓦吉拉隆功放棄掌控去年起由他統率的兩個軍團。示威活動進行前，泰國首都已經舉行了好幾天的抗議集會，由學生主導的民主運動自七月便開始，對該國政府和君主制度施加越來越大的壓力。

In the early days of the protests, [3]**demonstrators** called for the [4]**drafting** of a new constitution and the removal of **Prime Minister Prayuth Chan-ocha**, a former army general who came to power in a 2014 *coup. In recent months, however, they've shifted their focus to the monarchy, demanding that King Vajiralongkorn give

Vocabulary

1. **rally** [ˋræli] (n.)（政治）集會

2. **pro-democracy**
[ˋprodɪˋmækrəsi] (a.)
支持民主的，泛民主的，字首
pro- 表「贊成」

3. **demonstrator**
[ˋdɛmənˏstretə] (n.) 示威者，
名詞 **demonstration**
[ˏdɛmənˋstreʃən] 抗議，示威，動
詞 **demonstrate**

4. **draft** [dræft] (v.) 起草，草擬

up some of his vast power and wealth. In response, **royalists** in **yellow shirts** have marched to show their support for the king.

抗議活動初期，示威群眾呼籲起草新憲法，並要求總理帕拉育占奧差下臺，這位前將軍是在 2014 年政變時上台。然而近幾個月示威者將重心轉移到君主制上，要求泰王瓦吉拉隆功放棄自己的部分大權和財富。為回應此訴求，保皇黨穿著黃衫遊行，以表示對泰王的支持。

On Sunday evening, protesters marched to the headquarters of the 11th *__Infantry__ Regiment, one of the two army units brought under the king's control in October 2019. The entrance to the barracks was 5)**blockaded** with buses, which were quickly removed by protesters, as well as *__razor wire__. Some wore gas masks for protection, while others carried *__inflatable__ yellow ducks, which have become a symbol of the movement since demonstrators used them to 6)**shield** themselves from *__water cannons__ at a November 7 protest.

週日晚上，示威群眾遊行至第 11 步兵團總部，該步兵團是泰王自 2019 年 10 月掌控的兩個部隊之一。兵營的入口被公車和鐵絲網封鎖，示威群眾很快將公車移走。有些人戴著防毒面具以自保，另有一些人則舉著充氣的黃色小鴨。示威者自從在 11 月 7 日的示威活動中用黃色小鴨保護自己以免受水砲車攻擊後，黃色小鴨就成為抗議運動的象徵。

In a statement, protesters called the king's direct control of the two regiments a threat to democracy, and demanded that they be placed back under Thai Army command. Copies of the statement were folded into paper airplanes and thrown at **riot** police who 7)**stood guard** at the entrance. Protesters later splashed red paint on the ground, a 8)**reference** to the deadly army **crackdown** on 9)**anti-government red shirt** demonstrators in 2010.

示威群眾在聲明中聲稱，泰王直接掌控這兩個軍團是對民主構成威脅，並要求將軍團交回由泰國陸軍指揮。示威群眾將聲明稿折成紙飛機，並扔向在入口處站崗的鎮暴警察。示威群眾隨後在地上潑灑紅色油漆，象徵 2010 年軍隊血腥鎮壓反政府的紅衫軍示威群眾。

The government has responded to the recent protests by applying Thailand's 10)**harsh lèse-majesté** law, which makes 11)**Insulting** the

黃色小鴨已經成為這次泰國抗議行動的象徵，示威者頭頂黃色塑膠小鴨，抵擋高壓水砲。

Suptar©Shutterstock

kan Sangtong©Shutterstock

示威者冒雨抗議泰王揮霍他們的納稅錢，高舉「It's our tax」。

* **barracks** [ˋbærəks] (n.)
（恆用複數）兵營

* **regiment** [ˋrɛdʒəmənt] (n.) 軍團

* **monarchy** [ˋmɑnəkɪ] (n.)
君主政體

* **coup** [ku] (n.)（軍事）政變

* **infantry** [ˋɪnfəntrɪ] (n.)
步兵（部隊），步兵團

* **razor wire** (phr.)
（用來防止外人闖入的）尖利鐵
絲網

* **inflatable** [ɪnˋfletəbəl] (a.)
可充氣的

* **water cannon** (phr.)
（用來驅散人群的）高壓水柱

* **subject** [ˋsʌbdʒɛkt] (n.)
（君主國）臣民

king punishable by up to 15 years in prison. Vajiralongkorn, who [12]**succeeded** his father, **King Bhumibol Adulyadej**, in 2016, has also come under criticism for taking control of royal funds worth billions of dollars and spending most of his time in Germany while his ***subjects** are suffering under the coronavirus.

泰國政府對最近的示威活動採取了嚴厲的冒犯君主法，按此法，侮辱泰王最高可判處 15 年徒刑。瓦吉拉隆功於 2016 年繼承父親蒲美蓬阿杜德的王位，因掌控數十億元的王室資金，並在他的臣民受到新冠疫情所苦的期間大多待在德國而飽受批評。

Grammar Master

介系詞 to 當所有格表示

英文裡有一類名詞的所有格，既不是加 of，也不是加 's，而是以介系詞 to 來表示，如文中的 an entrance to「⋯的入口」，以下是更多例子：

1. the key to the door 這扇門的鑰匙
2. the secretary to the managing director 總經理的秘書
3. the right to the throne 王位的繼承權
4. a solution to a problem 解決之道
5. an approach to solving cases 破案的方法
6. access to the information 獲取資訊的管道

介系詞 to 所連接的兩個名詞之間有「屬於」的意義在裡面（如例子 1、2）。以 to 連接的兩個名詞也可以表示「與⋯有關」（如例子 3~5）。介系詞 to 後面如果接動詞時，應改為動名詞 Ving 的形式，如例子 5 就要寫 solving。

1. King Maha Vajiralongkorn & King Bhumibol Adulyadej 泰王瓦吉拉隆功與蒲美蓬大帝

2006 年政變後，泰王權力一直擴張，除了是國家元首，也是皇家部隊最高總司令，為目前君主立憲國家中權力最大的君主。蒲美蓬大帝 King Bhumibol Adulyadej 是在位時間最久的泰王，頗得民心，其資產據富比士在 2000 年所做的調查約為 300 億美元，為世界皇族第一。蒲美蓬於 2016 年駕崩，傳位給唯一兒子，也就是目前泰王瓦吉拉隆功 King Maha Vajiralongkorn。然瓦吉拉隆功長期居住德國，經常遙控治國，愛好女色，生活奢侈無度，引發民怨。

▲ 右為現任泰王 King Maha Vajiralongkorn，左為其父 King Bhumibol Adulyadej。此圖為泰銖上的肖像。

feelphoto©Shutterstock

▲ 現任泰國總理 Prayuth Chan-ocha 帕拉育。

2. Prime Minister Prayuth Chan-ocha 泰國總理帕拉育

2014 年，時任泰國陸軍總司令的 Prayuth Chan-ocha 帕拉育發動政變（coup），推翻當時以紅衫軍為主的政府，當上臨時總理，廢除泰國憲法，改由「國家和平秩序委員會」成為最高統治機構，並實施戒嚴、限制言論與集會。軍政府執政五年期間，他改組國會席次，修改新憲法，拖延大選數次，確保軍方在國會地位之後，推遲至 2019 年 3 月 24 日才舉行全國大選，選出 500 名眾議員與新任總理，結果親軍的公民力量黨取得 117 席，紅衫軍為泰黨取得 135 席，新興政黨取得 80 席。但由於國會有 250 軍方保留席，因此帕拉育仍當選為泰國總理。帕拉育也是堅定的保皇黨，就任期間擴張王室權力。

3. yellow shirts, red shirts 泰國黃衫軍與紅衫軍

泰國紅衫軍跟黃衫軍是支持與反對前總理塔克辛（Thaksin Shinawatra）的兩股勢力，「反獨裁民主聯盟 United Front for Democracy Against Dictatorship，簡稱 UDD」支持塔克辛，受到泰國北部與東北部農民支持。「人民民主聯盟 People's Alliance for Democracy，簡稱 PAD」反對塔克辛，由傳統政商菁英為主，反對「票票等值」的選舉制度，提出政權回歸王室，常身穿象徵王室的黃色抗議，稱黃衫軍。塔克辛原是電信大亨，1997 年金融風暴後成立泰愛泰黨成為黨主席，上任後實施公共醫療計畫，在農村發放發展基金，實施農民貸款前三年免息，鞏固佔多票數的農民票倉，同時限制媒體言論，利用職務將自家集團擴張成泰國最大電信集團，媒體大亨頌提（Sondhi Limthongkul）因此組成人民民主聯盟，成為反塔克辛勢力的主要領袖。2006 年反對塔克辛勢力越來越多，泰國軍方發動政變。軍政府統治期間，支持塔克辛的勢力成立反獨裁民主聯盟，抗議軍政府，抗議時他們多穿紅色，稱紅衫軍。

▲ 2005 年時任泰國總理的 Thaksin Shinawatra 塔克辛。

4. royalist 保皇黨

指擁護王室的人，泰國史上多數軍政府都是擁護泰國王室的人，現任總理帕拉育與泰國黃衫軍就是知名保皇黨，任職期間數次擴大泰王權力。

▶ 泰國黃衫軍代表保皇黨派，身穿象徵王室的黃色，手上拿著裱框的泰王照片表示隊王室的支持。

5. riot & crackdown 暴動與鎮壓

常見於新聞英文中，**riot** [ˋraɪət] 指涉及暴力的「暴動」。而 **unrest** 與 **turmoil** 則是敘述「局勢上的不安混亂」。針對暴動的「鎮壓」行為，就用 **crackdown** 表示。

◀ 泰國紅衫軍參加在泰國曼谷舉行的大型集會，紀念對反政府抗議進行血腥鎮壓（crackdown）三週年。

6. lèse-majesté 冒犯君主罪

Lèse-majesté 是法文字，指「對國王做了不敬的事情」（to do wrong to majesty），也稱「不敬罪」，在中國古代對帝王不敬會判死罪，在現代社會中，多數國家已廢除此罪，目前只剩下泰國仍有此罪行。

泰國採君主立憲，泰王在人民心目中地位崇高，不能輕易批評泰王或王室。泰國自 1908 年立《冒犯君主罪》一法，凡毀謗、侮辱或威脅王室成員（包含已故王室），最高可判 15 年囚禁，甚至有重判 35 年的例子，也有人因為批評王室養的寵物狗而入獄。

▶ 今日仍有許多泰國人民將已故泰王 Bhumibol Adulyadej 當做神一般的地位敬拜。

Entertainment 娛樂

The Unofficial Biography

#K-pop #South Korea
#Pop Star Power Rankings
#YG Entertainment #Blackpink
#BTS

Zety Akhzar©Shutterstock

YG 旗下女團 Blackpink 2020 年聲勢大漲，左起分別是 Jennie、Rosé、Lisa、Jisoo。

全文朗讀 ♪ 023 單字 ♪ 024

K-Pop Act Is World's Biggest Band
韓流藝人團體成為世上最成功的樂團

🕐 **November 17, 2020**

Who do you think the world's biggest pop ***act** is? If you were to guess Taylor Swift, Justin Bieber or Billie Eilish, you'd be wrong. According to the latest [1]**ranking** by **Bloomberg**, **K-pop girl group** Blackpink are the biggest pop band in the world.

你覺得世上最成功的流行音樂藝人是誰？如果你猜是泰勒絲、小賈斯汀或怪奇比莉，那你就猜錯了。根據彭博社最新排行榜，韓流女子團體 Blackpink 是世上最成功的流行樂團。

This is the first time a South Korean act has topped the news [2]**agency**'s **Pop Star Power Rankings** since the ***chart** ℗**kicked off** in April this year. A fellow K-pop group, the seven-member **boy band** BTS, [1]**ranked** No. 10 on the November Power Rankings chart.

這是該通訊社自今年四月設立流行之星影響力排行榜以來，南韓藝人首次登上榜首。同樣也是韓國流行團體，由七名男孩組成的防彈少年團，則在 11 月的流行之星影響力排行榜上排名第十。

Vocabulary

1. **ranking** [ˋræŋkɪŋ] (n.)
   排名，動詞 **rank**「將⋯分級，排名」

2. **agency** [ˋedʒənsɪ] (n.)
   代理公司，**news agency**「新聞社，通訊社」

南韓團體 BTS 防彈少年團於 2019 年獲頒第 26 屆 Billboard Music Award 的最佳團體獎與最佳社群媒體藝人。

Who else ℗ **made the cut**? American *rappers Pop Smoke—³⁾**tragically** killed in a home ⁴⁾**invasion**, his ⁵⁾**debut** album was released **posthumously** in July—and Cardi B filled the second and third ⁶⁾**slots** ⁷⁾**respectively**. Canadian superstar Justin Bieber and *late American rapper Juice WRLD—who died of a drug *overdose in December 2019—⁸⁾**rounded out** the top five.

還有誰登上排行榜？美國饒舌歌手波普斯莫克和卡蒂 B 分別排名第二和第三，前者在一場入室搶劫事件中慘遭殺害，他的首張專輯是在他過世後的七月發行。加拿大超級巨星小賈斯汀和已故的美國饒舌歌手朱斯沃爾德也進入前五名，後者於 2019 年 12 月因吸毒過量而過世。

3. **tragically** [ˋtrædʒɪklɪ] (adv.)
   悲慘地，不幸地

4. **invasion** [ɪnˋveʒən] (n.)
   入侵，侵略，動詞 **invade**

5. **debut** [deˋbju / ˋdebju] (n./v.)
   首度演出，初次登台

6. **slot** [slɑt] (n.)（名單中所佔的）
   位置，投幣孔，插槽

7. **respectively** [rɪˋspɛktɪvlɪ]
   (adv.) 分別地，個別地

8. **round out** (phr.)
   完成，常用在榜單，指「進入前⋯名」

9. **calculate** [ˋkælkjəˌlet] (v.) 計算

10. **criterion** [kraɪˋtɪrɪən] (n.)
    標準，準則，複數 **criteria**
    [kraɪˋtɪrɪə]

11. **stream** [strim] (n./v.)
    串流，直播

12. **groom** [grum] (v.)
    （為了特定目標）培養，訓練

13. **comprise (of)** [kəmˋpraɪz] (v.)
    由⋯組成，包含

Unlike traditional music charts like the **Billboard Hot 100**, which is ⁹⁾**calculated** by record sales and radio *airplay, Bloomberg's Pop Star Power Rankings are based on a combination of six ¹⁰⁾**criteria**. These include album sales, concert ticket sales, digital song ¹¹⁾**streams**, YouTube views and interactions on **Instagram**.

告示牌百大單曲榜等傳統音樂排行榜是由唱片銷售量和廣播播放量計算得出，而彭博社的流行之星影響力排行榜則是基於六項標準的整合統計，其中包括專輯銷售、演唱會門票銷售、數位歌曲串流量、YouTube 點閱率和在 Instagram 上的互動量。

Formed by **YG Entertainment**—the South Korean entertainment company responsible for ¹²⁾**grooming** K-pop acts like **Big Bang** and **PSY**—Blackpink is ¹³⁾**comprised** of Jisoo, 25, Jennie, 24, Rosé and Lisa, both 23. Unlike most K-pop acts, Blackpink is a relatively ¹⁴⁾**diverse** group. Rosé was raised in Australia, Jennie was raised in New Zealand and Korea, Lisa grew up in Thailand, and Jisoo is a Seoul native. Among them, the *charismatic *quartet can speak Korean, English, Mandarin, Thai and Japanese.

Blackpink 是由南韓娛樂公司 YG 娛樂培養出道，該公司也培養了 Big Bang 和江南大叔 PSY 等韓流藝人。Blackpink 是由 25 歲的金智秀、24 歲的金珍妮、23 歲的朴彩英和麗莎組成，與大多數韓團不同，Blackpink 是相對多元化的團體。朴彩英在澳洲長大，珍妮在紐西蘭和南韓長大，麗莎在泰國長大，金智秀是首爾土生土長。這具有魅力的四人團體會說韓語、英語、中文、泰語和日語。

Newsenstar1©WikiCommons

Blackpink 在 2020 年先後與 Lady Gaga、Selena Gomez 合作單曲，也與 Netflix 合作拍攝紀錄片《BLACKPINK: Light Up the Sky》，是 Spotify 上最多人關注的女團。

14. **diverse** [dɪˋvɝs] (a.)
多元的，不同，名詞 **diversity**
[dɪˋvɝsəti] 多元性，不同

15. **subscribe** [səbˋskraɪb] (v.)
訂閱

16. **generate** [ˋdʒɛnəˏret] (v.)
產生，引起

進階字彙

* **act** [ækt] (n.) 藝人，團體

* **chart** [tʃɑrt] (n./v.)
排行榜；登上排行榜

* **rapper** [ˋræpɚ] (n.)
饒舌歌手，**rap** 為「饒舌音樂」

* **posthumously** [ˋpɑstʃəməsli]
(adv.) 於死後出版地

* **late** [let] (a.) 已故的

* **overdose** [ˋovɚˏdos] (n./v.)
（藥物）過量

* **airplay** [ˋɛrˏple] (n.)
（廣播或電視上的）播放

* **charismatic** [ˏkærɪzˋmætɪk] (a.)
有魅力的，有吸引力的

* **quartet** [kwɔrˋtɛt] (n.)
四重奏，四人合唱團

* **drop** [drɑp] (v.)
（新曲、專輯）推出

Blackpink has been the most ¹⁵⁾**subscribed** musical act on YouTube for several months now, ¹⁶⁾**generating** over a billion views in October alone. The group is also the most popular female act on **Spotify**, and their latest album, The Album, which ***dropped** on October 2, debuted at No. 2 on the **Billboard 200**. Elsewhere, The Album reached No. 1 in New Zealand, Mexico and South Korea. With all these achievements, it's easy to see why Blackpink is the world's biggest pop act.

這幾個月來，Blackpink 一直是 YouTube 上最多人訂閱的音樂藝人，單單在十月就有超過十億的點閱率。該團體也是 Spotify 上最受歡迎的女藝人，她們的最新專輯〈專輯〉於 10 月 2 日問世，首次登上告示牌二百大專輯榜就名列第二。〈專輯〉在其他地方如紐西蘭、墨西哥和南韓排名第一。有這些成就，就不難理解為什麼 Blackpink 是世上最成功的流行音樂藝人。

Grammar Master

強調「不太可能實現」的假設語氣

本句 If you **were to** guess Taylor Swift, Justin Bieber or Billie Eilish, you**'d be** wrong. 用到了假設語氣，這裡的假設語氣是為了強調該假設「與事實或真理截然不同」，或是「該事發生可能性極低」。

● 句型：**If S + were to + VR, S + would/could/might/should + VR.**

例：If I were to reborn, I would want to be a boy. 如果我能重新投胎，我會想當男生。[真理是，人無法重新投胎。]

1. Bloomberg Pop Star Power Rankings 彭博社流行之星音樂榜

彭博有限合夥企業 Bloomberg L.P.（L.P. 為 limited partnership 縮寫）為美國大眾傳播媒體企業，跨足各種產業類型，包括財經、新聞、體育、廣播、電視等，**Pop Star Power Rankings**「流行之星影響力排行榜」則是旗下的音樂排行榜，於 2020 年 4 月開設，每月選出全球最受歡迎的前 25 名流行藝人團體，入圍標準參考演唱會門票銷售、演唱會獲益、實體與數位專輯銷量，社群媒體 Instagram 互動量與 YouTube 觀看次數。

2. K-pop 韓國流行音樂

K 即 Korean 縮寫，K-pop 專指南韓特有的流行音樂文化，特色是唱跳俱佳的 **boy band** 男團與女團 **girl group**，其舞蹈類型、穿著風格等往往帶起流行風潮，成為全球青少男女的流行指標。南韓經紀公司會先徵選練習生，讓他們進行團體生活同時訓練舞蹈與歌藝，從中挑出合適人選組團出道，也因為嚴格的訓練過程，南韓流行音樂在近幾年也打進海外音樂榜。南韓三大經紀公司分別是 SM Entertainment、YG Entertainment 與 JYP。SM Entertainment 是出產爆紅偶像團體的搖籃，男團元祖 H.O.T、東方神起、EXO，女團元祖 S.E.S.、BOA、少女時代、都是出自 SM。知名男團 Big Bang、PSY 便是 YG 出身。

▲ PSY 憑〈江南 style〉一曲紅遍全球，橫掃 2012 年許多音樂獎項，也讓更多海外人士認識 K-pop。

Dutchmen Photography©shutterstock

◀ 南韓團體的粉絲相當團結也很有影響力，圖片為參加 BTS 海外演唱會的 BTS Army 們。

3. Phrase kick off 開始

kick off 原本是足球賽以開踢第一球作為比賽開始，後來則借指「某事開始進行」。

A: So should we head straight to the club and go dancing?
　 我們要直接去夜店跳舞嗎？
B: I say we kick off the evening with margaritas at our favorite bar.
　 就在我們最愛的那間酒吧點杯瑪格麗特為今晚揭開序幕吧！

4. `Phrase` **make the cut** 達到標準

這個慣用語和切東西或縮減一點關係也沒有，而是指「達到標準」，如參加選秀比賽的選手必須達到某個特定分數才能晉級下一關。

A: How did the job interview go? 面試狀況如何？
B: Great! Out of ten applicants, I was the only one to make the cut.
很棒！十個求職者中，我是唯一達到標準的。

5. Billboard 美國告示牌排行榜

Billboard「美國告示牌」是娛樂雜誌起家，後來成為娛樂媒體品牌，其 **Billboard Hot 100**「告示牌百大單曲榜」和 **Billboard 200**「告示牌 200 專輯榜」分別公布最受歡迎的美國單曲與專輯，每週更新一次，榜單是由實際銷量與電台播放次數決定，可說是美國最具公信力的音樂排行榜。除了音樂排行榜之外，Billboard 每年也舉行 **Billboard Music Awards**「告示牌音樂獎」，為美國三大音樂獎項之一。

6. Instagram

社群媒體（**social media**）不斷推陳出新，目前最受年輕人歡迎的社群媒體已經不是 Facebook，而是介面更簡潔直覺、以圖片為主的 Instagram。只要上傳照片或十秒影片，就能輕鬆分享生活片段，而 Instagram 所帶起的風潮還有 hashtag。在台灣許多人會用「IG」來簡稱之，不過這個說法老外其實沒在用，老外常把 Instagram 簡稱叫做 Insta。

norazaminayob©Shutterstock

7. Spotify

2006 年成立於瑞典的音樂串流服務公司，是目前全球最大的音樂串流（streaming）品牌，提供方案分為免費及付費（premium）兩種，差別在於廣告的播放、切換歌曲的次數、離線收聽功能以及音質。費用各國不太一樣，台灣定價為每月新台幣 149 元。Spotify 專有的播放軟體使用數位版權管理（DRM，digital rights management），透過這項存取控制技術，防止音樂未經授權就被使用。

#BadGuy @billieeilish
#GRAMMYs

Ben Houdijk©shutterstock

Billie Eilish 怪奇比莉在 2019 年巡迴演唱會上熱唱。

全文朗讀 🎵 025　單字 🎵 026

Billie Eilish Sweeps the Grammys
怪奇比莉橫掃 2020 葛萊美獎

🕐 **January 26, 2020**

Vocabulary

1. **dominate** [`dɑmə,net] (v.)
   佔優勢；支配，主宰

2. **ceremony** [`sɛrə,moni] (n.)
   儀式，典禮

3. **category** [`kætɪ,gɔri] (n.)
   種類，範疇

4. **debut** [`debju / de`bju] (a./n.)
   首度演出（的）；(v.) 首度演出

5. **contemporary**
   [kən`tɛmpə,rɛri] (a.)
   當代的，同時代的

All the stars were out for the 62nd **Grammy Awards**, and none shone brighter than Billie Eilish. At only 18 years of age, Eilish ¹⁾**dominated** the ²⁾**ceremony**, taking home all four **awards** in the top ³⁾**categories**: Record of the Year, Album of the Year, Song of the Year and Best New Artist. She also won the award for Best Pop Solo Performance for her hit single "Bad Guy."

參加第 62 屆葛萊美獎頒獎典禮眾星雲集，但沒有人比怪奇比莉更亮眼。年僅 18 歲的怪奇比莉在葛萊美頒獎典禮上獨領風騷，抱回全部四大獎項：年度唱片、年度專輯、年度歌曲和最佳新人獎。她也憑藉單曲〈壞傢伙〉贏得最佳流行個人演出獎。

Eilish is the youngest artist to win all four top Grammys on the same night, and the first since Christopher Cross pulled off the *feat in 1981. She recorded her ⁴⁾**debut** album, When We Fall Asleep, Where Do We Go?, with her older brother **Finneas** in a bedroom studio in their parents' Los Angeles home. The ^**siblings** have developed a unique, ⁵⁾**contemporary** sound with ⁶⁾**minimal** electronic production. Eilish and Finneas, who also picked up Producer of the Year for his [7]**contributions**, were humble and gracious in their victory. The pair expressed surprise that they'd won anything, [8]**let alone** the most [9]**prestigious** awards. Finneas remarked that the lyrics on their album, which deal with [10]**gloomy** themes like **depression** and climate change, are usually not the type to find [11]**mainstream** success.

怪奇比莉是史上在同一屆同時抱回四大葛萊美獎的最年輕藝人，也是克里斯托夫克羅斯於 1981 年獨攬四大獎之後的首位藝人。她跟哥哥菲尼亞斯在洛杉磯父母家中的一間臥室錄製了她的出道專輯〈當我們睡了怪事發生了〉。兩兄妹用最少的電子設備錄製出獨特的現代音樂，菲尼亞斯也以此貢獻獲得年度製作人獎，怪奇比莉和菲尼亞斯懷著謙恭之心面對這次成就。兩人表示，不管獲得什麼獎項都令他們驚訝，更不用說是最負盛名的獎項。菲尼亞斯表示，專輯中的歌詞涉及憂鬱症和氣候變遷等令人沮喪的主題，通常不是能成功打入主流的類型。

Eilish has quickly Ⓟ**established herself as** both a singer-songwriter and a fashion icon. Her [12]**eccentric** look [13]**complements** her [14]**melancholy** music. Unlike most young female pop stars, who like to [15]**play up** their **sex appeal**, Eilish likes to wear loose, baggy clothes. She looked stylish at the Grammys in a black and green outfit that matched her black and green hair.

怪奇比莉很快建立起創作歌手和時尚偶像的地位。她古怪的外表與憂鬱曲風相得益彰。與多數喜歡凸顯性感外表的年輕女流行歌手不同，她喜歡穿寬鬆下垂的衣服。她在葛萊美獎典禮上穿著黑色和綠色衣服，搭配她的黑色和綠色頭髮，看起來很時髦。

6. **minimal** [ˋmɪnəməl] (a.)
最小的，最少的，相反詞
maximal「最大的」

7. **contribution** [ˌkɑntrəˋbjuʃən] (n.) 貢獻

8. **let alone** (phr.) 更不用說

9. **prestigious** [prɛsˋtɪdʒəs] (a.) 有名望的，負盛名的

10. **gloomy** [ˋglumɪ] (a.) 陰鬱的，陰沈的

11. **mainstream** [ˋmenˌstrim] (n./a.) 主流（的）

12. **eccentric** [ɪkˋsɛntrɪk] (a.) 古怪的，奇特的

13. **complement** [ˋkɑmpləmənt] (v.) 補足

14. **melancholy** [ˋmɛlənˌkælɪ] (n./a.) 憂鬱，鬱悶

15. **play up** (phr.) 強調，凸顯

Billie Eilish 與哥哥 Finneas 在 Corona Capital Fes 2019 的演出。

16. **tribute (to)** [ˋtrɪbjut] (n.)
（對～的）稱頌，表達敬意的
言辭或事物

17. **literally** [ˋlɪtərəli] (adv.)
確實地，簡直

進階字彙

* **feat** [fit] (n.) 功績，成就

* **sibling** [ˋsɪblɪŋ] (n.)
手足，簡稱 **sib**

* **diva** [ˋdivə] (n.)
女伶，一線女歌手

Staples Center 是洛杉磯湖人隊的主場，右側的大看板紀念 Kobe 這 20 年來替湖人隊打下一片江山。

The award ceremony, which took place at **L.A.'s Staples Center**, included performances by hip pop singer Lizzo, gay rapper Lil Nas X and pop ***divas** like Ariana Grande and Demi Lovato. There was also a special [16]**tribute** to basketball star Kobe Bryant, who died in a helicopter crash that same day. "We are [17]**literally** standing here heartbroken in the house that Kobe Bryant built," said Grammys host Alicia Keys. "We never imagined in a million years we'd have to start the show like this."

頒獎典禮在洛杉磯的史坦波中心舉行，表演嘉賓包括嘻哈歌手莉佐、同性戀饒舌歌手利爾納斯 X、流行天后莉亞安娜和黛咪洛瓦特等。典禮也特別向籃球明星柯比布萊恩致敬，他在那一天因墜機身亡。典禮主持人艾莉西亞凱斯表示：「我們傷心欲絕地站在柯比布萊恩所建立的球場，我們萬萬沒想到會以這樣的方式開場。」

Grammar Master

pull off

● 「辦到，完成困難的事情」，為非正式用法，即文章中的用法，也可說 pull it off：
例：We pulled off the deal. 我們終於談成交易。

● 「路邊停車」：
例：The man pulled off the road to make a phone call. 男子在路邊停車打電話。

● 「（車子）發動」：
例：The car pulled off and sped up the road. 車子發動後加速行駛在路上。

● 「脫下」，等同 take off：
例：I pulled off my sweater when the sun came out. 太陽出來後我把毛衣脫掉。

News Word 📖

1. Grammy Awards 葛萊美音樂獎

原名為 Gramophone [ˋgræməˌfon]（留聲機）Awards，或稱 Grammys，始於 1958 年，在音樂界的地位等同於電影界的奧斯卡金像獎。葛萊美獎由 Recording Academy 國家錄音藝術科學學院主辦，每年二月頒發，為美國音樂界最重要的獎項之一，和 Billboard Music Awards 告示牌音樂獎、American Music Awards 全美音樂獎並列「三大（獎）the Big Three」。

▲ Billie Eilish 與哥哥 Finneas 成為 2020 年第 62 屆葛萊美獎最大贏家。

「**Billboard Music Awards 告示牌音樂獎**」是由《Billboard 告示牌》雜誌贊助，每年十二月頒發。頒發對象為每種音樂類型的最佳專輯、藝人與單曲。

「**American Music Awards 全美音樂獎**」與葛萊美獎不同，是由歌迷票選決定得獎者，而且全美音樂獎並沒有設置最佳單曲與最佳唱片的獎項。

2. 各種「獎項」說法：award, prize, reward

award 當動詞指「頒贈，授與」，如 award a prize/medal/honor，當名詞，指「獎項，獎品，獎金」，如本文的 Grammy Award 葛萊美獎、The Academy Awards for Best Picture 奧斯卡最佳影片獎。當「獎項」時，prize 基本上意思等同 award，如 the Nobel Prize 諾貝爾獎，可與以下動詞連用：**give/present/hand out/bestow an award/a prize**。而 reward 當名詞則是指「酬勞，報酬，獎勵」。

3. Finneas O'Connell

怪奇比莉自小就受到音樂薰陶長大，母親 Maggie Baird 跟哥哥 Finneas 寫歌，爸爸彈奏鋼琴跟烏克麗麗，從小便參加兒童合唱團，精進歌唱技巧。怪奇比莉每次接受訪問必定會提到哥哥 Finneas，哥哥一直在她的音樂中擔任類似音樂監製的角色，可以說沒有 Finneas，就沒有今天的怪奇比莉。而怪奇比莉之所以爆紅，也是因為哥哥將本來做給自己樂團的歌〈Ocean Eyes〉給了妹妹唱，因為他認為妹妹的歌聲最適合這首歌，結果這首歌曲丟上 SoundCloud 之後一夕爆紅，因而促成兩兄妹簽進環球唱片旗下。

4. depression 憂鬱

指「憂鬱、沮喪」，在醫學上可以指「憂鬱症」。形容詞為 **depressed**，當有人說 I'm so depressed. 不是說他有憂鬱症，而是在表達他「好鬱卒」。

5. Phrase establish (oneself/sb./sth.) as sth. 確立（自己或某人物）作為…的地位

如果說一個人 establish oneself，表示他們因為擁有好品質、或成功完成成就，因此建立聲譽、達成成就。

例 **Mario's has established itself as one of the best Italian restaurants in the city.**
馬力歐連鎖餐廳是城裡最有名的義大利餐廳。

6. sex appeal 性感，性吸引力

即 sexual attractiveness，指對異性或同性散發性方面的魅力。

#South Korea
#Oscars #Feature Film
#Best Director #Best Picture
#Golden Globe

Kinocine PARKJEAHWAN4wiki©WikiCommons

《寄生上流》導演奉俊昊（左一）與全體演員現身於南韓首映會上。

全文朗讀 ♪ 027　　單字 ♪ 028

South Korea's *Parasite* Sweeps the Oscars
南韓電影《寄生上流》橫掃奧斯卡金像獎

🕐 **December 14, 2020**

Vocabulary

1. **stunning** [ˈstʌnɪŋ] (a.)
   令人震驚的，（精采或美到）
   令人屏息的

2. **shrewd** [ʃrud] (a.) 精明聰穎的

3. **spectrum** [ˈspɛktrəm] (n.)
   （物理）光譜，幅度，範圍

4. **collide** [kəˈlaɪd] (v.)
   （移動的物體）相撞

5. **formidable** [ˈfɔrmɪdəbəl] (a.)
   令人敬畏的，難以對付的

6. **opponent** [əˈponənt] (n.)
   對手，反對者

In a ¹⁾**stunning *upset**, the black comedy *Parasite* from South Korean director Bong Joon-ho won Best Picture at the 2020 Academy Awards, becoming the first non-English language film to capture the top prize in the ceremony's 91-year history. *Parasite* had a big night on "the biggest night in Hollywood," taking home a total of four awards, including Best Director, Best International Feature Film, and Best Original Screenplay, a prize that recognized the film's ²⁾**shrewd** script, which tells the tragicomic story of two families at opposite ends of the *socioeconomic ³⁾**spectrum** whose lives ⁴⁾**collide**.

南韓導演奉俊昊的黑色幽默電影《寄生上流》大爆冷門，在 2020 年奧斯卡金像獎頒獎典禮上獲得最佳影片獎，成為奧斯卡獎 91 年來史上首部奪得最高獎項的非英語電影。《寄生上流》在「好萊塢最輝煌的一夜」中度過盛夜，共抱回四大獎項，包括最佳導演獎、最佳國際長片獎、最佳原創劇本獎，這是肯定電影劇本優異的獎項，本劇是悲喜劇，講述各處於社會經濟光譜兩端兩個家庭的人生衝突。

Bong faced [5]**formidable** [6]**opponents** in all categories for which *Parasite* was nominated, but particularly in the Best Director race. Of the four other nominees—Sam Mendes for **war epic** *1917*, Todd Phillips for **psychological thriller** *Joker*, Quentin Tarantino for **comedy-drama** *Once Upon a Time in Hollywood*, and Martin Scorsese for **crime film** *The Irishman*—Mendes and Scorsese had previously won Best Director, and all four have received many other top *accolades. In his [7]**acceptance** speech, Bong [8]**acknowledged** the [9]**legendary** company he now finds himself in, pointing out that he studied Scorsese's films in school. Bong also thanked Tarantino for promoting his films to American audiences—support that helped lead to Bong's current moment in the [10]**spotlight**.

在《寄生上流》獲得提名的所有獎項類別中，奉俊昊面臨強勁對手，尤其是最佳導演獎的競爭。其他四位提名人中——山姆曼德斯的戰爭史詩《1917》、陶德菲利普斯的心理驚悚片《小丑》、昆汀塔倫提諾的喜劇劇情片《從前有個好萊塢》和馬丁史柯西斯的犯罪片《愛爾蘭人》——曼德斯和史柯西斯都曾獲得最佳導演獎，且四人都拿過許多頗具盛名的獎項。奉俊昊在獲獎感言中向這幾位知名導演致敬，並指出他在學校學習過史柯西斯的電影。奉俊昊也感謝塔倫提諾向美國觀眾宣傳他的電影，由於他的支持，促成了奉俊昊此時此刻成為眾人矚目的焦點。

Parasite was the first South Korean film to be nominated for Best International Feature Film as well as the first film to win the prize in this newly renamed category, which was known as Best Foreign Language Film until last year. While the category still honors films produced outside the United States that feature *predominantly non-English dialogue, the new name shifts the focus away from the "foreignness" of such films, perhaps to encourage greater acceptance among American [11]**viewers**, who often avoid movies with [12]**subtitles**.

《寄生上流》是南韓首部獲得最佳國際長片獎提名的電影，也是此獎項改新名稱後第一個獲獎的作品，此獎項在去年以前都稱為最佳外語片。此獎項仍頒給美國以外地區所製作的電影，主要為非英語對白，新名稱是為了避免將焦點放在這類電影的「外來性」上，或許能鼓勵更多美國觀眾接受，因為他們往往會避開觀看需看字幕的電影。

tania volobueva©WikiCommons

《寄生上流》也拿下 2019 年 Cannes Film Festival 坎城影展最高榮譽金棕櫚獎（法語：Palme d'Or）。右為導演奉俊昊，左為男主角宋康昊。

7. **acceptance** [əkˋsɛptəns] (*n.*)
接受，承認，**acceptance speech** 指「獲獎感言，受命演說」

8. **acknowledge** [əkˋnɑlɪdʒ] (*v.*)
感謝，向…致敬

9. **legendary** [ˋlɛdʒən͵dɛri] (*a.*)
傳說中的，著名的

10. **spotlight** [ˋspɑt͵laɪt] (*n.*)
聚光燈，公眾注意的焦點

11. **viewer** [ˋvjuə] (*n.*) 觀看者

12. **subtitle** [ˋsʌbtaɪtl] (*n.*)
（固定用複數）字幕

13. open-minded [ˋopənˋmaɪdɪd]
(a.) 心胸開放的，無偏見的，也寫做 **openminded**

14. overcome [ˌovɚˋkʌm] (v.)
克服，戰勝

15. barrier [ˋbærɪɚ] (n.)
障礙（物），阻礙

16. inspire [ɪnˋspaɪr] (v.)
賦予⋯靈感，激勵

進階字彙

* **upset** [ˋʌpˌsɛt] (n.)
爆冷門，指結果出乎意料

* **socioeconomic**
[ˌsosɪoˌɛkəˋnɑmɪk] (a.)
社經地位相關的

* **accolade** [ˋækəˌled] (n.)
盛讚，榮譽，嘉獎

* **predominantly** [prɪˋdɑmɪnəntli]
(adv.) 主要地

* **moviegoer** [ˋmuviˌgoɚ] (n.).
常看電影的人，亦做 **filmgoer** 或 **cinemagoer**。

Sharon Hahn Darlin©WikiCommons

美國洛杉磯影廳內的《寄生上流》海報。

On receiving the Best Director award at the **Golden Globes** in January, Bong used his acceptance speech to encourage audiences to be more [13]**open-minded**. "Once you [14]**overcome** the one-inch tall [15]**barrier** of subtitles, you will be introduced to so many more amazing films," Bong said. The success of *Parasite*, which overcame many barriers on a historic **Oscars** night, will no doubt [16]**inspire** more ***moviegoers** to give international films a chance.

奉俊昊於一月在金球獎頒獎典禮上獲得最佳導演獎時發表感言，鼓勵觀眾以更開放的態度觀影。奉俊昊說：「一旦你克服了一英寸高的字幕障礙，你就能觀賞更多精彩的電影。」《寄生上流》的成功，克服了奧斯卡之夜史上許多障礙，無疑將鼓勵更多電影愛好者給國際電影一個機會。

Grammar Master

關係代名詞所有格 **whose**.

關係代名詞所有格 whose 具有「關係代名詞」與「所有格」的特性，在句子上連接前後兩個子句，後方如同所有格只能接名詞。「...which tells the tragicomic story of two families at opposite ends of the socioeconomic spectrum **whose** lives collide.」句中的 which 為本句主詞，指逗點前面的那件事情。動詞為 tell，受詞則是 the tragicomic story of two families。從 at 到 spectrum 則是修飾受詞的介系詞片語，可省略不看。因此，whose 就是代替受詞 the tragicomic story of two families 中的 two families「兩個家庭」，由於 whose 後方的 lives 為名詞，這裡使用所有格代名詞 whose 才是正確的。還原本句就是：two families' lives collide。

1. Academy Awards (Oscars) & feature film 奧斯卡金像獎與電影長片

Academy Awards「學院獎」，更為人所知的名稱是 **Oscars**「奧斯卡金像獎」或「奧斯卡獎」，設立於 1929 年，由美國電影藝術與科學學院頒發，於每年的二月下旬舉辦頒獎典禮。奧斯卡獎的評選委員是由學院中的會員和學院邀請的貴賓產生。

Den Miami©Shutterstock

小寫 **feature film** 指「電影長片」，標準是至少 75 分鐘的片就歸類為長片，相對地 **short film** 就是「電影短片」。2020 年的奧斯卡將原本的 Best Foreign Language Film「奧斯卡最佳外語片」改名為 Best International Feature Film「奧斯卡最佳國際影片獎」。

2. screenplay & script 劇本

screenplay 也能寫作兩個字 screen play，與 script 都是「劇本」，兩者差在 screen play 專指電影或電視劇的劇本，撰寫 screenplay 的人叫 **screenwriter**「編劇」，而 script 則是指戲劇劇本，撰寫 script 的人則稱 **playwright**「劇作家」。

電影《從前有個好萊塢 Once Upon a Time in Hollywood》拿下 2020 年金球獎 Best Screenplay 最佳劇本。

Joaquin Rafael Phoenix 在《小丑 Joker》中的出色表現，拿下 2020 年金球獎與奧斯卡獎最佳男主角。Renée Zellweger 也因《茱蒂 Judy》拿下同屆奧斯卡與金球獎最佳女主角獎。

由 Netlifx 製作的《婚姻故事 Marriage Story》則獲得最多金球獎獎項提名。

3. Golden Globes 金球獎

為美國年度電視及電影盛會，由近百位外籍娛樂記者組成的 Hollywood Foreign Press Association（好萊塢外國記者協會，簡稱 HFPA）所舉辦，由協會成員投票選出得獎者。與電影奧斯卡金像獎 (Academy Awards) 和電視艾美獎 (**Emmy Awards**) 不同的是，金球獎因受限於缺乏專業投票團，故略過技術方面的獎項，只頒發普通獎項。頒獎日期落在每年的一月中旬，距離三月的奧斯卡頒獎典禮頗近，故被稱「奧斯卡的風向球」。

4. 各種電影類型

本文中提及了許多電影類型，以下一一介紹：

· **black comedy 黑色喜劇**：《寄生上流》就是黑色喜劇代表，這類影片的幽默與單純搞笑的幽默不同，常帶濃重的荒謬、絕望與陰暗，甚至有點殘忍。劇中會誇大某種不協調感，如本片透過畫面、人物設定與情節，誇大上流社會與下層階級的差距，使之更加荒誕不經到可笑，同時令人感到沈重苦悶。

· **war epic 戰爭史詩片**：epic 史詩片通常用來講述歷史英雄事蹟或故事，特色是反映那個時代的場景與規模，並使用背景音樂給人身歷其境感。epic 可以跟不同電影種類如 **sci-fi** 科幻片結合，如《星際大戰 *Star Wars*》即是。war epic 則是描繪戰爭的史詩片。

· **tragicomedy 悲喜劇**：由 tragedy+comedy 而來，出現在文中的是形容詞 **tragicomic**，悲喜劇其實是批著喜劇皮的悲劇，常透過一連串的喜劇情節，凸顯出現實人生的沈重或悲哀。如義大利電影《美麗人生 *Life is Beautiful*》、《剪刀手愛德華 *Edward Scissorhands*》等。

· **psychological thriller 心理驚悚片**：thriller 驚悚片常與其他電影類型結合，如 **action thriller** 動作驚悚片，而這裡的 **psychological thriller** 利用心理變態或精神分裂的角色或情節製造懸疑驚悚，代表作為《沉默的羔羊 *The Silence of the Lambs*》、《控制 *Gone Girl*》等。

· **comedy-drama 劇情喜劇**：又稱 **dramedy**，也就是帶有戲劇性的喜劇片，融合了嚴肅的劇情片元素與搞笑歡樂的喜劇元素，如 Tom Hanks 的《阿甘正傳 *Forrest Gump*》。

· **crime film 犯罪片**：也稱「警匪片」，是最普遍的電影類型之一。

《剪刀手愛德華 *Edward Scissorhands*》海報。

《沉默的羔羊 *The Silence of the Lambs*》海報。

《控制 *Gone Girl*》海報。

《阿甘正傳 *Forrest Gump*》海報。

10

#LGBTQ #transgender
#Netflix #Umbrella Academy
#Ellen Page #Elliot Page

lev radin©Shutterstock

曾經是 Ellen Page 的 Elliot Page（圖左）於 2014 年公開出櫃，2018 年與 Emma Portner
（圖右）結婚，2020 年公開自已是跨性別者（transgender）。

全文朗讀 ♫ 029　　單字 ♫ 030

Umbrella Academy Star Comes Out as Transgender

《雨傘學院》明星公開跨性別身分

⏲ December 1, 2020

Fans of Ellen Page who follow the actress on social media got a big surprise when they [1]**logged on** Tuesday. "Hi friends," Page wrote in a message posted on several social media platforms, including Instagram and Twitter, "I want to share with you that I am **trans**, my **pronouns** are **he/they** and my name is Elliot."

追蹤艾倫佩吉的粉絲週二登入社群媒體時收到驚人消息。佩吉在 Instagram 和推特等幾處社群媒體張貼這則訊息：「嗨，朋友們，我想跟你們分享一件事，我是跨性別者，我的代名詞是他或他們，我的名字是艾略特。」

"I feel lucky to be writing this. To be here. To have arrived at this place in my life," Page continues, before thanking the people who helped him on his path. "I feel [2]**overwhelming** [3]**gratitude** for the [4]**incredible** people who have supported me along this journey. I can't begin to express how [5]**remarkable** it feels to

Vocabulary

1. **log on/in** *(phr.)*
   登入（電腦系統）

2. **overwhelming**
   [`ovɚˌhwɛlmɪŋ] *(a.)*
   壓倒性的，勢不可擋的

3. **gratitude** [`grætɪˌtud] *(n.)*
   感恩，感激之情

4. **incredible** [ɪn`krɛdəbl̩] *(a.)*
   不可思議的，驚人的

5. **remarkable** [rɪ`mɑrkəbl̩] *(a.)*
   非凡的，特別的

6. **authentic** [ɔˈθɛntɪk] *(a.)*
   道地的，純正的，真正的

7. **community** [kəˈmjunəti] *(n.)*
   社群，社區，社會

8. **generosity** [ˌdʒɛnəˈrasəti] *(n.)*
   慷慨，大方

9. **inclusive** [ɪnˈklusɪv] *(a.)*
   具包容性的

10. **compassionate**
    [kəmˈpæʃənət] *(a.)*
    有同情心的，有同理心的

11. **statistic** [stəˈtɪstɪk] *(n.)*
    統計資料，統計數字

12. **discrimination**
    [dɪˌskrɪməˈneʃən] *(n.)*
    差別對待，歧視，偏袒

13. **consequence** [ˈkɑnsəˌkwɛns]
    (n.) 後果，結果

14. **pregnant** [ˈprɛgnənt] *(a.)*
    懷孕的，懷胎的 **pregnancy**
    [ˈprɛgnənsi] *(n.)*

進階字彙

* **ceaselessly** [ˈsislɪsli] *(adv.)*
  不停地，孜孜不倦地

* **staggering** [ˈstægərɪŋ] *(a.)*
  驚人的，難以置信的

* **rife** [raɪf] *(a.)* 充斥的

* **insidious** [ɪnˈsɪdʒəs] *(a.)*
  陰險狡詐的，暗中為害的

* **horrific** [hɔˈrɪfɪk] *(a.)*
  極其可怕的；令人震驚的

* **acclaim** [əˈklem] *(n./v.)*
  （尤指對藝術成就的）稱譽，高
  度評價

* **renew** [rɪˈnju] *(v.)*
  延長期限，更新

Ellen Page 與眾多演員出席 Netflix 於 2019 年製作的迷你劇集（miniseries）《城市故事 *Tales of the City*》首映。此劇描繪多元性別者在舊金山爭取平權的故事。

finally love who I am enough to pursue my [6]**authentic** self." The 33-year-old actor reserves special praise for fellow members of the **transgender** [7]**community**: "I've been endlessly inspired by so many in the trans community. Thank you for your courage, your [8]**generosity** and *ceaselessly** working to make this world a more [9]**inclusive** and [10]**compassionate** place."

在感謝這一路有大家幫助之前，佩吉繼續寫道：「我很幸運能寫這則訊息，也很幸運能身在這裡，並在我的生命中走到這一步。對於在這趟旅程中支持我的那些了不起的人，我不勝感激。我終於足夠愛自己，得以讓我追求真正的自己，我無法形容這感覺有多美妙。」這位 33 歲的演員特別讚揚跨性別族群的同志：「我在跨性別族群中不斷受到許多人啟發。感謝你們的勇氣、寬容和不懈的努力，讓這世界變得更具包容和慈悲。」

While Page's overall tone is positive, he also addresses the difficulties faced by his community. "The [11]**statistics** are *staggering**," he writes. "The [12]**discrimination** towards trans people is *rife**, *insidious** and cruel, resulting in *horrific** [13]**consequences**. In 2020 alone it has been reported that at least 40 transgender people have been murdered, the majority of which were Black and **Latinx** trans women."

佩吉的整體語氣是積極正面的，但他也道出了其族群所面臨的困境。他寫道：「統計數字令人震驚。對跨性別者的歧視程度猖獗、陰險而殘酷，造成了可怕的後果。據報導，光是在 2020 年至少就有 40 名跨性別者遇害，其中大多數是非裔和拉丁裔的跨性別女性。」

Page began acting at the age of ten, appearing in Canadian films and TV shows until his **breakout role** in the 2005 thriller *Hard Candy* launched his Hollywood career. Two years later, Page's performance as a [14] **pregnant** teenager in hit dramedy *Juno* brought the young actor an Oscar nomination and international ***acclaim**. Other big roles include Araidne in the sci-fi thriller *Inception* and Kitty Pride in the **X-Men** series. Page **came out** as **gay** in a 2014 speech in support of **LGBTQ** youth. Following the actor's trans announcement on Tuesday, **Netflix** confirmed that his character in the popular superhero series *The Umbrella Academy*—just ***renewed** for a third season—will not be changing **genders**.

Ellen Page 因演出情節喜劇（dramedy）《鴻孕當頭 *Juno*》一炮而紅，並入圍當年奧斯卡最佳女主角。

佩吉從十歲開始當演員，演出加拿大電影和電視節目，直到他在 2005 年的驚悚片《水果硬糖》中演出突破性角色之後，展開了好萊塢職業生涯。兩年後，佩吉在爆紅劇情喜劇片《鴻孕當頭》中飾演懷孕青少女的表現，為這位年輕演員帶來奧斯卡獎提名和國際讚譽。他參演過的其他重要角色還包括科幻驚悚片《全面啟動》中的亞麗雅德和《X 戰警》系列電影中的幻影貓。佩吉在 2014 年一次多元性別青年的演講中公開同性戀身分。這位演員於週二宣布跨性別身分後，Netflix 已證實他在人氣超級英雄系列影集《雨傘學院》中的角色將不會改變性別，此劇集已續訂第三季。

Grammar Master

平行結構

本新聞引述了 Elliot Page 的 tweet，裡頭用到許多的平行結構，如「I feel lucky **to be writing** this. **To be here**. **To have arrived** at this place in my life」連用三個 to V 結構，這種結構讓句子更簡潔有力，讀起來順暢並令人印象深刻，常用在演說中。平行結構運用標點符號或連接詞，將相同的文法結構做連結，逗點或連接詞前後所接的結構要一樣才行。

● **形容詞的平行結構**

例：Early to bed and early to rise makes a man healthy, wealthy and wise. 早睡早起讓人身體健康、富裕、且聰明。

● **動詞的平行結構**

例：To be, or not to be, that is the question. 做與不做都是問題。

● **介系詞的平行結構**

例：I promise to be true to you in good times and in bad, in sickness and in health. 我承諾，無論順境或逆境、疾病或健康，我都會對你忠誠。

1. LGBTQ 多元性別族群

七〇年代平權運動盛行，少數族群開始尋求認同，因而出現 LGBT 一詞，作為少數性別認同族群的集合稱呼，以示尊重。近年加上 Q，而成為 LGBTQ，這五個字母分別指：**lesbian**（女同性戀）、**gay**（男同性戀）、**bisexual**（雙性戀）、**transgender**（跨性別者）以及 **queer**（酷兒）或 **questioning**（對自己性傾向尚不清楚的人）。其中，transgender [ˋtrænsˌdʒɛndə] 是指不認同自己性別（**gender**），或認為自己是屬於另一個性別的人，可作名詞與形容詞，口語上常簡稱 **trans**。

bakdc©Shutterstock

在性別認同運動中，pronoun「代名詞」不再只是生理性別「sex」的代表，也是性別認同「gender」的代表，因此出現了去性別化的 **ze/hir/hirs** 取代傳統用來指稱第三人稱的男性代名詞 he/him/his 與女性代名詞 she/her/hers，而韋氏大辭典也於將 **they** 的定義改成可以用在單數，用來指不以二元性別做為自我認同的人的代稱，如：I use they as pronouns.（我用 they 當成我的代名詞。）

2. Latinx 拉丁美洲裔

念作 [ləˋtinɛks]，指生活在美國的拉丁美洲（Latin American）人。這個字不分性別都可以使用，字尾 -x 取代了原本的 Latino 與 Latina 的 -o 與 -a，各自代表男性與女性的詞尾。換言之，Latinx 含括了 **Latino**（拉丁美洲裔男性）與 **Latina**（拉丁美洲裔女性）。不過這個字在多數仍用 Latino/Latina 的族群中並不被接受。

DFree©Shutterstock

3. breakout role 突破性角色演出

也稱 **breakthrough role**，指演員所演出的角色對其職涯有重大突破，獲得廣大影迷認可。白話一點來說，就是該角色使得原本默默無名的小演員成為家喻戶曉的一線明星（**A-list star**）。

◀ Gal Gadot 演出《神力女超人 *Wonder Woman*》一角，使她成功在好萊塢站穩腳步，紅遍全球。

4. come out (of the closet) 出櫃

多元性別族群常因社會規範，選擇向親友大眾隱藏自己的性向，可用 **in the closet**「在衣櫃裡」來比喻。因此，當他們公開坦承自己的性向時，就可以說 **come out of the closet**「走出衣櫃」，簡稱 **come out**「出櫃」。

5. X-Men film series X 戰警電影系列

X-Men 原本是美漫，敘述一群擁有特殊能力的變種人（mutant），以 Professor X（X 教授）與 Magneto（萬磁王）分成兩派之間的爭鬥，前者主張與人類共存，後者則主張向人類宣戰，這部漫威漫畫陸續改編成卡通與影集，2000 年首部系列電影《X 戰警 *X-Men*》上映，可說是近代超級英雄電影先驅（漫威 Marvel 超級英雄電影第一部《鋼鐵人 *Ironman*》上映時間已經是 2008 年），拍攝三部電影之後，便推出 Woverine（金剛狼）的獨立電影。目前與 X 戰警有關的電影有 12 部，包含金剛狼與

▲ X 戰警前三部曲（trilogy）的 DVD 封面。

▲ 2017 年《羅根 *Logan*》電影海報。

Deadpool（死侍）的獨立電影，評價褒貶參半。其中《羅根 *Logan*》不以變種人的無所不能為拍攝視角，呈現金剛狼人性一面（電影名稱 Logan 便是金剛狼的本名），不同於其他 X 戰警電影風格，獲得一致好評。

6. Netflix 網飛

Netflix 成立於 1997 年，原本是郵寄出租 DVD 公司，2008 年推出網路影片串流服務，讓會員能透過手機或平板觀看影劇，Netflix 更進一步開始自製節目，推出

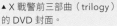

Netflix Original 網飛原創，包含影集、節目、電影與紀錄片，引領全球串流影片風潮，改變人們觀劇方式與電影業界生態。現在在超過 190 個國家都可收看 Netflix。

知名 Netflix Original 包括人氣最高的經典影集《紙牌屋 *House of Cards*》，2013 年推出第一季就替 Netflix 增加了三百萬的新訂戶。《埃及廣場 *The Square*》甚至是 Netflix 原創中首度獲奧斯卡提名的電影作品。近年 Netflix 作品不斷，除了美劇《怪奇物語 *Strange Things*》《后裔棄兵 *The Queen's Gambit*》外，也與多國合作戲劇如韓劇《李屍朝鮮》、台劇《罪夢者》等，而 2020 年奧斯卡獎入圍名單中也有 Netflix Original 作品：《愛爾蘭人 *The Irishman*》《婚姻故事 *Marriage Story*》等。

7. *The Umbrella Academy* 《雨傘學院》

為 Netflix Original 所製作的美劇，描述一群擁有超能力的人處理自己人生問題，同時面對即將來臨的世界末日，類型涉足黑色喜劇 black comedy、科幻 sci-fi 與超級英雄 super hero，目前已經上映兩季，2020 年 11 月 Netflix 確定續訂第三季。

Sports 運動

#FIFA World Cup #soccer
#Barcelona
#Hand of God #Goal of the Century
#Lionel Messi #Pelé

©WikiCommons

1986 年世界盃 Maradona 率領阿根廷隊奪冠，手中握著 Golden Ball 與隊友歡慶。

全文朗讀 ♫ 031   單字 ♫ 032

Soccer Great Maradona Dies at 60
世紀球王馬拉度納逝世，享年 60 歲

🕐 **November 26, 2020**

Soccer legend Diego Maradona died on Wednesday at the age of 60. The [1]**beloved** Argentine *succumbed to heart failure at his home in Buenos Aires. Millions of fans around the world [2]**mourned** his death and celebrated his life.

足球傳奇人物迪亞哥馬拉度納週三逝世，享籌 60 歲。這位備受喜愛的阿根廷人在他位於布宜諾斯艾利斯的家中死於心臟衰竭。世界各地無數球迷在哀悼他過世的同時，也頌揚他的人生。

Maradona [3]**attained** celebrity [4]**status** after leading Argentina to victory in the 1986 **FIFA World Cup**. It was during the **quarterfinal** game against England that Maradona scored his [5]**notorious** **"Hand of God"** goal, punching the ball into the net. This was a *flagrant [6]**violation** of the rules, and should have resulted in a **yellow card**. But because the [7]**referee** didn't see the [8]**foul**, the goal was counted. Later in the same game, Maradona [9]**dribbled**

Vocabulary

1. **beloved** [bɪˋlʌvɪd / bɪˋlʌvd] *(a.)*
   深受喜愛的

2. **mourn** [mɔrn] *(v.)* 哀悼，哀痛

3. **attain** [əˋten] *(v.)* 獲得，達到

4. **status** [ˋstætəs] *(n.)* 地位，身分

5. **notorious** [noˋtorɪəs] *(a.)*
   惡名昭彰的

6. **violation** [ˏvaɪəˋleʃən] *(n.)*
   違反，侵犯

7. **referee** [ˏrɛfəˋri] *(n.)* 裁判員

Maradona 逝世，阿根廷舉國上下降半旗哀悼。

8. **dribble** [ˋdrɪbəl] (v.)
盤球，帶球

9. **foul** [faʊl] (n.)（比賽）犯規

10. **defender** [dɪˋfɛndə] (n.)
後衛，防守者，動詞 **defend**

11. **trophy** [ˋtrofɪ] (n.)
獎盃，獎品

12. **pitch** [pɪtʃ] (n.)（英）足球場

13. **addiction** [əˋdɪkʃən] (n.)
上癮，癮

14. **ban** [bæn] (v./n.) 禁止，取締

15. **eternal** [ɪˋtɜnəl] (a.)
永恆的，永久的

past seven English [10]**defenders** to score a remarkable goal later voted **"Goal of the Century"** in a FIFA poll. After leading his team to beat West Germany in the final, he also won the **Golden Ball** as best player of the **tournament**.

馬拉度納在帶領阿根廷贏得 1986 年世界盃後享譽盛名。當時在對戰英格蘭的八強賽中，馬拉度納踢出了惡名昭彰的「上帝之手」進球，用手將球推進球門。這是公然違反規則，應給一記黃牌，但由於裁判沒看到犯規，所以算進球一分。稍後在同一場比賽中，馬拉度納帶球盤過七名英格蘭守衛，踢進一記卓越的進球，後來此球在國際足球總會的票選中獲選為「世紀進球」。在總決賽帶領球隊擊敗西德後，馬拉度納也獲頒該賽事最佳球員的金球獎榮譽。

Maradona started his professional career with the Buenos Aires **club** Argentinos Juniors and later *transferred to the Boca Juniors, helping them win a **league** title. The rising star's next two moves set transfer fee records—to Barcelona for $7.6 million in 1982, and then Napoli for $10.5 million in 1984. Maradona's seven-year *stint with Napoli was marked by highs and lows. The talented **midfielder** led the Italian *side to five [11]**trophies**, including their first two ever **Serie A** titles. Off the [12]**pitch**, however, he struggled with *cocaine [13]**addiction**, and left Napoli in 1992 after serving a 15-month [14]**ban** for failing a drug test.

馬拉度納是在布宜諾斯艾利斯的阿根廷青年體育會展開職業生涯，後來轉到博卡青年競技俱樂部，幫助該隊贏得一次聯賽冠軍。這位閃亮新星接下來兩次轉隊創下了轉會費紀錄——1982 年以 760 萬美元身價轉至巴塞隆納，然後在 1984 年以 1050 萬元轉至拿坡里。馬拉度納在拿坡里的七年職涯歷經了高潮和低谷。這位才華橫溢的中場球員帶領這支義大利球隊贏得五座獎杯，包括頭兩座義大利足球甲級聯賽冠軍。然而在場外，他為古柯鹼毒癮所困，在因藥檢不合格而被禁賽 15 個月後，於 1999 年離開拿坡里。

A career in club management followed Maradona's playing years, taking him from Argentina and Mexico to the United Arab Emirates. He became manager of Argentina's national team in 2008 and led them to the 2010 World Cup in South Africa. But after Argentina's 4-0 *rout by Germany in the quarterfinal, the team decided not to renew his contract.

馬拉度納結束球員職涯後，開始從事足球俱樂部經理工作，待過阿根廷、墨西哥與阿拉伯聯合大公國。他於 2008 年成為阿根廷國家隊經理，並帶領他們打入 2010 年南非世界盃。但阿根廷隊在四強賽以 4 比 0 敗給德國後，球隊決定不續約。

©WikiCommons

Maradona 在繞過英格蘭七名守衛後，踢出「Goal of the Century 世紀進球」的一刻。

Upon Maradona's *passing, fellow soccer greats ⓟ**paid tribute to** the player many consider the greatest of all time. "Diego is ¹⁵⁾eternal," wrote **Lionel Messi**. "The world has lost a legend," tweeted Brazilian icon **Pelé**. The Argentine government declared three days of mourning for their national hero.

馬拉度納逝世後，許多足球大人物都向這位公認史上最偉大球員致敬。萊納爾梅西寫道：「迪亞哥永恆不朽。」巴西足球偶像比利推文：「世界失去了一位傳奇人物」。阿根廷政府也宣布為這位民族英雄哀悼三天。

Grammar Master

以 it 為首的強調句型

當我們想強調句子裡某事件、某時、某人等的時候，可把欲強調事物前面加上虛主詞 it，並將剩餘句子置於句尾，如本句「It was **during the quarterfinal game against England** that Maradona scored his notorious "Hand of God" goal...」就是強調 Maradona 於「該場賽事上」踢出聞名全世界的一球。

● 強調主詞：
例：It was **Dr. White** who/that made me fall in love with literature. 是懷特教授讓我愛上文學。

● 強調受詞：
例：It was **the antique vase** that the boy broke accidentally. 男孩不小心打破的是古董花瓶。

● 強調地方：
例：It was **the restaurant** where her boyfriend proposed to her. 就是在那餐廳她男友和她求婚的。

1. FIFA & World Cup 國際足球協會與世界盃

FIFA 國際足球總會，為法語 Fédération Internationale de Football Association 的縮寫，足球國際體育組織，負責主辦國際足球賽事，最著名的就是四年舉行一次的 World Cup 世界足球盃，2018 年世界盃由法國奪得，下一屆世界盃將在 2022 年 11 月 21 日於阿拉伯國家卡達舉行。

2. tournament & quarterfinal 錦標賽與四強賽

tournament [ˈtɜnəmənt]「錦標賽」指大規模的運動比賽，參與球隊眾多，所以 tournament 會先舉行 **qualifying stage**「資格賽」，勝出的球隊就能進入 **knockout/elimination stage**「淘汰賽」爭奪冠軍。如 FIFA 世界盃就選出前八強打淘汰賽。淘汰賽的最後一場比賽叫 **final**「決賽」，決賽前的四爭二的比賽就叫 **semifinal**「半決賽」，半決賽前的比賽就稱 **quarterfinal**「四強賽」，即八隊爭四強的比賽。

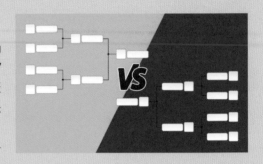

3. Hand of God 上帝之手
Goal of the Century 世紀進球

這兩個傳奇稱號都是 Maradona 在 1986 年墨西哥世界盃的八強賽所獲得。得分的第一球經賽後慢動作檢視，球是由他的右手撥進而非頭錘頂進，但由於角度關係，裁判未發現而誤判。賽後馬拉度納表示，「有的進球是靠馬拉度納的頭，但有些則是靠上帝的手」，Hand of God 從此成為他的代名詞。第二個進球便是足球迷口中的 Goal of the Century「世紀進球」，Maradona 先以上帝之手拿下第一分後，接著獨自一人帶球 68 公尺，繞過英格蘭隊防守者並將守門員騙倒在地，成功射門入網。這顆進球被足球迷選為「世紀進球」，至今仍是。

▲ Maradona 當年被稱為「上帝之手」的進球。

4. yellow card 黃牌

足球比賽中，若球員違反規則、延誤比賽，或擅自進出球場，裁判員 **referee** 就會對犯規球員舉黃牌作為警告，拿到一張黃牌警告的球員可繼續比賽。但若是嚴重犯規或語言無禮等，裁判就會舉紅牌直接驅逐球員離場，停賽一場。累積兩張黃牌等於一張紅牌。傳統上裁判員會拿出小記事本記錄球員犯規，因此 yellow card 也稱 **booking**「記名」。

Dziurek©Shutterstock

5. Golden Ball 世界盃金球獎

Golden Ball 金球獎是頒發給當屆世界盃中表現最優秀球員的獎項，始於 1982 年的西班牙世界盃，由國際媒體投票選出。1986 年 Maradona 帶領阿根廷二度拿下世界盃，以 5 球進球獲頒 Golden Ball 殊榮。

6. club 足球俱樂部

在運動界中，club 指一個組織，就像公司一樣，擁有完整的球隊、球場、設備、人員教練與粉絲，一個 club 底下可能有好幾支球隊 team。許多足球隊名中的縮寫 FC 便是指 football club。

7. midfielder 中場

根據足球員在比賽中的位置與功能，可分為 **goalkeeper** 守門員、**defender** 後衛、**midfielder** 中場、**center forward** 或 **striker** 前鋒四個位置。midfielder 負責控球、阻擋對方進攻，為己方進攻，是核心位置。

8. Serie A 義大利足球甲級聯賽

Lega Serie A 義大利足球甲級聯賽，簡稱義甲，是義大利最高等級的職業足球聯賽（league）。目前參賽球隊有 20 隊。義甲特色為注重防守，曾經是世界上水準最高的職業足球聯賽之一，在 1990 年世界盃足球賽過後，更被譽為「小世界盃」。

Christian Bertrand©Shutterstock

9. Lionel Messi 梅西

現年 33 歲的梅西是足球迷公認的最偉大球員之一，也被 Maradona 視為「完美接班人」，現效力於 Barcelona 巴塞隆納，同時擔任阿根廷國家足球隊與巴塞隆納足球隊隊長。梅西的勤奮與自律，讓他在長達十年持續有超人表現，並持續締造新紀錄，目前共獲得 10 次聯賽冠軍，4 次歐冠冠軍，6 座歐洲金靴獎，6 次歐聯神射手，以及 6 次 FIFA 足球先生。

John Mathew ©WikiCommons

10. Pelé 球王比利

全名為 Edison Arantes do Nascimento 的比利（比利 Pelé 是他的暱稱），現年 80 歲，是已退役的巴西知名足球員，專職前鋒，是二十世紀最偉大的體育明星之一，他最具特色的踢球技巧就是倒掛金鉤（bicycle kick 或 scissors kick），曾帶領巴西國家足球隊拿下三次世界盃，是世上唯一一位三次奪得世界盃的球員，被 FIFA 授與 The King of Football「球王」稱號。

▲ 1995 年的 Pelé。

11. `Phrase` pay tribute to sb./sth. 向某人致意

tribute 指「頌詞，表達敬意的言詞」，因此 pay tribute to sb./sth. 就是對我們所敬愛的人物表達敬意，可以是「讚揚某人，稱頌某人」，或是在本文中指「悼念過世的人」。

例 The man paid tribute to the firemen who saved his daughter's life.
男子向那位拯救了他女兒性命的消防員致意。

2020 NBA 決戰泡泡圈

Barack Obama
@BarackObama

Always look forward to watching the NBA Finals—and tonight I had the chance to thank a great group of first-time poll workers with @morethanavote.

It's critical that everybody votes In this election—by mail or in person if you can. Register to vote at vote.org/obama.

12:09 PM · Oct 1, 2020

98.5K   14.7K people are Tweeting about this

▲ 疫情原因，今年的 NBA Finals 採取虛擬觀眾，美國前總統 Obama 也現身在第一排觀看湖人隊與熱火隊爭奪 NBA 總冠軍。

有在關注體育新聞的讀者，應該對「bubble」這個字不陌生，bubble 這個概念起始於 support bubble「社交泡泡」一詞，因應這次疫情而出現。疫情使得各群體或國家之間接觸之前需進行檢疫或居家隔離，而 bubble 便是指「確保雙方安全之後，省去這些檢疫跟隔離的程序」，也就是 quarantine-free 之意。因此，support bubble 就是「居家泡泡」，用在親密的一小群人中，符合條件的家庭不用保持社交距離，而 travel bubble「旅遊泡泡」就是兩國間的旅遊無需檢疫與隔離，只需確保無感染 Covid-19 就可入境。而體壇上如 NBA bubble，也是同樣意思。

在這個 NBA Bubble 中，參加球隊需限制在同一場地進行比賽，而非在各自主場比賽，並且從練習開始就要隔離到賽事結束，因此對每個球員來說，身心上都是不小挑戰。2020 年 NBA 季後賽曾一度取消，最後在七月選定佛羅里達州奧蘭多的迪士尼世界復賽。因比賽場地就在迪士尼世界裡舉行，又稱 the Disney Bubble。

NBA 賽季介紹

Regular Season 例行賽

NBA 分東、西兩區（Conference），各有三組（Division），每組五隊，因此全聯盟共有 30 支球隊。每支球隊在季賽要打 82 場例行賽，例行賽季一般於 10 月打到隔年 4 月。

10 月	11 月	12 月	1 月	2 月	3 月	4 月	5 月	6 月	7 月	8 月	9 月

Playoffs & Finals
季後賽與總決賽

四月例行賽季結束後，按例行賽成績，東西兩區各選出八隊、共 16 隊進入季後賽（playoffs，也稱 postseason），進行賽季最後爭霸。季後賽於例行賽打完兩三天後開始，為期約兩個月。而 NBA Finals 總決賽就是指季後賽的最後一輪比賽，每年六月初舉行，六月中旬產生總冠軍 champion。

offseason 休賽期間

沒有舉行比賽的期間就統稱為 offseason「休賽期間」，season「賽季」前面加上 off，就是沒有比賽的意思。這段時間通常就是 NBA 各球隊養精蓄銳，同時進行選秀（draft）或交易球員的期間。

籃球各個位置說法

籃球一隊五個人，雖然沒有固定的位置，但有其分工跟責任：

photoyh©Shutterstock

- **控球後衛（point guard，簡稱 PG）**：通常是身材最小巧的球員，負責組織攻勢，要具備優異的運球與傳球能力，加上良好的視野，多做助攻（assist）將球傳給隊友製造得分。代表球星有 Stephen Curry 與退役的 Isiah Thomas。

- **得分後衛（shooting guard，SG）**：顧名思義是負責得分的位置，通常在外圍等待機會，一拿到隊友傳球快速跳投得分，因此得分後衛常是精準的三分球射手，出手也要夠快夠準。代表球星有籃球大帝 Michael Jorden、黑曼巴 Kobe Bryant。

▲ Stephen Curry（右）

- **小前鋒（small forward，SF）**：雖然名稱有 small 一字，但是擔任小前鋒的球員通常身材高大，主要任務是得分，他是隊上的頭號攻擊手，有好速度與突破能力，以突破重圍切入得分。前文爭奪 2020 年 NBA Finals 的兩大球星 LeBron James、Jimmy Butler 就是小前鋒。

- **大前鋒（power forward，PF）**：平均身高都在 200 公分以上的長人，負責抓籃板、卡位、鞏固禁區，通常是搶籃板球搶最多的人，較常中距離射投。知名大前鋒有 Kevin Durant。

- **中鋒（center，C）**：主要工作是埋伏在底線跟禁區附近，搶籃板跟近籃攻擊，防守時中鋒常常給對方蓋火鍋（block），也稱 the five「第五人」或 big man「大個子」。知名中鋒有 Nikola Joki 、姚明。

▲ Michael Jordan

籃球比賽的各種時間說法

看籃球比賽時經常會聽到「第四節下半」等的時間說法，這裡一次整理如下：NBA 一節有 12 分鐘，一場共四節，「一節」就稱 quarter（取「一場中的四分之一」的意思）。因此，第一到第四節分別是 the 1st/2nd/3rd/4th quarter。前兩節可合稱 first half「上半場」，後兩節 second half「下半場」，播報時經常省略 quarter 一字，如 five minutes into the 3rd (quarter)「第三節開打五分鐘」。其他說法還有：

- **中場休息**：halftime break，break 可省略。
- **加時賽**：overtime，簡稱 OT。NBA 加時賽是 5 分鐘，次數沒有上限。

其他籃球相關單字

名詞：

三分球：three-pointer　　罰球：free throw
壓哨球：buzzer-beater，buzz 指蜂鳴器，在讀秒時間到時會響起。
麵包球：air ball，指連碰到籃板都沒碰到的球，就是俗稱肉包（台語）。
籃板球：rebound，搶到籃板球的動詞可用 grab。
擦板球：bank shot　　助攻：assist
地板傳球：bounce pass

動詞：

傳球：pass，make a pass　●　運球：dribble
投籃：shoot、shoot the ball、take a shot
投球沒進：miss。
進球（得分）：drain，nail，sink，score
上籃：shoot a layup　●　灌籃：slam-dunk，dunk
投進空心球：swish，其發音類似球空心入網的聲音，也可說 hit nothing but net
卡位：box out

#NBA #The Lakers
#LeBron James #Kobe Bryant
#Immunity Bubbles

©WikiCommons

全文朗讀 🎵 033   單字 🎵 034

Lakers Beat Heat for 17th NBA Title
湖人隊擊敗熱火隊拿下第 17 個 NBA 冠軍

🕐 October 12, 2020

Vocabulary

1. **champagne** [ʃæmˋpen] (n.)
   香檳

2. **ambiguity** [ˏæmbɪˋgjuəti] (n.)
   模棱兩可，意義不明確

3. **decisive** [dɪˋsaɪsɪv] (a.)
   決定性的，斷然的

4. **versus** [ˋvɝsəs] (prep.)
   對，對抗，與⋯相對

5. **let up** (phr.) 減輕，停止

6. **urge** [ɝdʒ] (v.) 催促，力勸

Last night Los Angeles Lakers superstar **LeBron James** playfully sprayed reporters with ¹⁾**champagne**, then called his mother. The Lakers had just won the **NBA Finals**, and James and his teammates were celebrating as **champions**. The final score of the Lakers' *showdown** with the **Eastern Conference** champion **Miami Heat** was 106-93.

昨晚洛杉磯湖人隊的超級明星雷霸龍詹姆士調皮地朝記者灑香檳，接著打電話給他母親報喜。湖人隊剛贏得 NBA 總決賽，詹姆士和隊友開香檳慶祝。湖人隊與東區聯盟冠軍邁阿密熱火隊的對決，最終以總分 106 比 93 收場。

By *halftime** of Game 6, there was little ²⁾**ambiguity** about who would take the trophy. The Heat never took the lead, and by the break, the Lakers were up 64-36. The only other time there's been a lead more ³⁾**decisive *midway** through a Finals game was the Lakers ⁴⁾**versus** the Celtics in 1985. The Lakers refused to ⁵⁾**let up** in dominating Miami, with James ⁶⁾**urging** his teammates on toward a

◀ 奧蘭多迪士尼世界的空拍圖，藍色線
以南就是此次 NBA 季後賽的隔離泡泡
區，季後賽期間球員不得跨出藍色線。

certain victory. Sunday's **championship** win put the Lakers in a tie with the Boston Celtics for the most in NBA history.

比賽進行到第六場中場時，勝負可以說早已底定。熱火隊一直無法取得領先，中場休息前湖人隊就以 64 比 36 大幅領先。另一次在總決賽中場前就取得明確領先的是 1985 年湖人隊對戰塞爾提克隊。儘管明顯領先邁阿密，但湖人隊並沒有因此放鬆，詹姆士敦促隊友勢必要奪冠。湖人隊在週日的奪冠，使得該隊獲得的冠軍次數與波士頓塞爾提克隊並駕齊驅。

James, who finished the game with 28 points, 14 *rebounds and 10 *assists, had reason to be joyous. The 35-year-old was named Finals **MVP**, taking home the fourth **championship ring** of his career. He previously won two NBA Finals while playing for the Heat and once with the Cleveland Cavaliers, [7)]**delivering** the *franchise its first championship.

詹姆士為這場比賽貢獻了 28 分 14 個籃板球與 10 次助攻，完全有理由慶祝。35 歲的詹姆士獲封為總決賽最有價值球員，抱回職涯第四枚冠軍戒指。他先前獲得的 NBA 總決賽冠軍，兩次是在熱火隊，一次則是在克里夫蘭騎士隊，並為該隊奪得第一次冠軍。

Gold and white *confetti rained down on the [8)]**triumphant** Lakers on the [9)]**court** at the AdventHealth [10)]**Arena** near Orlando, Florida. The arena is located entirely within Walt Disney World, where both teams *quarantined for over three months to [11)]**safeguard** against COVID-19. Players had to live, train and compete within strict safety [12)]**guidelines**.

金色與白色彩帶雨在佛羅里達州奧蘭多附近的健保運動場落下，慶祝湖人隊的勝利。這座運動場位於迪士尼樂園內，兩支球隊在這裡隔離三個多月以防範新冠病毒。球員都必須在嚴格的安全規定下生活、訓練和比賽。

7. **deliver** [dɪˋlɪvɚ] (v.)
   履行（承諾），成功完成

8. **triumphant** [traɪˋʌmfənt] (a.)
   取得巨大成功的

9. **court** [kort] (n.)
   （籃球等）球場

10. **arena** [əˋrinə] (n.)
   （運動比賽或表演）場地

11. **safeguard** [ˋsef͵gɑrd] (v.)
   保護，捍衛，守護

12. **guideline** [ˋgaɪd͵laɪn] (n.)
   準則，規範

13. **acknowledge** [əkˋnɑlɪdʒ] (v.)
承認，接受

14. **retirement** [rɪˋtaɪrmənt] (n.)
退休。動詞 **retire**

15. **dedicate (to)** [ˋdɛdɪ͵ket] (v.)
以…獻給

進階字彙

* **showdown** [ˋʃo͵daʊn] (n.)
對決；攤牌

* **halftime** [ˋhæf͵taɪm] (n.)
（球賽）中場休息時間

* **midway** [͵mɪdˋwe] (adv./a.)
中間（的），中途（的）

* **rebound** [ˋri͵baʊnd] (n.) 籃板球

* **assist** [əˋsɪst] (n.)
（籃球、足球等）助攻

* **franchise** [ˋfræntʃaɪz] (n.) 球隊

* **confetti** [kənˋfɛti] (n.)
慶典時拋灑的彩色碎紙

* **quarantine** [ˋkwɔrən͵tin] (v./n.)
隔離，檢疫

* **mentor** [ˋmɛntɔr / ˋmɛntə] (n.)
精神導師，師父

* **legion** [ˋlidʒən] (n.)
（常用複數）眾多，大量（+ of）

©WikiCommons
2015 年 Kobe（右）穿著湖人隊隊服。

Lakers coach Frank Vogel said training had been difficult this year and [13)]**acknowledged** that the tragic death of **Kobe Bryant** had been hard on the team. Bryant led the Lakers to five championships before his [14)]**retirement** in 2016. He remained a hero and ***mentor** to the team until his death in a helicopter accident in January. After their victory last night, many Lakers players paid tribute to Bryant and [16)]**dedicated** the win to his memory. It was a night to remember for the Lakers and their ***legions** of fans.

湖人隊教練法蘭克沃格爾說，今年的訓練很辛苦，並承認柯比布萊恩的不幸過世對球隊造成沉重打擊。布萊恩在 2016 年退休前帶領湖人隊贏得五次冠軍。他於一月在一場直升機墜機事故中過世，此前一直是球隊的英雄和良師益友。球隊昨晚獲勝後，許多球員都向布萊恩致敬，並把冠軍獻給他。對於湖人隊和其眾多球迷來說，這是一個難忘的夜晚。

Grammar Master

過去完成式

過去完成式「had + Vp.p.」用法單純，只會出現在敘述「有先後發生次序的兩件事件」，其中使用到「過去完成式」的事件會比另一件「過去」發生的事情要早發生。本句「The Lakers **had** just **won** the NBA Finals, and James and his teammates **were celebrating** as champions.」中的第二件事 were celebrating 使用過去進行式，在慶祝「前」發生了「贏得總冠軍」，因此第一句的動詞用更早發生的過去完成式 had won 表示。

例：The train **had** just **left** when I **arrived** at the station. 我到了車站火車才剛走。

例：I **had saved** my file before the computer **crashed**. 我在電腦當機前存好檔案。

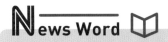
1. champion 和 championship 有什麼不同？

champion 指「拿到冠軍的人或球隊」，而 **championship** 則是「冠軍地位或頭銜」，也指「冠軍賽，錦標賽」，即不同地區或競賽組之間的一系列決賽制，如 NBA Finals（NBA 總冠軍賽）就是一種 championship。**championship ring** 則是 NBA 總冠軍的個人榮譽冠軍，獲得總冠軍的球隊除了能抱回獎盃，無論是否有在季後賽名單上的所有球員均可獲得一枚冠軍戒指。

2. NBA & Eastern Conference 美國職籃 NBA 與東區聯盟

美國國家籃球協會（NBA，National Basketball Association，簡稱美國職籃）由 30 支球隊組成（其中僅一支球隊位於加拿大，其他位在美國），這 30 支球隊分屬 **Eastern Conference**「東區聯盟」與 **Western Conference**「西區聯盟」。東區聯盟共有 15 支球隊，主要分布在大西洋及五大湖沿岸城市，包含紐約、芝加哥跟費城，聯盟分成大西洋組、中央組跟東南組三個賽區（**division**）。多倫多暴龍 Toronto Raptors 是唯一不在美國境內的東區聯盟球隊。

▲ 圖左跟圖右分別是 NBA 東西區聯盟常勝隊伍的標誌。

Western Conference「西區聯盟」同樣也有 15 支球隊，分散在密西西比河以西地區，如加州、洛杉磯，分成西南組、西北組與太平洋組。洛杉磯是唯一同時擁有兩隻球隊 Lakers 湖人隊與 Clippers 快艇隊的城市。在西區聯盟中，洛杉磯湖人隊堪稱戰績最為輝煌的球隊，在東區則是波士頓賽爾提克 Boston Celtics 表現最佳。

NBA 賽季每年 10 月開打，分為例行賽（**NBA Regular Seasons**）與季後賽（**NBA Playoffs**）兩大部份。每支球隊都要先完成 82 場比賽，也就是例行賽，為循環賽制，例行賽會打到隔年 4 月，接著每個聯盟的前八強將有資格進入季後賽，季後賽採七戰四勝制，共分四輪，最後一輪比賽稱 **NBA Finals**「準決賽」。

▲ Kobe 與 13 歲小女兒搭機前往訓練途中失事。
spatuletail©Shutterstock

3. Kobe Bryant 黑曼巴柯比

NBA 傳奇球星柯比布萊恩於 2020 年 1 月 27 日飛機失事意外身亡，但他的 the Black Mamba「黑曼巴精神」永遠不滅。Kobe 自稱 Black Mamba，他在紀錄片《*Muse*》提到，這是他從電影《追殺比爾 *Killing Bill*》的刺客用黑曼巴蛇殺死對手時所獲得的靈感，他認為自己就像條快速又致命的黑曼巴蛇。2003 到 04 年是 Kobe 人生的低谷，他捲入性侵官司，雖然最終以和解收場，但他也因此身敗名裂，於是他創造「黑曼巴」這個分身，讓自己在心態上抽離當下困境；場外的個人家庭問題，由 Kobe Bryant 來面對，在球場上就由黑曼巴來大開殺戒。最能體現 Kobe 黑曼巴精神的比賽之一，是 2004 年 3 月 25 日與奧蘭多魔術隊的比賽，他在該場比賽第四節拿下 24 分，整場貢獻 38 分，幫助湖人隊以 113 比 110 分奪得冠軍。

MLB SUPERSTITIONS

美國職棒
的各種魔咒

在歷史悠久的美國職棒文化中,流傳了許多 baseball curse「棒球魔咒」,當有強隊一直無法晉級世界大賽,或是多次與冠軍頭銜失之交臂,球迷與球隊就會開始出現迷信說法,將無法奪冠但又無法解釋原因的現象用 curse 稱之。

Chicago White Sox 芝加哥白襪隊:
Curse of the Black Sox 黑襪魔咒

1

FIX THESE FACES IN YOUR MEMORY

EIGHT MEN CHARGED WITH SELLING OUT BASEBALL

未奪冠記錄／魔咒時間 **88** 年

◀ 打假球的八個白襪隊球員,右上角的 Joe Jackson 人稱 Shoeless Joe,是大聯盟史上安打率第三高的球員,因醜聞遭終身禁賽。因此此咒又稱 Curse of Shoeless Joe。
©WikiCommons

白襪隊曾在 1919 年打進世界大賽,當時一次世界大戰剛結束,換言之,這是戰後的第一場職棒世界大賽,因此有賭徒便趁此機會大撈一筆,賄賂薪資不高的白襪隊球員打假球。這個詛咒之所以用 black 取代 white,就是暗指白襪隊球員收賄打假球。

當時職棒球員待遇並不好,尤其白襪隊的老闆是出了名的小氣,最後白襪隊有八名球員同意在世界大賽打假球,最後白襪以 3 勝 5 敗輸給 Cincinnati Reds 辛辛納堤紅人隊。這起「黑襪醜聞 Black Sox scandal」讓美國職棒人氣跌落谷底。1988 年電影《陰謀密戰 *Eight Men Out*》與 1989 年以 *Shoeless Joe* 小說改編的《夢幻成真 *Field of Dreams*》,就是以此事件為背景。

▲ Eight Men Out 的 DVD 封面／*Field of Dreams* 的電影海報,由凱文科斯納主演。©WikiCommons

一直到 2005 年打敗 Houston Astros 休士頓太空人,白襪隊才拿到總冠軍,終結詛咒。

Chicago Cubs 芝加哥小熊隊：
Curse of the Billy Goat 山羊魔咒

未奪冠記錄 **108** 年／魔咒時間 **71** 年

目前等待封王最久的就是現在要介紹的芝加哥小熊隊，距離上次封王已經是 1908 年（清光緒年間！）的事。阻擋小熊隊封王的魔咒發生在 1945 年，那年小熊隊和 Detroit Tigers 底特律老虎隊在小熊主場爭奪世界大賽冠軍，當地小酒館的老闆 Billy Sianis 買了兩張票，一如往常要帶著他的山羊 Murphy 進場觀賽，幫小熊隊加油。

▲2016 年小熊隊贏得世界冠軍，大家歡欣鼓舞的樣子。

門票人員勉強放 Billy 與 Murphy 進場，但比賽途中因山羊味道太重遭觀眾抗議，Billy 跟他的山羊被趕了出去。事後小熊隊老闆說「人可以進去，動物不准」，還補上一句「因為山羊太臭了」，惹得 Billy 氣得說：「因為你們污辱我的山羊，以後小熊隊不會打進世界大賽，也不會拿冠軍。」過了一百多年，小熊隊才終於在 2016 年打敗道奇隊，拿下世界冠軍。

◀場外還販賣破除山羊詛咒的小熊隊餅乾。

Arturo Pardavila III©WikiCommons

Boston Red Sox 波士頓紅襪隊：
Curse of the Bambino 貝比魯斯魔咒

紅襪隊在 1919 年把隊上扛霸子 Babe Ruth 貝比魯斯（暱稱 Bambino，義大利語「baby」的意思）高價賣給洋基隊，讓原本已經拿了五屆總冠軍的紅襪隊從此與冠軍無緣，反而是買下貝比魯斯的洋基隊成了當今拿下總冠軍最多次的球隊。這也是讓紅襪與洋基球迷成為世仇、常起衝突的原因。

據說貝比魯斯相當熱愛波士頓，還曾立下要為紅襪隊奮戰 20 年的宏願，顯見他對這個城市與這隻球隊的熱愛，因此當他被球隊售出，可想見他有多失望。

未奪冠記錄／魔咒時間 **86** 年

為了破除魔咒，紅襪隊多次去到貝比魯斯出生地巴爾的摩朝拜，也在球場上舉辦了幾十年的除咒大會，連巫師都請來了，甚至甚至有球迷帶著波士頓小熊隊球帽登頂聖母峰，祈求好運。直到 2004 年，紅襪隊總算擺脫魔咒，拿到總冠軍。

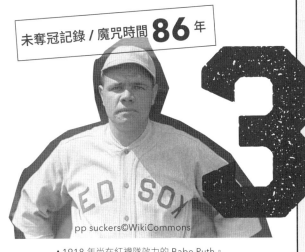

pp suckers©WikiCommons

▲1918 年尚在紅襪隊效力的 Babe Ruth。

#MLB #WorldSeries
#Dodgers #Rays
#break the curse

Joseph Sohm©Shutterstock

圖片為 2018 年道奇隊在世界大賽第三戰打敗 Red Sox 紅襪隊，但該年仍由紅襪隊拿下冠軍頭銜。

全文朗讀 🎵 035　　單字 🎵 036

Dodgers Win First World Series in 32 Years
道奇隊 32 年來首次贏得世界大賽

🕐 **October 28, 2020**

Vocabulary

1. **celebration** [ˌsɛləˋbreʃən] (n.)
   慶祝活動，慶典

2. **reward** [rɪˋwɔrd] (v./n.)
   報答，獎賞；獎勵，報酬

3. **loyalty** [ˋlɔɪəltɪ] (n.)
   忠誠，忠心

4. **competition** [ˌkɑmpəˋtɪʃən] (n.)
   競爭，競賽

5. **fierce** [fɪrs] (a.)
   激烈的，強烈的

6. **lead** [lid] (v.)
   領先，過去式與過去分詞分別為 **led**，**led**

The streets of Los Angeles exploded in [1]**celebration** Tuesday night after **the Dodgers *clinched** their win in game 6 of the 116th **World Series**. Long-suffering Dodgers fans were [2]**rewarded** for their [3]**loyalty** when the Dodgers achieved victory over the Tampa Bay Rays, with a final score of 3-1. It was the first Series win for the Dodgers in 32 years.

週二晚上，道奇隊在第 116 屆世界大賽第六場比賽最終奪勝，洛杉磯街道一片歡欣鼓舞。道奇隊最後以比分 3-1 擊敗坦帕灣光芒隊，長年飽受煎熬的道奇隊忠實球迷終於獲得回報。這是道奇隊 32 年來首次贏得世界大賽。

The [4]**competition** was [5]**fierce**, but the Rays had reason to be optimistic early in the game. They [6]**led** the Dodgers 1-0 until the bottom of the sixth **inning**, when the Rays [7]**switched** out starting **pitcher** Blake Snell. It was then that Mookie Betts put the Dodgers on the path to [8]**triumph** by **hitting a double**. Betts followed with a home run in the eighth inning, [9]**ensuring** the Rays' defeat. Players and fans barely contained their excitement as the Dodgers

[10]**reversed** what many believed was a decades-long curse on the team—the so-called "**curse of '88**." On Wednesday, Dodgers **shortstop** Corey Seager—who **batted .400** in the Series with two home runs and five **RBIs**—was named World Series **MVP**.

賽況激烈，不過光芒隊在比賽前半其實前景看好。他們原先以 1-0 領先道奇隊，直到六局下半光芒隊換下先發投手布萊克史內爾，緊接著穆奇貝茲便擊出一記二壘安打，將道奇隊推向奪勝之路，貝茲接著在第八局轟出一支全壘打，確定擊敗光芒隊。道奇隊球員和球迷都難掩興奮之情，因為許多人認為該球隊推翻了幾十年來的所謂「1988 年詛咒」。道奇隊游擊手柯瑞席格於週三獲封為世界大賽最有價值球員，他在世界大賽中擊出兩支全壘打並貢獻五分打點，打擊率為 .400。

The pandemic made training for the series difficult. The teams had to stay within "***immunity** bubbles," which meant limiting contact with the outside world to avoid [11]**infection**. In addition, none of the games took place on either team's home **diamond**. The entire Series was played in Arlington, Texas. This was also an attempt to limit [12]**exposure** to the virus. Despite the unusual [13]**circumstances**, both teams displayed the skill and [14]**sportsmanship** expected in the World Series.

這次疫情讓世界大賽的訓練變得艱辛。球隊必須待在「隔離泡泡」中，這表示要限制與外界的接觸以避免感染。此外，世界大賽的每場球賽並不在兩隊的主場舉行，而是在德州阿靈頓舉行，這也是為了避免接觸病毒的機會。儘管是非常時期，但兩隊在世界大賽中展現的技巧和運動家精神，仍如預期。

7. **switch** [swɪtʃ] (v./n.)
   更換，替換

8. **triumph** [ˈtraɪəmf] (n./v.)
   成功，勝利

9. **ensure** [ɪnˈʃur] (v.)
   確保，保證

10. **reverse** [rɪˈvɝs] (v.)
    逆轉，反轉

11. **infection** [ɪnˈfɛkʃən] (n.)
    傳染，感染

12. **exposure** [ɪkˈspoʒə] (n.)
    暴露，遭受 (+ to)

13. **circumstance** [ˈsɝkəmˌstæns] (n.) (當此定義固定用複數) 情況，情勢

14. **sportsmanship** [ˈsportsmənˌʃɪp] (n.) 運動家精神

Keeton Gale©Shitterstock

Corey Seager 於 2018 年的比賽照片。

15. **authority** [əˈθɔrətɪ] *(n.)*
（多為複數）當局，管理機關

進階字彙

* **clinch** [klɪntʃ] *(v.)*
獲得勝利，最終贏得

* **immunity** [ɪˈmjunətɪ] *(n.)*
免疫，文中指「避免感染」

* **roster** [ˈrɑstə] *(n.)*
球員名單

All-Pro Reels©WikiCommons

受疫情影響，觀眾席上擺出各國球迷紙板充當觀眾。

Earlier this year, fans were worried there might not be an **MLB** season at all. Games were delayed for months as [15]**authorities** tried to determine the safest way to proceed during the global pandemic. The Dodgers were concerned that their *****roster** of highly talented players would ⓟ**go to waste**. Their victory proves that the spirit of Major League Baseball is still alive in America, ⓟ**despite all odds**.

球迷原本擔心今年職棒大聯盟賽季不會舉行，全球大流行期間，由於當局想確定最安全的舉行方式，而將球賽推遲數月。道奇隊原本擔心球技高超的球員陣容到時無用武之地。他們的勝利證實，儘管困難重重，但美國的職棒大聯盟精神仍不滅。

Grammar Master

until vs. not until

until「直到」，有時候與 not 連用，有時卻不用，以下整理 until 的兩種用法與分別。

● **until 指一個動作持續「直到（某時間點）為止」，即本文用法。**

例：I was up until three in the morning writing my report. 我寫報告寫到凌晨三點才睡。

● **not until 強調某行為「在（某時間點）之前尚未發生」，也就是「直到（某時間點）之後才開始進行」，等於 not before。not until 放句首須倒裝。**

例：Not until our daughter called us did we stop worrying. 直到女兒打電話來，我們才停止擔心。

例：I didn't start studying until the night before the exam. 我一直到考試前一天晚上才開始唸書。

1. MLB & World Series 美國大聯盟與世界大賽

美國職棒大聯盟 MLB（Major League Baseball）的世界大賽又稱 Fall Classic「秋季經典大賽」，由每年 American League 美國聯盟與 National League 國家聯盟的冠軍隊組成（美聯與國聯合起來就是 MLB），是七戰四勝的系列賽，贏家又稱為 World Champions「世界冠軍」。世界大賽於 1903 年開辦後立即獲得廣大球迷支持，是美國最重要的體壇盛事之一。目前為止，贏得最多世界大賽的球隊是 the Yankees 紐約洋基隊，共拿下 27 次冠軍。

2. **Phrase** go to waste 浪費，無用武之地

waste 在這裡當名詞用。這組片語的用法就是 sth. + go to waste，指該物被浪費掉了。

A: You didn't finish your meal. Do you want a doggy bag? 你沒吃完，你需要廚餘袋嗎？
B: Sure. It would be a shame to let good food go to waste. 好啊。不然把好食物浪費掉就太可惜了。

3. **Phrase** despite all odds 儘管困難重重

也可說 **against all odds**，all 可以改成 the。odds 指成敗的機率。如果要說「克服重重困難、力抗萬難」，可說 **defy/overcome the odds** 或 **battle/struggle against the odds**。

A: Did you hear that Mike got accepted to Harvard? 你有聽說麥可被哈佛錄取了嗎？
B: Yeah. Against all odds, he made it into the Ivy League.
　　是啊，儘管困難重重，他還是進了常春藤盟校。

360b©Shutterstock

4. Dodgers & curse of '88 洛杉磯道奇隊與「1988 年詛咒」

Dodgers 道奇隊自 1884 年成軍以來奪下 23 次聯盟冠軍、六次世界冠軍，是 MLB 的名門球隊。不過上次奪冠已經是 1988 年的事，當時打敗奧克蘭運動家隊拿下世界冠軍後，便長達 32 年與世界冠軍擦身而過。由於道奇隊在分區連續八年稱霸，新秀養成、交易補強都做得相當出色，多次拿到世界大賽門票仍拿不到冠軍獎盃，因此球迷便將此稱為 Curse of '88，直到 2020 年對上光芒隊最後逆轉勝，才破除此咒。

5. inning 球局

這個字最早用於 cricket 板球運動，現常見於棒壘球運動。在棒壘球運動中，一局 inning 用單數，複數才加上 s，棒壘球賽一般打九局，除非比分相同才會延長局數（**extra inning**）。板球運動中則沒有單數用法，一律使用 innings 指單複數球局。

6. hit a double 擊出二壘安打

double 指「二壘安打」，**triple** 與 **home run** 分別是「三壘安打」以及「全壘打」。

7. pitcher& shortstop 投手與游擊手

棒球運動中共有九個位置，分別是：投手 **pitcher**，捕手 **catcher**，一壘／二壘／三壘手 **first/second/third baseman**，游擊手 **shortstop**、**left/center/right fielder** 左外／中外／右外野手，除了後三個位置之外，其餘屬內野手 **infielder**。shortstop 常縮寫成 SS，是棒球賽中負責防守二、三壘間的球員。除了要接捕擊球，也要跑到二壘接捕其他守備球員的傳球，由於打者多半是右撇子，所以擊到二三壘的球通常較多，所以游擊手通常是內野手中守備能力最優異的。

8. batting average 打擊率

指打者打出安打的機率，如一名打者打了 18 個打數（打擊次數）中擊出 9 次安打，該打者的打擊率就是五成。

9. RBI 打點

run batted in 的縮寫，指打者擊出球使壘包上的跑者（包含打者本身）跑回本壘的得分。白話一點來說，就是「幫球隊打回的分數」。打者靠擊出安打、犧牲打、野手選擇、內野滾地球出局而使跑者得分都計為打者打點；滿壘時因打者被四壞球保送、觸身球打擊妨礙或妨礙跑壘而使打者上一壘、擠回三壘跑者時，也算打者打點。最容易賺打點的方法，就是擊出全壘打。

10. MVP 單場最有價值球員

為 **most valuable player** 的縮寫，是給予各類球賽表現最為優秀成員的榮譽，近年也常見於非體育活動上。新聞中提到的 World Series MVP 是由媒體、大聯盟跟球迷投票決定，2020 年由道奇隊的席格拿下，為 MLB 史上第八人。

11. diamond 棒球場

diamond 是 baseball field 棒球場的別名，因棒球場外形似鑽石而來。

不同球類運動的球場用字也不同，如前文使用 **court** 稱「籃球場」，足球場則說 **football/soccer field** 或 **pitch**，高爾夫球場則是 **golf course**，冰上曲棍球場 **ice rink**。拳擊雖然不是球類，不過拳擊擂臺稱 **boxing ring**。此外，體育文章中的 **arena** 與 **stadium** 都是「體育場」，但 arena 指密閉空間，如籃球場就是 arena，而 stadium 為開放式，如 MLB 紐約洋基隊主場就稱 Yankee Stadium。

Society 社會

#Taiwan #Taichung
#suicide #lawsuit
#haunted house

全文朗讀 ♫ 037　　單字 ♫ 038

Parents of Suicide Victim Liable for Damages

🕐 **March 13, 2020**

輕生死者父母承擔賠償責任

Vocabulary

1. **commit** [kə`mɪt] (v.)
   犯下（過失、罪等）

2. **rental** [`rɛntəl] (n./a.)
   租賃（的）

3. **landlord** [`lænd͵lord] (n.)
   房東，地主

4. **moreover** [mor`ovə] (adv.)
   而且，再者

5. **compensation**
   [͵kɑmpən`seʃən] (n.) 補償，薪資。
   動詞 **compensate** [`kɑmpən͵set]

The Tainan District Court has **ruled** that the parents of a woman who ¹⁾**committed** suicide in a ²⁾**rental** apartment must pay the ³⁾**landlord**, *surnamed Hsieh, NT$2.86 million in **damages**. According to the **plaintiff**, the *deceased, surnamed Yang, should have been aware that committing suicide in a rental property would turn it into a "**haunted house**," making it difficult to rent or sell.

一名女子在承租公寓內自殺，台南地方法院裁定，其父母必須向謝姓房東賠償 286 萬元新台幣。據原告稱，楊姓死者應知道在承租屋中自殺，會使房屋成為「凶宅」，以至於難以出租或出售。

Hsieh claimed that Yang **intentionally** committed suicide in her apartment, and was therefore **liable** for damages. ⁴⁾**Moreover**, because Yang was no longer alive, her parents should be required to pay ⁵⁾**compensation**. Hsieh said the losses she suffered included

NT$2.3 million in property ***depreciation** and NT$238,000 due to early [6]**termination** of rental contracts.

謝姓房東聲稱，楊女是故意在她的公寓自殺，因此應承擔賠償責任。此外，由於楊女已死，她的父母理應付賠償金。謝姓房東說，她的損失包括 230 萬元的房價貶損和 23 萬 8000 元的提早解約金。

Yang [7]**leased** one of Hsieh's rooftop rental ***units** in January of last year, and committed suicide the following December. This caused her other [8]**tenants** to move away out of fear, and she was unable to find new tenants after news of the suicide spread, said Hsieh. When the value of her property also began to [9]**decline** because it was now seen as a haunted house, she decided to sue Yang's parents for the losses ***incurred**.

楊女於去年 1 月承租謝姓房東的其中一間頂樓套房，並於同年 12 月自殺。她表示，這件事造成其他房客因恐懼而搬離，自殺消息傳開後，她也找不到新的房客。由於她的房子現在被視為凶宅，房價也開始貶損，因此她決定以造成損失為由控告楊女的父母。

Yang's parents [10]**countered** that because their daughter had no **intention** to cause financial losses to Hsieh, she had no right to be **compensated**. [11]**Furthermore**, because Hsieh's rooftop rental units were **illegal structures** and should therefore be ***demolished**, their daughter wasn't liable for any lost rent or decline in property value.

楊女的父母反駁，由於他們的女兒無意為謝姓房東造成財務損失，因此她無權獲得賠償。此外，由於謝姓房東的頂樓出租套房是違章建築，理應拆除，因此他們的女兒不需對租金損失或房價貶損承擔任何責任。

The Taiwan District Court, however, ruled that because Yang was an adult, she should have been aware that her suicide would make the rental unit a haunted house, and so there was reason to believe her actions showed **indirect intent**. The judges also said that the illegal [12]**construction** of the rental units was a separate question from the property depreciation caused by Yang's suicide.

不過台灣地方法院裁定，由於楊女已成年，她應該知道自殺會導致租屋變成凶宅，因此有理由相信她的舉動有間接意圖。法官也表示，租屋為違章建築與楊女自殺造成房價貶損是兩回事。

---

6. **termination** [ˌtɝmɪˈneʃən] (n.)
終止，結束。動詞 **terminate**
[ˈtɝmɪ.net]

---

7. **lease** [lis] (v./n.) 出租；租約

---

8. **tenant** [ˈtɛnənt] (n.) 房客

---

9. **decline** [dɪˈklaɪn] (v./n.)
下跌，衰退

---

10. **counter** [ˈkaʊntə] (v.)
反駁，反擊

---

11. **furthermore** [ˈfɝðəˌmor]
(adv.) 此外，再者，
同 **moreover**

---

12. **construction** [kənˈstrʌkʃən]
(n.) 建設，營造工程；建造物

13. **estimate** [ˈɛstəmət / ˈɛstəˌmet]
(n./v.) 估計

14. **real estate** (phr.)
房地產，不動產，同 **realty**
[ˈriəlti]

* **surname** [ˈsɝˌnem] (v./n.)
姓；姓氏，同 **last name** 和
family name

* **deceased** [dɪˈsist] (a.)
已故的，**the deceased** 指「死
者」（為複數名詞，需與複數動
詞使用）

* **depreciation** [dɪˌpriʃiˈeʃən] (n.)
貶值，掉價
depreciate [dɪˈpriʃiˌet] (v.)

* **unit** [ˈjunɪt] (n.)
（公寓大樓的）公寓、套房

* **incur** [ɪnˈkɝ] (v.) 招致，惹來

* **demolish** [dɪˈmɑlɪʃ] (v.)
拆除，毀壞

示意圖。

Because Hsieh's claim for compensation were based on an [13]**estimate** made by [14]**real estate** professionals, the court ordered the **defendants** to pay her NT$2.86 million in compensation. The January 7 **ruling** can be appealed.

由於謝姓房東的索賠是根據房地產專業人士的估算得出，因此法院下令要求被告賠償她 286 萬元。這項於 1 月 7 日做出的裁決可再上訴。

Grammar Master

各種「控告」的英文表達

英文表達「控告」的動詞包括 sue，accuse，charge 跟 prosecute，這四個字在用法稍有不同：

● **accuse**：用法是 accuse sb. of doing sth.「指控某人某行為」。

例：The employee was accused of stealing company funds. 該員工被指控竊取公司基金。

● **sue**：指「對某人提出訴訟」，常用 sue sb. for sth.「以⋯罪名控告某人」。在法律上，sue 尤指金錢賠償相關的提告。

例：The actress sued the magazine after it published naked photos of her.
女演員向刊登她裸照的雜誌提出訴訟。

● **charge** 與 **prosecute**：charge sb. with sth.「以⋯罪行起訴某人」，意同 prosecute [ˈprɑsɪˌkjut] sb. for sth.，兩個字皆用在刑事訴訟上。prosecutor 指「檢察官」。

例：The police have charged the suspect with murder. 警方以謀殺罪起訴該嫌犯。

例：Shoplifters will be prosecuted. 竊賊將被起訴。

1. rule 裁決，裁定

rule 當動詞在法律上有「（法官，法院或主管機關）做出裁定，裁決」的意思，名詞為 **ruling**。

2. damages 損害賠償金

在法律用語中，**damage** 指因過失（negligence [`nɛɡlɪdʒəns]）、故意或意外事故而非法侵害他人人身財產造成的損害。複數形式 damages 指「損害賠償金」。

3. plaintiff & defendant 原告與被告

plaintiff [`plentɪf] 指「原告，起訴人」，就是提出訴訟的一方。與之對立的則是「被告」**defendant** [dɪ`fɛndənt]，共同被告人可以說 **co-defendant**。

4. haunted house 鬼屋，凶宅

haunted [`hɔntɪd] 當形容詞，指「鬧鬼的」。在台灣，只要是傳出兇殺案的屋子，幾乎就會變成空城。不過在部分國家如英國，鬧鬼的房子由於多半是歷史悠久的古堡，建築物本身與周遭景色優美，反而成為觀光景點，有人甚至會特意詢問房子是否鬧鬼，如果不鬧鬼偏不住。而在日本，由於發生過兇殺事件的房子房價會便宜許多，因此不少日本人為了省錢並不在意，甚至還有專門網站清楚列出發生兇殺案的住房（兇殺時間、手法都清楚詳細列出）供找房參考。

5. intention vs. intent 「意向」與「意圖」

在一般英文中，intention 跟 intent 是可以交替互用的，然而在法律中，兩個字意思大不相同。intention「意向」跟當名詞使用的 intent「意圖」都有「想執行某事」的意思，intention 偏向想做某事，但不一定會做；相較起來，intent 更有積極要達成某事，因此 intent 常出現在法律中，指對方「故意，有犯罪意圖」。此外，刑法中的「間接故意」英文說法是 **indirect intent**。

🗩 He was carrying a gun with intent to commit robbery. 他持槍意圖搶劫。

🗩 It was not my intention/intent to hurt your feelings. 我無意傷害你的感受。

6. liable 應負法律責任的

念作 [`laɪəbəl]，指「應負法律責任的」，「有義務（納稅等）的」。在本文中，**be liable for** 等於 **have to pay**，指「需承擔（因法律所規定的）費用」。

7. illegal structure 違章建築

illegal 為「非法的」，illegal structure 即「違章建築」，也可說 **illegal building**。所有違例的建築工程都算，如頂樓加蓋、陽台外推都算。

CTITV NEWS CHANNEL 52

#Taiwan #NCC
#Want Want China Times
#freedom of speech #freedom of press

取自 youtube

NCC 自 2006 年成立以來，首度對新聞台做出不予換照的決議。

全文朗讀 ♫ 039　　單字 ♫ 050

CTi News to Go Off the Air
中天新聞臺關臺

⏰ **December 11, 2020**

Chung Tien Television (CTi), a **pro-China** cable news station in Taiwan, must [1]**cease** broadcasting at midnight on Dec. 11, 2020. This decision by Taiwan's Supreme [2]**Administrative** Court [3]**upheld** the earlier ruling by the **National Communications Commission** (NCC) in November that CTi's [4]**license** not be renewed.

台灣的親中有線新聞臺中天電視必須在 2020 年 12 月 11 日午夜停播。這項裁決由台灣最高行政法院的裁定，維持國家通訊傳播委員會（後簡稱 NCC）先前於 11 月做出中天新聞臺不予換照的決議。

The NCC had fined CTi 25 times over the previous six years for spreading [5]**inaccurate** information. In announcing its decision, the NCC [6]**cited** CTi's "repeated violations of [7]**regulations** and a failure of its internal [8]**discipline** and control [9]**mechanisms**." The Supreme Administrative Court's decision is final and can't be appealed by Chung Tien.

NCC 在過去六年以散佈不精確消息為由對中天新聞臺罰款 25 次。NCC 在宣佈這項決議時，舉出中天新聞臺「不斷違規，且內部控管與自律機制運作失靈」。最高行政法院的裁決已定案，中天無法上訴。

Following the court's ruling, officials from Taiwan's [10]**opposition** Kuomintang (KMT) held a [11]**press conference** to draw attention to the NCC's decision, which they believe was politically [12]**motivated**. While Taiwan claims to be an open, democratic society, argued KMT Party [13]**Chairman** Johnny Chiang, this move proves that the current government is against freedom of speech and freedom of the press.

法院做出裁決後，在野黨國民黨舉行新聞記者會以吸引大眾關注 NCC 的決議，他們認為這項決議是出於政治動機。國民黨主席江啟臣認為，儘管台灣自稱是開放的民主社會，但此舉證明當前政府違反言論自由和新聞自由。

CTi is owned by the **Want Want China Times** media group, which has extensive business interests in China. In its ruling, NCC Chairperson Chen Yaw-shyang did not mention the station's **pro-China slant**, but did say that the channel may be ***susceptible** to outside influence. The ruling DPP rejected the KMT's claims, arguing that the NCC arrives at its decisions independently, no matter which party is currently in power.

中天電視由旺旺中時媒體集團擁有，該集團在中國有深厚的商業利益。NCC 主委陳耀祥在決議中並未提到該電臺的親中傾向，但表示該頻道可能容易受外界影響。執政的民進黨否認國民黨的主張，辯稱 NCC 是獨立做出裁決，與目前是何政黨執政無關。

7. **regulation** [ˌrɛgjəˈleʃən] (n.)
法規，規則

8. **discipline** [ˈdɪsəplɪn] (n.)
紀律，風紀

9. **mechanism** [ˈmɛkəˌnɪzəm] (n.)
機制，機構

10. **opposition** [ˌɑpəˈzɪʃən] (n.)
反對，在野黨

11. **press conference** (phr.)
記者會

12. **motivated** [ˈmotɪˌvetɪd] (a.)
有目的，動機的

13. **chairman** [ˈtʃɛrmən] (n.)
主席，議長

14. **journalist** [ˈdʒɜnəlɪst] (n.)
新聞記者

15. **impact** [ˈɪmpækt] (v./n.)
影響，衝擊 (+ on)

16. **accessible** [ækˈsɛsəbəl] (a.)
可得到的，有途徑的（+ to）

17. **retain** [rɪˈten] (v.) 保持，保有

在新冠肺炎開始爆發之際，中天新聞臺曾於報導中打出「封臺倒數六天」字樣，引起社會恐慌，遭 NCC 罰鍰。

中天新聞臺關臺之後，轉型成為網路新聞頻道。

International media **watchdog Reporters Without Borders**, which has been monitoring the situation, said in a statement released on Nov. 18 that the decision didn't go against press freedom. The group did, however, express regret that the ***livelihood** of some CTi [14)]**journalists** will be [15)]**impacted** by the decision not to renew the station's broadcast license.

一直關注局勢的國際媒體監督團體無國界記者在 11 月 18 日發表聲明，表示此決議不違反新聞自由。但因電臺的廣播執照不予換發一決議使部分中天記者生計受影響，該組織表示遺憾。

18. **pledge** [plɛdʒ] *(v./n.)*
承諾，保證

19. **application** [ˌæpləˋkeʃən] *(n.)*
應用程式

進階字彙

* **susceptible** [səˋsɛptəbəl] *(a.)*
易受影響的

* **livelihood** [ˋlaɪvlɪˌhud] *(n.)*
生活，生計

* **jurisdiction** [ˌdʒurɪsˋdɪkʃən] *(n.)*
管轄權，管轄範圍

While this ruling means that CTi will no longer be [16)]**accessible** to cable TV subscribers in Taiwan, the station still [17)]**retains** a strong online presence. Its official YouTube channel, for instance, has over a million subscribers, and the station has [18)]**pledged** to continue its work through various mobile and Internet [19)]**applications**. These platforms don't fall under the ***jurisdiction** of the NCC or any other government body.

儘管這項裁決表示台灣的有線電視訂戶將無法再收看中天新聞臺，但該電臺在網路上仍有全方位的能見度。例如該電臺的官方 YouTube 頻道擁有逾一百萬訂閱數，該電臺也已承諾，將透過各種行動裝置和網路應用程式繼續運作。這些平臺不受 NCC 或任何其他政府機構管轄。

Grammar Master

自由有兩種

英文中有兩種表達自由的用法，一是「追求…的自由」，可以用 freedom of N 或 freedom to V 表達，本文中提到的 freedom of speech「言論自由」與 freedom of the press「新聞自由」就屬此例，後者的 press 指「媒體報導、新聞界」。

● **freedom to V「追求…的自由」：**
例：freedom to express 表達意見的自由

● **freedom from Ving「免於…的自由」：** 為第二種自由，介系詞 from 有「遠離」之意：
例：freedom from want 免於匱乏的自由

1. pro-China (slant) 親中傾向

字首 pro- 有「支持」之意，pro-China 在台灣政治上指「親中的」。中天新聞臺於 2009 被中資旺旺中時媒體集團買下，因此中天新聞臺被歸類為親中新聞頻道。**slant** 本指「傾斜、偏向」，常用來特定「政治或言論傾向」。

2. National Communications Commission, NCC 中華民國國家通訊傳播委員會

是台灣管理電信通訊、廣播電視等訊息流通事業的最高主管機關，於 2006 年成立，為受行政院監督的獨立機關，目的希望能使通訊與傳播事業管理能不受政治影響。除了管理如電視台的執照外，如 4G 等通訊設備的發照也是由 NCC 管理發放。

3. Want Want China Times 旺旺中時集團

常被媒體稱作「旺中集團」的旺旺中時媒體集團，前身是中國時報集團，於 2009 年被中資旺旺集團買下，旺旺集團從此跨足台灣媒體領域。旺旺集團原本是食品產銷業起家，由蔡明衍創立，之後進軍中國大陸、新加坡等市場，由於獲利來源主要是在中國大陸，之後發展重心便轉向大陸。2010 年 10 月，傳出旺旺中時集團打算出資併購有線電視中嘉網路，擴大其媒體版圖，專家學者與公民團體擔心此併購案恐會讓中國控制台灣媒體，因此舉行多次抗議與公聽會，主管機關 NCC 最後於 2013 年認定旺旺中時集團併購中嘉案因未達其附帶條件而不予通過，此事件後來通稱「旺中案」，與此次的中天電視台關臺一樣，NCC 的決議同樣引起擁護抑或壟斷媒體言論自由的正反意見。

4. watchdog 監督組織、機關

國外媒體常以 watchdog 一字指各種監管機關，此詞並沒有任何貶意。

▲ 中天電視總部位於臺北市內湖區「時報廣場大樓」裡頭，此為大樓正面的旺仔。

5. Reporters Without Borders 無國界記者

由 Robert Ménard 於 1985 年於法國創立，法文名稱為 Reporters sans frontières，縮寫為 RSF，是致力保護記者免受迫害、並致力於推動新聞自由的國際非營利組織。

#BLM #Black Lives Matter
#US #Minnesota
#African American
#racial equality #police brutality
#George Floyd

Tverdokhlib©Shutterstock

全文朗讀 ♫ 041　單字 ♫ 042

The Death of George Floyd

白人警察殺害黑人佛洛依德，引發群憤

⏱ May 30, 2020

Vocabulary

1. **convenience** [kən`vinjəns]
   (n.) 方便，便利設施，
   convenience store 即「便利
   商店」

2. **cruiser** [`kruzɚ] (n.)
   警車；巡洋艦

3. **restrain** [rɪ`stren] (v.)
   抑制，遏制

4. **kneel** [nil] (v.)
   跪下，用膝蓋頂

On the evening of May 25th, an **African-American** man named **George Floyd** lost his life in Minneapolis, Minnesota. Suspected of using a ***counterfeit** $20 bill at a [1]**convenience** store, Floyd was arrested and placed inside a police [2]**cruiser**. After a short struggle, a white officer named **Derek Chauvin** pulled Floyd out of the car, causing him to fall onto the street, where he lay face down in handcuffs. Chauvin then [3]**restrained** Floyd by [4]**kneeling** on his neck.

五月 25 日晚上，一名叫喬治佛洛伊德的非裔美國人在明尼蘇達州的明尼阿波利斯市喪命。佛洛伊德疑似使用 20 美元假鈔在便利商店買東西，因而被逮捕，並壓入警車內。經過一陣掙扎，一名叫德瑞克蕭文的白人警察將佛洛伊德拉出車外，讓已上手銬的他臉朝下倒在地上。接著，蕭文用膝蓋壓住他的脖子，限制他的行動。

Over the next eight minutes, Chauvin kept his knee on Floyd's neck, while three other officers [5]**looked on**. Despite the fact that Floyd said "I can't breathe" at least 16 times, and several ***bystanders** expressed concern for his condition, Chauvin only removed his knee from the man's neck when an ambulance arrived. For his last three minutes on the ground with a knee in his neck, Floyd appeared to be [6]**unconscious**. An hour later, he was [7]**pronounced** dead at a local hospital.

蕭文持續壓住佛洛伊德的脖子長達八分鐘，在此期間其他三名警察就站在一旁觀看。儘管佛洛伊德說了十六次「我不能呼吸」，好幾名旁觀者也出聲關心，但直到救護車到場之前，蕭文還是持續壓住該男子的脖子。在佛洛伊德被膝蓋壓住脖子伏在地上的最後三分鐘，他似乎已經失去意識。一小時之後，他在當地醫院宣不治。

A video of Floyd on the ground repeating "I can't breathe" and "Don't kill me" taken by a bystander quickly went viral on social media, and the next day Chauvin and the other three officers were fired from the police department. That same day, protests against Floyd's killing began in the Minneapolis-St. Paul area. They started out peacefully, but later became violent as buildings were [8]**set on fire**, stores were ***looted** and ***vandalized**, and some protesters [9]**clashed** with police.

一名旁觀者拍下佛洛伊德被壓制在地上重複呼喊「我不能呼吸」「不要殺我」的影片，在社群媒體上迅速延燒開來，隔天蕭文和其他三名警察立即被解職。同一天，多場佛洛伊德之死的抗議行動便在明尼阿波利斯聖保羅地區展開。他們一開始以和平方式抗議，但稍晚演變成暴動，許多大樓被縱火，商店被洗劫一空並遭破壞，部分示威者與警方發生衝突。

The demonstrations have now spread to over 75 cities around the country, and the news is filled with scenes of violence and [10]**destruction**. Chauvin was arrested on May 29 and charged with **third-degree murder**, but the fires continue to burn.

Hayk_Shalunts©Shutterstock

示威者舉著「Stop Police Brutality」（停止警方暴力），抗議警察對黑人施暴。

5. **look on** *(phr.)* 站在一旁觀看

6. **unconscious** [ʌnˋkɑnʃəs] *(a.)* 失去意識的

7. **pronounce** [prəˋnaʊns] *(v.)* 宣告，公布

8. **set on fire** *(phr.)* 縱火，起火

9. **clash** [klæʃ] *(v./n.)* 發生衝突；衝突

10. **destruction** [dɪˋstrʌkʃən] *(n.)* 毀滅，破壞

* **counterfeit** [ˋkaʊntɚˌfɪt] *(a.)*
  偽造的

* **bystander** [ˋbaɪˌstændɚ] *(n.)*
  旁觀者，路人

* **loot** [lut] *(v.)* 洗劫，搶劫

* **vandalize** [ˋvændəlˌaɪz] *(v.)*
  任意破壞

佛洛依德之死，造成美國全國大規模警方與民眾間暴力衝突。

示威行動至今已延燒到全美超過 75 個城市，新聞充斥著暴力與破壞畫面。蕭文在五月 29 日以三級謀殺罪被逮捕起訴，但這股怒火仍持續延燒。

Grammar Master

as 用法整理

本文中「They became violent **as** buildings were set on fire...」（隨著建築物焰火燃燒，示威者也變得暴力）的 as 當連接詞，表達「隨著、當…」，用法與意思同 **when**：

例：I witnessed a car accident as I was walking on the street. 我走過馬路時目睹了一場車禍。

● as 也可以用來「比較」：as...as「和…一樣…」，與形容詞或副詞原級連用：

例：I can't run as fast as you do. 我沒辦法像你跑得一樣快。

● as 也可以表達「作為…身分」：

例：Sally works as a flight attendant. 莎莉的職業是空服員。

● as 也可當作「因為，由於」，用法等同 because：

例：As she is interested in art, Kate often visits museums. 因為對藝術有興趣，凱特時常參觀博物館。

● as 指「如…一樣」：

例：Please follow the steps as written in the manual. 請依照手冊上的步驟操作。

● as 也可以與形容詞連用：adj. + as + S + V，表達「儘管，雖然」：

例：Frustrated as he was, he strived to overcome the difficulty. 儘管很挫折，他依然努力克服困難。

1. African American 非裔美國人

17 至 18 世紀美國從西非引進人口強迫奴役，19 世紀中期，美國南北戰爭雖解放黑奴，社會對非裔依舊充斥歧視，南方仍實行種族隔離政策。20 世紀中，以 Martin Luther King, Jr. 為首的民權運動以及美國總統甘乃迪的努力促成 1964 年民權法案（Civil Rights of 1964）的通過，禁止種族隔離與歧視。2008 年歐巴馬贏得總統選舉，成為美國歷史上首位非裔總統。2020 年非裔美國人口約有 4 千 4 百萬人，佔美國總人口 14%，位居白人 60%、拉丁裔 18% 後。

African American「非裔美國人」一字帶有平等、尊重的意味，中間加上連字號 **African-American** 則成為形容詞。

2. George Floyd & Derek Chauvin

George Floyd，46 歲，非裔美國人，生於北卡羅來納州。2009 年 Floyd 曾因持械行搶而在德州監獄服刑 5 年。出獄後，他搬到明尼蘇達州，在明尼亞波利斯（Minneapolis）一家餐廳當了五年保全，因 Covid-19 疫情失去工作。他有五名子女，住在休士頓。2020 年 6 月官方最終驗屍報告顯示，Floyd 生前曾感染新冠肺炎，但無症狀，也非死亡原因。致死原因為頸部受壓，窒息而心臟驟停，不過報告中也指出 Floyd 的潛在健康問題，如心臟病和使用類鴉片止痛劑「吩坦尼」（fentanyl）也可能是致死原因。

白人警察 Derek Chauvin。

Chauvin 射殺 Floyd 除了引起種族爭議，也引起美國民眾對於警方濫用權力的不滿。

Derek Chauvin，44 歲白人，是此事件中單膝跪在佛洛伊德頸部的白人警官。Chauvin 自 2001 年擔任明尼亞波利斯警官，在他的記錄中共有 18 項被投訴記錄，甚至因其中 2 項而被記警告（reprimand）。發生此案之前，Chauvin 已有 3 起案件開槍紀錄，其中一次還對對方擊斃。2020 年 10 月 7 日，Chauvin 交保釋放，該案審判預定在 2021 年 3 月進行。蕭文的辯護律師以疫情出庭人數為由，要求將審判延 7 月，法官予以駁回。

3. third-degree murder 三級謀殺

murder「謀殺罪，殺人罪」是美國律法上規定的一種罪行，屬於重罪（**felony**）。murder 分成三級，與 first-degree murder 一級謀殺和 second-degree murder 二級謀殺相比，third-degree murder 三級謀殺罪行最輕，指沒有預謀殺害動機的作案，美國各州針對謀殺的定罪各有不同，在明尼蘇達州可判處最高 25 年有期徒刑。

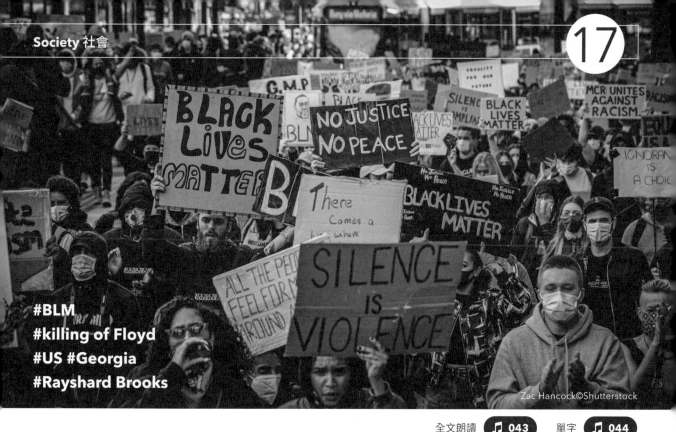

#BLM
#killing of Floyd
#US #Georgia
#Rayshard Brooks

Zac Hancock©Shutterstock

全文朗讀 🎵 043　單字 🎵 044

Atlanta Man Fatally Shot
繼佛洛依德之後，亞特蘭大一名黑人又被射殺

🕐 **June 13, 2020**

Vocabulary

1. **fatally** [ˋfetəli] *(adv.)*
   致命地，形容詞為 **fatal**

2. **in response (to)** *(phr.)*
   作為⋯的回應

3. **backup** [ˋbæk͵ʌp] *(n.)*
   支援，支持

Just weeks after George Floyd lost his life at the hands of Minneapolis police officers, another African-American man has been [1]**fatally** shot by police outside of a Wendy's restaurant in Atlanta, Georgia.

喬治佛洛依德死在明尼阿波利斯市警手上的事情才過去沒幾週，在喬治亞州的亞特蘭大，又發生一起非裔美國人在溫蒂漢堡外面被警察射殺的事件。

On the evening of June 12, police arrived at the Wendy's parking lot [2]**in response to** a call about a car blocking the **drive-through lane**. Finding 27-year-old Rayshard Brooks asleep in his car, Officer Devin Brosnan woke him up and asked him if he'd been drinking. Brooks admitted that he had, and after checking his driver's license, Brosnan called for [3]**backup**.

六月 12 日晚上，警察抵達溫蒂漢堡的停車場，因為他們收到一通電話，通報有台車擋住了得來速車道。原來是 27 歲的雷沙德布魯克斯睡在車內，警察迪文布洛斯南將他叫醒，問他是否有喝酒。布魯克斯承認自己有喝，而在查看他的駕照之後，布洛斯南呼叫支援。

When Officer Garrett Rolfe arrived several minutes later, he **ⓟpatted** Brooks **down** and gave him a sobriety test, which he failed. "I think you've had too much to drink to be driving," Rolfe told Brooks. "Put your hands behind your back." But when Rolfe tried to handcuff Brooks—who was calm and ⁴⁾**cooperative** up till then—he began resisting arrest.

警察對 Brooks 做酒測當時的監視器畫面。

警察葛瑞特羅爾夫幾分鐘內抵達現場，他對布魯克斯搜身，並讓他做酒測，而布魯克斯酒測沒過。「我覺得你喝太多，不能開車。」羅爾夫告知布魯克斯，「把雙手放在背後。」正當羅爾夫將布魯克斯上銬時，布魯克斯開始掙扎拒捕，而在這之前，一直表現得相當平靜且合作。

After a *scuffle with the two officers, Brooks ⁵⁾**managed** to get hold of Brosnan's **Taser** and escape. As Rolfe chased Brooks, he turned around and fired the Taser at the officer. Rolfe then ⁶⁾**drew** his gun and fired three shots, two of which hit Brooks in the back. An ambulance arrived for Brooks several minutes later, but he died during ⁷⁾**surgery** shortly ⁸⁾**thereafter**. Brosnan was treated for a *concussion

與兩名警察經過一番扭打之後，布魯克斯試圖拿到布洛斯南的電擊槍並逃跑。羅爾夫追捕布魯克斯時，布魯克斯轉身以電擊槍攻擊警察，接著羅爾夫拔槍朝他射了三槍，兩發擊中布魯克斯的背部。救護車在幾分鐘內到達，然而布魯克斯稍後在手術中死亡。布洛斯南也因腦震盪接受治療。

ⓟOpinions about the shooting **are divided**. Many believe the use of *lethal force against Brooks wasn't ⁹⁾**justified**, while others feel that Rolfe made the right decision in shooting a ¹⁰⁾**fleeing** criminal who'd just taken a police weapon and fired it at him.

針對這起槍殺事件的意見分歧。許多人認為，運用致死手段制服布魯克斯並不合理，而部分人則認為，羅爾夫對一名搶走警察武器並朝他開槍的逃犯做出開槍的決定是正確的。

4. **cooperative** [koˋɑprətɪv] (a.)
   （樂意）合作的，配合度高的

5. **manage (to)** [ˋmænɪdʒ] (v.)
   設法做到、完成

6. **draw** [drɔ] (v.) 拔出（武器）

7. **surgery** [ˋsɝdʒərɪ] (n.)
   手術，開刀

8. **thereafter** [ðɛrˋæftɚ] (adv.)
   之後，以後

9. **justified** [ˋdʒʌstəfaɪd] (a.)
   有正當理由的

10. **flee** [fli] (v.) 逃跑，逃離，過去式與過去分詞分別為 **fled, fled**

11. **resign** [rɪˋzaɪn] (v.)
請辭，下台

* **scuffle** [ˋskʌfəl] (n./v.)
扭打，亂鬥

* **concussion** [kənˋkʌʃən] (n.)
腦震盪

* **lethal** [ˋliθəl] (a.) 致命的

* **engulf** [ɪnˋgʌlf] (v.) 吞沒，捲入

arzualtincicek©Shutterstock

事發地點的溫蒂漢堡餐廳之後遭抗議者縱火燒毀。

In any case, the Atlanta police chief [11]**resigned** the next day, Rolfe was fired, and Brosnan was placed on **desk duty**. That same evening, protesters began gathering at the Wendy's where Brooks was shot, and within hours the restaurant was ***engulfed** in flames.
無論如何，亞特蘭大警察局長隔天請辭，羅爾夫被解雇，布洛斯南被調任文職。當天晚上，示威者開始聚集在布魯克斯被射殺的溫蒂漢堡前。數時內，那間餐廳便被火吞沒。

Grammar Master

in case 相關片語

本句「**In any case**, the Atlanta police chief resigned the next day...」的 in any case 代表「無論如何，反正」。

例：I don't want to go to the party and in any case, I haven't been invited. 我才不想去派對，反正也沒人邀請我。

● **in that case** 「既然如此，如果這樣的話」
例：There's no Coke left? In that case I'll have a Sprite. 沒有可樂了嗎？如果這樣，我點雪碧。

● **In case of + N** 「萬一，如果…」
例：In case of fire, the alarm will go off. 萬一發生火災，警報鈴會響起。

● **(just) in case…** 「以免；萬一」
例：Bring an umbrella with you just in case it rains. 帶把傘以免會下雨。

1. drive-through lane 得來速通道

亦可拼作 **drive-thru**。顧客開車駛入餐廳，無需下車，直接透過窗口點餐結帳，快速取餐。該服務最先出現在 1930 年代的美國，從此便傳遍全世界。台灣「得來速」一詞首見於麥當勞，該公司在 2006 年將「得來速」註冊為商標，其他食品業者改用「點餐車道」（如肯德基）、「車道門市」（如星巴克）等字眼。

FREELY ART©Shutterstock

2. `Phrase` **pat sb. down 搜某人身**

pat 本是「輕拍」的意思，pat down 就是從頭拍到尾的意思，也就是「搜身」的意思，名詞寫法：pat-down 或 patdown。

例 It's standard for police officers to pat down suspects before handcuffing them.
警察將嫌犯上手銬之前，需先搜身，這是標準程序。

3. Taser 泰瑟電擊槍

Taser 一詞 為 Thomas A. Swift Electric Rifle 的縮寫，式由美國泰瑟公司製造的電擊槍。命名靈感來自發明人美國太空總署的核物理學博士傑克科弗（Jack Cover）童年最喜歡的一本青年科幻讀物《Tom Swift and His Electric Rifle》。因非致命性與方便使用之特性，泰瑟槍為多國保安警隊、航空公司常用之做為防暴武器，具有極高知名度。

4. `Phrase` **opinions (about...) are divided （有關…的）意見分歧**

divided 指「意見分歧的」，整個片語也可寫成單數 opinion (about...) is divided。

例 Opinions about U.S. pork imports are divided.
大眾對美國豬肉進口一事意見分歧。

5. desk duty 文職

desk 原本指「辦公桌」，延伸為文書工作，而 duty 為「工作職責」，因此 desk duty 代表在辦公室工作、不需出勤的文職，也可說成 **desk job**。

#international #US #NFL
#affirmative movement
#BLM #brand activism

dean bertoncelj©Shutterstock

圖為 Washington Redskins 原本的隊徽。

全文朗讀 ♫ 045　　單字 ♫ 046

Washington Redskins Name Under Review

美國平權爭議燒向美式足球：華盛頓紅人隊隊名惹議

🕐 July 7, 2020

Vocabulary

1. **patriot** [ˋpetrɪət] *(n.)* 愛國的人

2. **appearance** [əˋpɪrəns] *(n.)*
   出席，現身

If you're a fan of American football, you're sure to be familiar with the **Washington Redskins**. Since joining the **NFL** in the early 1930s, the Redskins have won two NFL Championships and three **Super Bowls**. Only five teams have appeared in more Super Bowls than the Redskins—the New England [1]**Patriots**, Dallas Cowboys, Pittsburgh Steelers, Denver Broncos and **San Francisco 49ers**.

如果你是美式足球迷，想必對華盛頓紅人隊不陌生。從 1930 年代初期加入美國職業美式足球聯盟 NFL 以來，紅人隊拿下兩次 NFL 冠軍以及三次超級盃冠軍。目前參加超級盃的次數能超越紅人隊的只有五個球隊——新英格蘭愛國者隊、達拉斯牛仔隊、匹茲堡鋼人隊、丹佛野馬隊，以及舊金山 49 人隊。

In recent years, however, the Redskins have come under increasing criticism. Although the Redskins' last Super Bowl [2]**appearance** was in 1992, this criticism isn't about their performance on the field, but rather their name.

不過，紅人隊近年遭受的批評聲浪不斷，儘管他們最近一次現身在超級盃已經是 1992 年的事，但是針對他們的批評跟他們球場上的表現無關，而是跟他們的隊名有關。

Where does the term "redskin" come from? In the 18th century, French [3]**settlers** in the Mississippi River Valley [4]**translated** a word used by local Indians to [5]**refer** to themselves into *peau rouge*. This was later translated into English as redskin, a term that was used for many years with no negative meaning, even by Indians themselves. But during **the civil rights movement of the 1960s**, American Indian [6]**activists** began to feel that words like redskin promoted negative [7]**stereotypes** about Native Americans.

隊名中的「redskin 紅皮膚」一字是怎麼來的？這要追溯到十八世紀移居到密西西比河流域的法國人，他們先將當地印地安人用來自稱的字翻成 peau rouge，這個法文詞後來就翻成了英文字 redskin「紅皮膚」。當時，這個字並沒有任何負面含意，也相安無事用了許多年，連印地安人自己也在用。不過，到了一九六〇年代人權運動時期，美國印地安社運人士開始覺得，這個字會引起大眾對美國原住民的負面刻板印象。

Today, most dictionaries define redskin as an [8]**offensive** term, but it's not that simple. A number of polls have shown that the majority of football fans, the general public, and even American Indians, don't find the word redskin offensive. And Redskins owner Dan Snyder has said the name was chosen back in 1933 to honor **Native Americans**, including the head coach—who was part **Sioux**—and four of the team's players.

如今，多數字典都將 redskin 這個字定義成歧視字眼不過事情可沒這麼簡單。一連串的民意調查顯示，美式足球觀眾、一般大眾、甚至是美國印地安人，都不覺得 redskin 這個字有歧視意味。而且，紅人隊老闆丹史耐德也說了，這個隊名是他們在 1933 年為了表彰隊上的美國原住民隊員而選定的，包含印第安蘇族出身的總教練以及其他 4 名球員。

3. **settler** [ˈsɛtələ] (n.)
拓荒者，移民，殖民者

4. **translate** [ˈtrænslet] (v.)
翻譯，轉譯

5. **refer (to)** [rɪˈfɝ] 稱為，提及

6. **activist** [ˈæktəvɪst] (n.)
社運人士

7. **stereotype** [ˈstɛrɪəˌtaɪp] (n.)
刻板印象

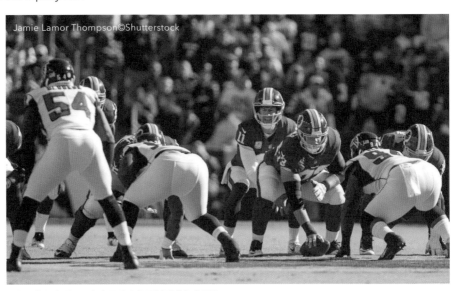

Jamie Lamor Thompson©Shutterstock

球場上的紅人隊，酒紅色配上金色是該隊的經典配色。

8. **offensive** [əˈfɛnsɪv] (a.)
   冒犯的，歧視的

9. **investor** [ɪnˈvɛstə] (n.)
   投資者，出資者

10. **sponsor** [ˈspɑnsə] (n./v.)
    贊助者，贊助商；贊助，資助

11. **call on** (phr.) 呼籲，訴求

12. **merchandise** [ˈmɜtʃən͵daɪs]
    (n.) 商品，為不可數名詞

13. **logo** [ˈlogo] (n.)
    商標，徽章，標誌

But following the police killing of George Floyd, a group of ⁹⁾**investors** wrote letters to Redskins ¹⁰⁾**sponsors** like FedEx, Nike and PepsiCo urging them to put pressure on the team to change its name. On July 2, FedEx publically ¹¹⁾**called on** the team to change its name, and Nike removed all Redskins ¹²⁾**merchandise** from its website. The next day, the team announced that it would be reviewing its name, and on July 13 made an official statement that they would retire the Redskins name and ¹³⁾**logo**.

然而，發生佛洛依德之死事件之後，一群投資人寫信給 FedEx、Nike、百事可樂等紅人隊的贊助商，希望他們對紅人隊施加壓力更改隊名。7 月 2 日，FedEx 公開呼籲紅人隊改名，Nike 則是撤下官網上所有有紅人隊隊徽的產品。隔日紅人隊宣布會審慎檢討隊名，並在 7 月 13 日做出官方說明，表示他們會讓 Redskins 紅人這個名字與隊徽走入歷史。

miker©Shutterstock

◀ 紅人隊隊名爭議越演越烈，一名印地安女子高舉「換掉隊徽」的抗議牌子。

Grammar Master

加上補語才會完整的動詞 find + it + OC

動詞中有不少不完全及物動詞，即使後面接了受詞，意義仍不完整，必須再接補語 OC，才能補充說明受詞的完整性，find 就是這類動詞，因此句中的受詞 the word redskins 後方還要接形容詞 offensive 作為補語，才能完整說明受詞。

● **類似的動詞還有：call、make、consider、think：**
例：The crying baby made me crazy. 哭泣的寶寶使我抓狂。[形容詞 crazy 補充說明 me 的狀況]
例：I consider Tom a good friend. 我把湯姆當好朋友。[名詞 a good friend 補充說明 Tom]

● **如果受詞是不定詞 to V，則會以虛主詞 it 代替，將不定詞挪到補語之後：**
例：Lisa found it hard to take days off during the busy season. 麗莎覺得旺季很難請假。
[不定詞 to take days off 挪到後面，以虛主詞 it 代替]

1. NFL and Super Bowl 美式足球聯盟與超級盃

National Football League 是世界最大的職業美式足球聯盟，而 NFL 的年度冠軍賽可說是全美國的全民運動，一般在每年 1 月最後一個或 2 月第一個禮拜天舉行，參賽球隊就是爭奪 Super Bowl，所以當天也稱為 Super Bowl Sunday，這一天連美國總統也不用上班，就是為了觀看超級盃足球賽！

EQRoy©Shutterstock

Hard Rock Stadium 被選為 2020 年 Super Bowl 舉辦場地。

2. Washington Redskins 華盛頓紅人隊

紅人隊自 1932 年成立以來已經打了 1000 多場比賽，是 NFL 中唯一一支常規賽和季後賽連勝超過 600 場的球隊之一，其球隊主場是 FedEx Field。目前球隊先暫時以 Washington Football Team 的隊名參加 2020 年賽季，內部正在商討新的隊名與隊徽，據說隊徽將保留酒紅色跟金色，改用球員的球衣號碼取代頭盔上印第安頭徽標。

3. San Francisco 49ers 舊金山 49 人隊

為 NFL 的招牌球隊，成立於 1946 年，隊名由來是為了紀念 1849 年舊金山的大量淘金潮，因此也稱舊金山掏金人。曾經是名人堂，出了如 Joe Montana、Jerry Rice、Steve Yang 等美足巨星。49 人隊的明星四分衛 Colin Kaepernick 曾在 2016 年國歌演奏時單膝跪地，抗議黑人受到警察不公對待，一時蔚為話題。

Uncle Leo©Shutterstoc

4. the Civil Rights Movement 美國民權運動

1960 年代是黑人平權運動的轉捩點，牧師馬丁路德金恩博士發表 I Have a Dream 演說，表達黑人對平等社會的憧憬，獲得數十萬黑人及白人支持。1963 年美國總統甘迺迪也在民權運動上做了許多努力，促成 1964 年民權法案（Civil Rights Act of 1964）的通過，成為南北戰爭後黑人平權的里程碑。

◀ 馬丁路德金恩 Martin Luther King, Jr. 的肖像。

5. Native Americans and Sioux 美國原住民與印地安蘇族

美國原住民在不同背景下也稱 **American Indians**、**Indigenous Americans** 或簡稱 **Indians** 印地安人。Sioux 蘇族是北美印第安人的一支，原本居住在北美五大湖以東地區，種植玉米，崇拜太陽。1990 年電影《與狼共舞》(*Dances with Wolves*) 就是描述南北戰爭末期北軍中尉與印地安蘇族的故事，電影中用到許多蘇族語言，獲得 7 座奧斯卡獎。

©Orion Pictures

KEVIN COSTNER

DANCES WITH WOLVES

▶ 《與狼共舞》的海報，男主角為 Kevin Costner 凱文柯斯納

#bullying #social justice
#Nike #BLM
#racial equality

示意圖，Nike 近日在日本推出廣告，議題觸及罷凌現象（bullying），在網上引發話題。

全文朗讀 ♫ 047　單字 ♫ 048

Nike Ad Draws Strong Response in Japan
耐吉日本廣告引發軒然大波

⏱ December 2, 2020

Vocabulary

1. **highlight** [ˋhaɪ.laɪt] (v.)
   強調，凸顯

2. **boycott** [ˋbɔɪ.kɑt] (v./n.)
   抵制，杯葛

3. **feature** [ˋfitʃɚ] (v./n.)
   以…為特色，以…為號召；特色

4. **ultimately** [ˋʌltəmɪtli] (adv.)
   最後，總而言之

5. **confidence** [ˋkɑnfɪdəns] (n.)
   自信，信心

6. **academic** [ˌækəˋdɛmɪk] (a.)
   學術的

A new Nike video ad [1]**highlighting racism** and **bullying** in Japan has sparked fierce debate online, including some calls to [2]**boycott** the company. The two-minute video, titled "The Future Isn't Waiting," [3]**features** three teenage girls from diverse backgrounds who are bullied in school, but [4]**ultimately** gain [5]**confidence** through their ***prowess** on the soccer field.

耐吉推出的新廣告因為強調日本種族歧視和霸凌現象，而在網路上引起激烈論戰，包括有些人要求抵制該公司。這段兩分鐘的影片名為「未來不等人」（日文為「動かしつづける。自分を。未来を。」），描述三名來自不同背景的青少女在學校遭霸凌，但最終在足球場上大展身手而獲得信心。

While one girl is a Japanese student who struggles with [6]**academic** pressure, the other two are bullied because of their ethnic and **racial** backgrounds. The second girl is a *zainichi*, or ethnic Korean, a group that has long faced **discrimination** in Japan. Shown being stared at when she wears traditional Korean clothing, the girl later proudly tapes the Korean surname Kim over the Japanese name on her soccer *****jersey**.

其中一名女孩是日本學生，飽受學業壓力之苦，另外兩名女孩則因族裔背景而遭到霸凌。第二名女孩是在日本長期遭受歧視的在日韓國人，或稱韓裔。她在影片中穿著傳統韓國服飾時引來旁人異樣眼光，後來該女孩自豪地將自己的韓國姓氏金貼在自己足球球衣的日本名字上。

日本職業網球選手大坂直美於 2018 年於決賽打敗小威廉絲，獲得生涯首個大滿貫女單冠軍，也是日本第一座大滿貫單打冠軍。

The third girl, a **mixed-race** teen with a black father and a Japanese mother, is shown surrounded by classmates touching her [7]**curly** hair. In another scene, she is seen watching a video of another mixed-race woman on her phone—a *****cameo** appearance by Japanese tennis champion Naomi Osaka, who is sponsored by Nike. Osaka, born to a Japanese mother and a Haitian-American father, **Ⓟ is no stranger to** racial **prejudice**. An ad from another sponsor, Nissan Foods, showed her with white skin and light brown hair, and a Japanese [8]**comedian** suggested she "needed some [9]**bleach**." Osaka has since become an [10]**advocate** for **racial justice**, showing her support for the Black Lives Matter movement at the U.S. Open in September.

影片中第三名女孩是混血少女，有非裔父親和日本母親，同學包圍著她並觸碰她的一頭捲髮。在另一個場景中，可以看到她用手機觀看另一個混血女孩的影片，影片中的女孩就是耐吉贊助的日本網球冠軍大坂直美，在這則廣告中客串演出。大坂的母親是日本人，父親是海地裔美國人，對種族偏見並不陌生。曾有另一個贊助商日清食品的廣告將她呈現為白皮膚和淺褐色頭髮，還有位日本諧星建議她「需要一些漂白劑」。此後大坂成為種族正義的倡導者，在九月的美國網球公開賽上表示對「黑人的命也是命」運動的支持。

Within days of its release on Twitter, the Nike ad had received 14 million views and over 60,000 likes, but also a flood of [11]**critical** [12]**comments** from Japanese posters, with some [13]**vowing** never to buy Nike products again. "Goodbye Nike, we won't be buying any more products from you," wrote one poster. "Every day you can see students of different [14]**nationalities** happily going to school together," said another. "It's Nike that's **prejudiced**."

耐吉的廣告在推特上發布後幾日內就獲得 1400 萬的點閱次數和逾六萬個讚，但也收到大量日本網友的批評，其中有些人發誓不再購買耐吉產品。一名網友寫道：「再見，耐吉，我們不會購買你的任何產品。」另一人說：「每天都能看到不同國籍的學生一起快樂地上學，有偏見的是耐吉。」

7. **curly** [ˈkɝli] (a.) 捲曲的

8. **comedian** [kəˈmidiən] (n.) 諧星，喜劇演員

9. **bleach** [blitʃ] (n./ v.) 漂白水；漂白（使頭髮顏色變淺）

10. **advocate** [ˈædvəkɪt / ˈædvə.ket] (n./v.) 提倡者，擁護者；提倡，擁護

11. **critical** [ˈkrɪtɪkəl] (a.) 批評的，挑剔的

12. **comment** [ˈkɑmɛnt] (n.) 意見，評論

13. **vow** [vau] (v./n.) 發誓；誓言

14. **nationality** [ˌnæʃəˈnæləti] (n.) 國籍，民族

15. controversy [ˋkɑntrə͵vɝsi] *(n.)*
爭議，爭論

* prowess [ˋprauɪs] *(n.)*
傑出的能力

* jersey [ˋdʒɝzi] *(n.)* 球衣

* cameo [ˋkæmi͵o] *(n.)* 客串演出

動かしつづける。自分を。未来を。The Future Isn't Waiting...
稍後觀看　分享

圖片為日本 Nike 引起熱議的廣告截圖。Nike 近年的廣告常以社會正義（social justice）作為訴求，為少數族群發聲，儘管引發正反兩方的論戰，也流失一些既有客群，但也讓 Nike 躍升話題焦點。Nike 也在美國發生 George Floyd 事件後於 Twitter 上發佈貼文「For once, don't do it.」表達對 social justice 的關注。

Nike Japan hasn't commented directly on the [15]**controversy**, but did post a statement on their website, reading: "Nike for a long time has listened to **minorities**, supported them and voiced our views about causes that meet Nike's values."
耐吉日本公司未對此爭議直接發表評論，但在官網上發表聲明，內容寫道：「耐吉長久以來一直在傾聽少數族裔的意見、支持他們，並針對符合耐吉價值觀的準則表達我們的看法。」

Grammar Master

到底是 one... another... 還是 one... the other... ？

其實區分這兩個用法的原則很簡單，只要使用到「定冠詞」the，就是「限定」用法。本句話前一段已經提到這個廣告中有三名女孩，因此到了這裡，就可以使用 the other two 來限定所提的是另外兩個女孩。

● （非限定的兩者）one...another... 一個…另一個…：

例：I had one cold beer, and it was so refreshing that I had another. 我喝了一瓶冰啤酒，實在太暢快了，就又再喝了一瓶。[本句話沒有前提限制我要喝的第二瓶啤酒是哪一瓶，因此使用 another。]

● （限定的兩者）one...the other... 一個……另一個……：

例：One of Charlie's feet sank into the mud, and then the other. 查理的一隻腳陷入了泥濘之中，接著另一隻也陷進去了。[查理只會有兩隻腳，一開始提到一隻，自然就剩下另一隻腳。]

1. 與「種族」、「歧視」相關的字

名詞 **race** 指「人種，種族」，如果說某人是 **mixed-race**，就是說他是「混血兒」。形容詞是 **racial**「跟種族有關的」，如 **racial discrimination/prejudice**「種族歧視，種族偏見」。**discrimination** [dɪˏskrɪməˋneʃən] 意思為「差別待遇，歧視，偏袒」。**prejudice** [ˋprɛdʒədɪs] 指「成見，偏見」，形容詞為 **prejudiced**。

而 **racism**「種族主義，種族迫害」是一個包含上述行為和態度的術語，認為每個人種的每個成員都具有某種「特別優異」的品質或能力，因而對其他人種產生優劣區分，最極端的 racism 就是希特勒對猶太人的屠殺。而抱持有種族主義的人就稱 **racist**。針對「種族歧視」起身反抗的行為則稱 **racial justice**。

2. bullying 霸凌

中文的「霸凌」兩字其實來自於英文 bully，當動詞，有「強欺弱、大欺小」的含意，bullying 則指霸凌行為。bullying 指透過惡意言語或行為欺凌他人，或是透過冷落排他的方式讓他人在身心上感到痛苦、恐懼憂鬱等心靈創傷，霸凌現象若是發生在校園，就稱作 **school bullying**，而社群媒體的普及也造成網路霸凌 **cyberbullying** 的現象。日本的霸凌現象相當普遍，從校園到成人社會皆有，對於不同國籍的人也常有霸凌現象。Nike 的這個廣告也引起大眾對於日本霸凌現象的關注。

3. Phrase **is no stranger to + N** 對…並不陌生

stranger 是「陌生人」，這個句子可以表示某人常聽說或常處理某事物，有很多相關經驗，或是經常光顧某個地方。

A: Kevin built his own PC from scratch?　凱文從無到有組裝出自己的電腦？
B: Yeah. He's no stranger to computers.　是啊。他很懂電腦。

4. zainichi 在日韓國人

zainichi 為日文羅馬拼音字，日本漢字寫作「在日韓国人、在日朝鮮人」。跟歸化為日本籍的韓裔日本人不同，zainichi 尚保有韓國籍身分。

jgolby©Shutterstock

5. minority 少數族群

名詞 minority [maɪˋnɔrətɪ] 由形容詞 **minor**「少數的」而來，相反詞為 **major** 與 **majority**。minority 就是跟 majority「多數人，多數黨，多數族群」相比之下是較少數、弱勢的一群，如 LGBTQ 也是 minority。

lev radin©shutterstock

#metoo
#Hollywood

2020 年 1 月 6 日，前電影大亨 Harvey Weinstein 聽完最高法院對其多件涉嫌性侵案宣判後離開法院。

全文朗讀 ♫ 049　　單字 ♫ 050

Harvey Weinstein Sentenced to 23 Years for Sexual Assault
哈維溫斯坦因性侵罪被判 23 年徒刑

🕐 January 8, 2021

Vocabulary

1. **publicize** [ˋpʌblɪͺsaɪz] (v.)
   宣傳，廣告，公布

2. **sentence** [ˋsɛntəs] (v./n.)
   判刑；徒刑，**life sentence** 指「無期徒刑」

3. **rape** [rep] (n./v.) 強姦罪；強姦

4. **impose** [ɪmˋpoz] (v.)
   加（負擔）於，實施法律

5. **publish** [ˋpʌblɪʃ] (v.)
   出版，發行

Following a much-[1]**publicized** trial that lasted several months, former Hollywood producer Harvey Weinstein has been [2]**sentenced** to 23 years in prison. Weinstein had earlier been **found guilty** of a **first-degree** criminal sex act against Mimi Haleyi, which took place in 2006, and **third-degree** [3]**rape** of Jessica Mann in 2013. Judge James Burke [4]**imposed** sentences of 20 and 3 years, respectively, against Weinstein at the New York Criminal Court in Manhattan. The two women **gave testimony** at the trial, with Mann stating, "I have found my voice and hope for a future where monsters no longer hide in our closet."

在歷經數月且廣為報導的審訊之後，前好萊塢製作人哈維溫斯坦被判處 23 年徒刑。溫斯坦於 2006 年對米米海利犯下一級刑事性犯罪，並在 2013 年對潔西卡曼恩犯下三級強暴罪，並於稍早定罪。詹姆斯伯克法官在位於曼哈頓的紐約刑事法庭上，分別就兩項罪行判處溫斯坦 20 年和 3 年徒刑。兩名女子出庭作證時，曼恩說：「我為自己發聲，希望未來不再有惡魔藏在我們的衣櫥裡。」

Since *The New York Times* and *The New Yorker* magazine [5)]**published bombshell** reports in 2017 of Weinstein's decades of [6)]**predatory** [7)]**behavior**, around 100 women have come forward to publicly accuse the former head of Miramax Studios. Their stories have not only Ⓟ**shed light on** Weinstein's patterns of criminal behavior, but also helped bring the **#MeToo movement** to national and then worldwide attention. In addition to Haleyi and Mann, four other women **testified** at the trial, describing how the producer sexually [8)]**assaulted** them at business meetings. All six women were present in the courtroom for Weinstein's sentencing.

自從《紐約時報》和《紐約客》雜誌在 2017 年重磅報導溫斯坦數十年來的惡行後，約一百名女性挺身而出公開譴責這位米拉麥克斯影業的前負責人。她們的故事不但揭露了溫斯坦的犯罪行為模式，也使全美發起 MeToo 運動，並引起全世界關注。除了海利和曼恩，另有四名女子出庭作證，形容這位製作人如何在商務會議中性侵她們。溫斯坦被判刑時，所有六名女子都有出席。

Weinstein's defense ***attorneys** expressed anger at the length of the sentence, pointing out that it's more than what most [9)]**murderers** receive. Weinstein, 68, who arrived in the courtroom in a [10)]**wheelchair**, recently [11)]**underwent** a heart [12)]**procedure** while in custody. His lawyers plan to appeal the **conviction**, arguing that 23 years [13)]**essentially *amounts to** a life sentence for someone in such poor health. Weinstein spoke for 10 minutes at the sentencing, saying "thousands of men are losing **due process**," and adding that "men are confused about this issue."

溫斯坦的辯護律師對刑期表達不滿，並指出這超出大部分殺人犯所獲判的刑期。現年 68 歲的溫斯坦坐在輪椅上出庭，他近期才在拘押期間接受心臟手術。他的律師打算對此判決提出上訴，並辯稱 23 年刑期對健康狀況不佳的人來說基本上相當於無期徒刑。溫斯坦在宣布判刑時說了十分鐘的話，他說「成千上萬的男人正喪失正當程序」，並補充說道「男人對這個議題感到不解」。

6. **predatory** [ˋprɛdə͵torɪ] (a.)
   侵略的，狩獵的

7. **behavior** [bɪˋhevjə] (n.)
   行為，舉止

8. **assault** [əˋsɔlt] (v./n.)
   侵犯，攻擊

9. **murderer** [ˋmɝdərə] (n.)
   謀殺犯

10. **wheelchair** [ˋwilˋtʃɛr] (n.)
    輪椅

11. **undergo** [͵ʌndəˋgo] (v.)
    接受（治療、檢查等），經歷

12. **procedure** [prəˋsidʒə] (n.)
    醫療程序，手術

13. **essentially** [ɪˋsɛnʃəlɪ] (adv.)
    實質上，基本上

lev.radin©Shutterstock

曾受害的女星如 Rosanna Arquette、Rose McGowan 等也在法院外的記者會上接受訪問。

14. **lengthy** [ˋlɛnθɪ] (a.) 冗長的

* **attorney** [əˋtɜnɪ] (n.)
  律師，等同 **lawyer**

* **amount to** (phr.) 等於，意味著

Erin Alexis Randolph©Shutterstock

New York Post 以斗大標題「Harv Time」暗指 Harvey Weinstein 之後要面臨漫長刑期會很難熬（Hard Time）。

And Weinstein's legal troubles aren't over yet. In addition to a [14]**lengthy** appeals process in New York, Weinstein also faces criminal charges in California related to two alleged sexual assaults in 2013. He's currently being held in Wende **Correctional Facility** in Erie County, New York.

溫斯坦的司法糾紛尚未結束。除了在紐約有漫長的上訴程序外，溫斯坦在加州也面臨 2013 年兩起涉嫌性侵的刑事訴訟。他目前被拘留在紐約州伊利的溫德監獄。

Grammar Master

現在完成式

since 的常用句型是「since + 過去的一個時間點」，後面再加上現在完成式 (have + Vp.p.)，表達「從過去持續到現在的行為」或是「經驗」；亦可使用現在完成進行式 (have been + Ving)，強調「持續至今」。

例：Michael has lived in Taiwan since 2002. 麥可從 2002 年起就住在台灣。

例：Pam has been studying French since last October. 潘從去年十月開始學法文。

● 現在完成式也可以和「for + 一段時間」連用：

例：Michael has lived in Taiwan for 15 years. 麥可已經住在台灣 15 年了。

● 現在完成式不一定有明確時間表達，可和 **not yet**「尚未」、**already**「已經」、**just**「剛剛」等副詞連用：

例：I haven't been to America yet. 我至今還沒去過美國。

1. find guilty & conviction 判有罪與定罪

形容詞 guilty 指「有罪的」，在美國法律中，在被證明有罪之前人人都是假定無罪（**innocent**），一旦裁定有罪，就會判刑，因此使用動詞 find 一字。最後的「定罪」則用動詞 **convict**，名詞 **conviction** [kən`vɪkʃən] 表示。

2. first-degree & third-degree criminal sex act 一級與三級性犯罪

根據紐約州強暴罪和性侵罪分級，third-degree「第三級」最輕、first-degree「第一級」最重，分別在於犯案情節的輕重。以 Jessica Mann 為例，有罪成立的三級強暴罪，是 Mann 指控的 2013 年旅館性侵事件，因屬不合意性交，而構成了三級強暴罪。同時 Mann 控訴的另一個一級強暴罪，須涉及對被害人的肢體暴力行為、因身體無力抵抗的強迫性侵等，法庭審理後判決不成立。

3. give testimony 出庭作證

「出庭作證」可以用動詞 **testify** [`tɛstə͵faɪ]，或是用片語 **give testimony** 表達。

4. bombshell 重磅新聞

此俚語通常用來形容某消息或新聞是具破壞性的、出乎意料的重磅爆料。

5. `Phrase` shed light on 釐清真相，讓真相大白

shed 有「散發，流洩」的意思，動詞變化三態同型，因此文中的 shed 為過去式。shed light on 字面上意思是「讓光線照射到⋯上」，表示使事情變得清晰。也可以說 **throw light on**。

例 Experts hope that the flight recording will shed light on the cause of the plane crash.
　專家希望飛航紀錄能釐清墜機的原因。

6. #metoo movement # 我也是運動

或寫做 #MeToo。Me too. 這個短語是社運人士 Tarana Burke 先使用，幫助性受害者說出受害經過，以平復傷痛。2017 年底，多位女性勇敢出面指控美國影業大亨 Harvey Weinstein 長期對女星施以性侵、騷擾，女星 Alyssa Milano 提議大家在 Twitter 上寫下 #MeToo 作為聲援，引發巨大迴響，許多人在寫下 #MeToo 的同時，也說出隱藏多年的遇害秘密，不再視為羞恥。#MeToo 激起的社會能量，

▲ #MeToo 這個 hastag 已經成為全球女性拒絕性騷擾的代名詞。

進而推動了 2018 年初的 Time's Up 反性騷擾運動，美國影藝界 300 位女性工作者加入並捐款，成立一個法律辯護基金，提供各界無權無勢的婦女所需的法律支援，以停止所有行業性別歧視。

7. due process (of law) 正當法律程序

Rebekah Zemansky©Shutterstock

是一個重要的法治觀念與憲法原則，主要用於英美法系國家，指政府必須尊重任何依據法律所賦予人民在法律上的權力。

8. correctional facility 監獄

在英文中，「監獄」的正式名稱其實是 correctional facility，翻成中文就是「矯正機關」，簡單來說，監獄的功能是希望犯罪的人能在裡面受到感化教化，達到矯正其偏行為與觀念。

Health & Medicine

健康醫療

★：Covid-19 New Words 因 Covid-19 出現的新字

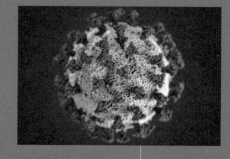

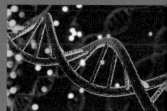

#B117 #UK
#Covid-19
#US #Colorado #California
#National Guard #nursing home

英國新冠肺炎變種病毒來勢洶洶，南韓、香港、新加坡、法國等國家相繼發現首例英國變種新冠病毒確診病患後，美國週二（29 日）確認了首起本土感染英國變種新冠病毒的案例。

全文朗讀 ♫ 051　單字 ♫ 052

New Covid Strain Found in U.S.
英國變種新型冠狀病毒 B117 現身美國

🕐 **December 29, 2020**

Two U.S. states have reported cases of a more [1]**contagious** new coronavirus **strain** that was first [2]**identified** in the United Kingdom. Colorado officials said Wednesday they were investigating a possible second case of the ***variant**—after discovering the first U.S. case on Tuesday—and California confirmed its first case in the southern city of San Diego.

美國兩個州通報了傳染性更強的新冠變種病毒案例，也就是首先在英國現蹤的變種病毒株。科羅拉多州官員於週三表示，週二在美國發現英國變種病毒株的首宗病例後，他們正在調查第二起疑似病例。而加州也確認在南方城市聖地牙哥出現了首宗病例。

"We are aware of one **confirmed case** and another possible case with the **B117** variant of the virus," said Colorado state **epidemiologist** Rachel Herlihy at a Wednesday morning news conference. Both cases are **National Guard** soldiers ***deployed** on Dec. 23 to support the **Good Samaritan** Society [3]**nursing home** outside of Denver. An [4]**outbreak** at the [5]**facility** began

Vocabulary

1. **contagious** [kənˋtedʒəs] (a.)
   傳染性的

2. **identify** [aɪˋdɛntəˌfaɪ] (v.)
   確認，識別，發現

3. **nursing home** (phr.)
   療養院，養老院

4. **outbreak** [ˋautˌbrek] (n.)
   （疫情）爆發

5. **facility** [fəˋsɪlətɪ] (n.)
   設施，設備（此定義用複數 **facilities**）

加州的 St. Jude Medical Center 加設臨時醫護站，因應因新冠病毒變種出現而短缺的 ICU 設施。

in mid-December, and 20 of 34 staff and all 26 residents tested positive for the coronavirus. Four residents died.

週三上午，科羅拉多州政府流行病學家瑞秋賀利希在新聞記者會上表示：「我們知道 B117 變種病毒株已有一例確診與一起疑似病例。」這兩宗病例都是國民警衛隊士兵受到感染，他們在 12 月 23 日到丹佛外支援善人協會養老院。該養老院於 12 月中爆發疫情，34 名員工中有 20 人和所有 26 名院民的新冠病毒檢測均為陽性。已有四名院民死亡。

The soldiers were given a *PCR test* the day after they arrived, and when scientists at the state [6]**lab** identified the B117 variant in one sample—by *sequencing* the viral **genome** and finding *mutations* specific to the variant's **spike protein gene**—they immediately [7]**notified** the **Centers for Disease Control and Prevention**. The confirmed case is a man in his 20s who experienced mild [8]**symptoms**. Both soldiers are currently undergoing **isolation**. Neither had traveled internationally in recent weeks, indicating possible **community transmission**.

士兵在抵達後第二天接受聚合酶連鎖反應檢測，州立實驗室科學家透過檢測病毒基因組序列，在病毒的棘蛋白基因上發現變種病毒株特有的突變，確認其中一個檢體是 B117 變種病毒株後，立刻通報美國疾病管制預防中心。確診病例是一名 20 多歲男子，有輕微症狀。兩名士兵目前都處於隔離狀態。最近幾週他們都沒有出國旅行，顯示可能是社區傳染。

In California, Governor Gavin Newsom confirmed the state's first case of the variant Wednesday afternoon in a video call with Anthony Fauci, the nation's top [9]**infectious** disease expert. San Diego County officials on Wednesday said a local man in his 30s with no travel history tested positive for the new strain. They believe there are other cases of the variant in the region that have not yet been detected. Southern California's hospitals are already [10]**strained** by the virus, with **intensive care units** in the region at full capacity.

加州州長葛文紐森週三下午與國家頂尖傳染病專家安東尼弗契進行視訊通話時，證實該州的第一宗變種病例。聖地亞哥郡政府官員週三表示，當地一名沒有旅行史的 30 多歲男子進行新冠變種病毒檢測的結果呈陽性。他們認為，該地區尚有其他變種病例未被發現。新冠病毒讓南加州的醫院疲於應付，該地區的加護病房已經人滿為患。

6. **lab** [læb] (n.) 實驗室，研究室，為 **laboratory** [ˋlæbrəˏtɔrɪ] 縮寫

7. **notify** [ˋnotəˏfaɪ] (v.) 通知，報告

8. **symptom** [ˋsɪmptəm] (n.) 症狀，徵兆

9. **infectious** [ɪnˋfɛkʃəs] (a.) 有感染力的

10. **strain** [stren] (v.) 給予沈重壓力，使緊繃

11. **account for** (phr.) 佔（比例）

12. **measure** [ˋmɛʒɚ] (n.) 措施，方法

Travers Lewis©Shutterstock

LONDON IS AT HIGH COVID ALERT LEVEL

Don't mix indoors with anyone you don't live with.

Hands　Face　Space

Download the NHS Test and Trace app at NHS.uk/coronavirus

City of Westminster

進階字彙

* **variant** [ˋvɛrɪənt] *(n.)* 變種，變體

* **deploy** [dɪˋplɔɪ] *(v.)* 部署，調動

* **PCR (polymerase chain reaction) test** 聚合酶連鎖反應檢測

* **sequence** [ˋsikwəns] *(v./n.)* 測定 DNA 的序列；序列

* **mutation** [mjuˋteʃən] *(n.)* 突變，變種，動詞 **mutate** [ˋmjutet]

* **virulent** [ˋvɪrjələnt] *(a.)* 致命的，劇毒的

U.K. scientists believe the variant strain to be more contagious than previously identified strains but not more ***virulent**. First spotted in September, the new variant [11)]**accounted for** 60% of cases in London by the week of Dec. 9. London and large areas of southern England are now under **lockdown** [12)]**measures**, and dozens of countries have banned travel from the U.K.

英國科學家認為，該變種病毒株比之前發現的病毒株更具傳染性，但毒性沒有更強。新變種病毒首先在 9 月發現，到了 12 月 9 日時已佔倫敦所有病例的六成。倫敦和英國南部多處地區目前都實行封城，已有數十個國家禁止來自英的旅客入境。

Grammar Master

表達「年齡」的說法

文章中表達「某人現在的年齡」的說法：in his 30s 表達「三十幾歲」，唸作 in his thirties。以此類推，in one's twenties, forties, fifties 等，就是指「二十幾、四十幾、五十幾歲」。如果要說二十「前半或後半」，則可以說 in one's early twenties 和 in one's late twenties，其餘以此類推。

● 注意，「十幾歲」的說法不是說 in one's tens，而是 in one's teens。

● 表達「過去幾歲的時候」就用：at the age of...：

例：He started his own business at the age of 20. 他在二十歲時開創自己的事業。

例：I started to play tennis at an early age. 我很小就開始打網球。

1. strain, B117 新型病毒

本新聞第一句的 **strain** 當名詞，指「動植物的品種，株」，這裡就是指病毒出現變異，產生新病毒株。最近在英國發現了新冠病毒的變種，此變種病毒傳染力更強，稱 B117。專門研究因病毒引發的疾病專家則稱 **epidemiologist** [ˌɛpɪˌdimɪˈælədʒɪst]「流行病學家」。

2. 新聞常見的疫情用字

本新聞中出現了幾個常見的疫情單字，如：confirmed case「確診病例」、community transmission「社區感染」、isolation「隔離」、lockdown「封城」。以下補充經常在新聞中到的其他單字：

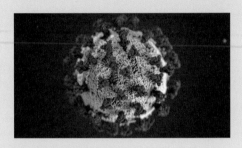

- epidemic 流行病，疫情
- pandemic 全球大流行
- herd immunity 群體免疫
- outbreak 疫情爆發
- WHO (World Health Organization) 世衛組織
- social distancing 社交距離
- contact tracing 接觸者追蹤
- contact/droplet transmission 接觸／飛沫傳染
- (home) isolation（居家）隔離
- (home) quarantine（居家）檢疫
- (mass) screening 篩檢／普篩
- tested negative/positive 檢驗呈陰性／陽性
- false negative/positive 偽陰性／偽陽性
- asymptomatic/symptomatic 無症狀的／有症狀的
- incubation period 潛伏期
- superspreader 超級帶原者
- loss of smell/taste 喪失嗅覺／味覺

3. U.S. National Guard 美國國民警衛隊

是指正規兵以外的後備部隊。美國各州與華府都有自己的國民警衛隊，工作是協助執法，多數人員是兼職，州長可以在緊急狀況下動用國民警衛隊，在天災或暴動時讓他們充當消防員、救護人員或鎮暴。如今年因 BLM 美國各地發生許多暴動行為，美國 20 多州與華府便出動國民警衛隊協助鎮壓。

▲ 美國國民警衛隊在新冠病毒大流行期間也協助發放物資。

4. good Samaritan 好撒瑪利亞人

Renata Sedmakova©Shutterstock

文中出現的 Good Samaritan Society 是美國知名療養機構，而名稱中的 Good Samaritan「好撒瑪利亞人」其實源自於聖經故事，故事中有個猶太人被打劫受傷倒在路邊，路過的祭司、利未人等高尚人士都對這個人不聞不問，只有一位身分低微的薩瑪利亞人向他伸出援手，因為這個故事，使得 Samaritan 變成了 good Samaritan，因此英文中便普遍使用 good Samaritan 來形容「見義勇為的人」。

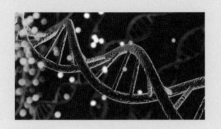

5. genome 基因組，染色體組

genome 念作 [ˋdʒinom]，指一個生物體的染色體當中完整的 DNA 序列。

6. spike protein 棘狀蛋白

病毒入侵人體的方式常是先附著在宿主合適的細胞上，然後增生，進而產生致病力，而 Covid-19 感染的方式，就是透過新型冠狀病毒（SARS-Cov-2）表面的 spike protein「棘狀蛋白」，又稱「s 蛋白」與宿主細胞表面受體 ACE2 結合，接著將病毒基因釋放到細胞中。

7. Centers for Disease Control and Prevention 美國疾病控制預防中心

bear_productions©Shutterstock

簡稱 CDC，指美國的疾病控制預防中心，為國家最高公共衛生單位，負責疾病預防控制、環境衛生、全民健康教育等提升國民健康有關的事務。台灣也有自己的 CDC，全名為「台灣衛生福利部疾病管制署」。

8. intensive care unit 加護病房

簡稱為 ICU，是醫院專為重症患者進行密集醫療照護的病房，為了避免外界干擾與傳染，加護病房採用密閉式設計，對訪客與會面時間都有嚴格限制，裡頭也有許多精密設備隨時監測患者身體變化，醫護人員會進行 24 小時輪班照護。

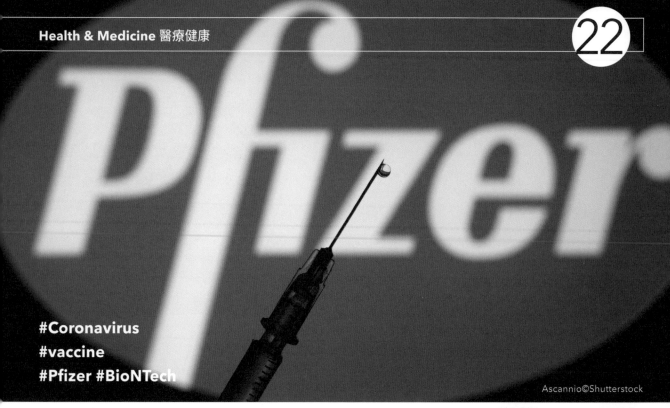

#Coronavirus
#vaccine
#Pfizer #BioNTech

Ascannio©Shutterstock

美國瑞輝與德國生技大廠合作開發的疫苗已經在 6 個國家、4 萬 3500 人身上試驗，目前尚未出現嚴重副作用。

全文朗讀 ♪ 053　　單字 ♪ 054

Coronavirus Vaccine Found 95% Effective
新冠病毒疫苗開發大有突破，效力達 95%

🕐 **November 10, 2020**

Vocabulary

1. **vaccine** [ˋvæksɪn] (n.)
    疫苗，動詞為 **vaccinate**
    [ˋvæksəˌnet] 接種疫苗

2. **clinical** [ˋklɪnɪkəl] (a.) 臨床的

3. **declare** [dɪˋklɛr] (v.)
    聲明，宣佈

4. **identical** [aɪˋdɛntɪkəl] (a.)
    完全相同的，一摸一樣的

5. **severe** [səˋvɪr] (a.)
    嚴重的，劇烈的

A new [1]**vaccine** has 🅿**shown great promise** in [2]**clinical** trials, leading public health officials to [3]**declare** "🅿**a light at the end of the tunnel**" of the **COVID-19 pandemic**. American **pharmaceutical** giant Pfizer and German partner BioNTech have produced a vaccine, called **BNT162b2**, which they say is 95% effective in preventing COVID-19. The drugmakers say the vaccine's high success rate is nearly [4]**identical** across all ages and ***ethnicities**. Even for the elderly, who are at high risk of [5]**severe** illness from the virus, the vaccine appears to be 94% effective.

一款新疫苗在臨床試驗中顯示大有希望，使公共衛生官員宣稱這是新冠病毒大流行中的「一道曙光」。美國製藥業巨頭輝瑞公司和德國合作夥伴 BioNTech 生物科技公司生產出一種名為 BNT162b2 的疫苗，他們說這種疫苗在預防新冠病毒上有 95％的效力。該製藥廠說，這種疫苗在不同年齡層與族裔間的成功率幾乎一樣高。即使是病毒導致重症的老年人高危險群，這種疫苗也似乎有 94％的效力。

Pfizer and BioNTech's vaccine makes use of **mRNA**, or **messenger RNA**, technology. Traditional vaccines use a weakened form of the virus they're targeting to [6]**provoke** the body to produce [7]**antibodies**, which protect against future infection. In contrast, mRNA vaccines use a piece of the virus' **genetic code** to [8]**accomplish** the same thing. This saves time and resources, because while it takes weeks to [9]**cultivate** and ship weakened forms of the virus, the code can be created in labs around the world immediately.

輝瑞和 BioNTech 的疫苗利用 mRNA，或稱信使核糖核酸技術。傳統疫苗使用弱型病毒，刺激人體產生抗體，繼而預防日後感染。相比之下，mRNA 疫苗使用病毒的部分遺傳密碼來達成相同目的。這可節省時間和資源，因為培養和運送弱型病毒需要數週時間，而遺傳密碼可在世界各地的實驗室立即生產。

The vaccine is [10]**administered** by [11]**injection**, with two [12]**doses** given at least three weeks apart. Full protection is achieved 28 days after the first dose. ***Side effects** may occur, but are usually very mild and go away within 48 hours. The drugmakers say they plan to produce over a billion doses in 2021. The U.K. approved the vaccine for widespread use on Wednesday, and the U.S. and the E.U. are expected to **ⓡfollow suit**.

疫苗是透過注射接種，兩劑間需至少隔三週。第一劑接種後滿 28 天即可獲得全面保護。可能會有副作用，但通常非常輕微，並會在 48 小時內消失。製藥廠表示，他們計畫在 2021 年生產逾十億劑疫苗。英國已於週三批准疫苗的廣泛使用，美國和歐盟預計跟進。

6. **provoke** [prəˋvok] (v.)
   激起（負面反應），激怒

7. **antibody** [ˋæntɪˌbɑdi] (n.) 抗體

8. **accomplish** [əˋkɑmplɪʃ] (v.)
   完成，實現，達到

9. **cultivate** [ˋkʌltəˌvet] (v.)
   培養，養成

10. **administer** [ədˋmɪnəstə] (v.)
    施行，給予

11. **injection** [ɪnˋdʒɛkʃən] (n.)
    注射，動詞 **inject**

12. **dose** [dos] (n.)
    一劑，一次劑量

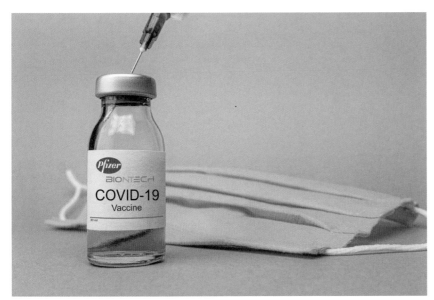

示意圖。

13. **approval** [əˋpruvəl] (n.)
批准，認可

14. **distribution** [ˌdɪstrəˋbjuʃən]
(n.) 分配，分發，經銷，動詞
distribute [dɪˋstrɪbjut]

15. **elsewhere** [ˋɛls͵wɛr] (adv.)
在別處，其他地方

16. **suspicious (of)** [səˋspɪʃəs] (a.)
可疑的，多疑的

17. **boost** [bust] (v.)
提升，促進

* **ethnicity** [ɛθˋnɪsɪtɪ] (n.)
族裔，民族

* **side effect** (phr.)
副作用

James R Poston©Shutterstock

第一批疫苗於美國當地時間 12 月 12 日抵達南卡羅納州哥倫比亞，準備分發到美國各地。

While the vaccine [13]**approval** is a positive development, it doesn't mean the pandemic is over. It will take time to produce enough doses, and [14]**distribution** may prove challenging. In addition, many in the U.S. and [15]**elsewhere** are [16]**suspicious** of the vaccine and may refuse to take it. To [17]**boost** public confidence in the vaccine, former presidents Obama, Bush, and Clinton have pledged to take their doses on camera.

儘管疫苗的批准是正面消息，但不表示大流行已結束。生產足夠的劑量需要時間，而且在分配施打方面具有挑戰性。此外，美國和其他地區有許多人對疫苗表示懷疑，可能拒絕接種。為加強公眾對這款疫苗的信心，前總統歐巴馬、小布希和柯林頓已承諾將在鏡頭前接種疫苗。

Grammar Master

contrast vs. contrary

contrast 可當動詞與名詞，指「對照，比對；差別，差異」，類似 compare。而 contrary 當名詞時指「相反，對立面」，形容詞指「相反的」，同 opposite。因此從定義來看，可看出 contrast 強調「差異」，而 contrary 強調「完全相反」。

● **in contrast 對照之下：強調前後兩件事的差異之處，也可以寫 by contrast。**

例：In contrast with his brother, Robert is quite tall. 在哥哥的對比之下，羅勃顯得很高。

● **on the contrary 恰恰相反地：表示前後看法完全相反。**

例：The economy isn't improving; on the contrary, it seems to be getting worse. 經濟沒有改善。恰恰相反，經濟似乎是越來越差。

1. Phrase **show promise 有成功的希望**

promise 這裡意思不是「承諾」，而是「有成功的跡象；有出息、前途」，當此定義時為不可數名詞。當你說某人 **show great promise** 就是說對方大有可為，作某事是很有希望成功的。

A: What do you think of the band that played the opening set? 你覺得開場演唱的那個團體如何？
B: I think they show a lot of promise. 我覺得他們大有可為。

2. Phrase **(a / the) light at the end of the tunnel 黑暗中的一道曙光**

tunnel [ˋtʌnəl] 為「隧道」，陰暗的隧道中射進一道光芒，就是形容在苦難或危急中出現的一絲希望。

A: Are you getting close to paying off your debt? 你終於要付清負債了嗎？
B: Yes. I can finally see light at the end of the tunnel. 是啊，我終於看到隧道中的一絲光明了。

3. COVID-19 新冠病毒

2019 年 12 月於中國武漢爆發，患者會出現類似肺炎如呼吸困難、肺部纖維化症狀，當時媒體以 Wuhan pneumonia [nuˋmonjə]「武漢肺炎」稱之。疫情很快蔓延全球，武漢、上海以及其他國家陸續封城，此疾病也正名為 COVID-19。WHO 世界衛生組織於 2020 年 3 月 22 日將 COVID-19 定義為 pandemic「全球大流行」。目前全球正致力研發有效疫苗。

4. pandemic 全球大流行

pandemic [pænˋdɛmɪk] 指「全球大流行」，指傳染病在多個國家出現重大且持續人傳人狀況，與 **epidemic** [ˌɛpɪˋdɛmɪk]「疫情流行」程度不同，此指在小範圍內有不尋常數量的人感染同種疾病。一當 WHO 宣布 COVID-19 為 pandemic，就代表世界各國將進行合作，以有效投注醫療資源控制疫情並研發疫苗，阻止疫情蔓延。

5. BNT162b2, pharmaceutical, drugmaker「製藥相關的」與「藥廠」
新冠病毒疫苗 BNT162b2 是由製藥界龍頭 Pfizer [ˋfaɪzə] 瑞輝與德國生技公司 BioNTech 共同研發，是目前對抗新冠病毒最早且號稱最有效的疫苗。**pharmaceutical** [ˌfɑrməˋsutɪkəl] 可當形容詞或名詞，指「製藥或藥品（相關的）」，**pharmaceutical company** 指「製藥公司」，也可以用較口語的說法 **drugmaker**。

6. mRNA, message RNA 信使 DNA
全球目前爭相研發新冠病毒的疫苗，由 Pfizer 與 BioNTech 共同研發的 BNT162b2 即屬於 mRNA 疫苗。mRNA 全名為 message RNA「信使 RNA」，可將特定蛋白質的製造指示送至細胞核糖體（ribosomes）進行生產。而 mRNA 疫苗就是利用 mRNA 的這個特性，將能製造新冠病毒棘狀蛋白的 mRNA 送至人體內，並不斷製造棘狀蛋白，藉此驅動免疫系統攻擊與記憶此類病毒蛋白，增加人體對新冠病毒的免疫力，使 mRNA 被細胞捨棄。由於 mRNA 疫苗並無攜帶所有能製造新冠病毒的核酸（nucleic acid），且不會進入人體細胞核，所以施打此疫苗並不會使人感染新冠病毒。

7. Phrase **follow suit 仿效，跟風**
follow 是「跟隨」的意思，而 suit 是指撲克牌四種花色，follow suit 就是說跟著出同樣花色，延伸為「有樣學樣，跟風」。

A: I hear United Airlines has decided to cut ticket prices. 我聽說聯合航空的機票要降價了。
B: Good. Hopefully the other airlines will follow suit. 太棒了，希望其他航空公司也能跟風一下。

Covid-19

因 COVID-19 而出現的新字

新冠肺炎（Coronavirus，或稱 COVID-19）的出現不只改變了我們生活的各方面，也帶來許多英文新字，一起來看看吧！

doomscroll
doomsurf

[n.] ☐ [v.] ☑ [adj.] ☐

無止盡地瀏覽負面新聞

doom [dum] 意思是「厄運、世界末日」，scroll [skroʊl] (the page) 指「滑手機」的動作，所以 doomscroll 這個動作就是說在疫情期間，許多人會持續看負面且令人沮喪的疫情新聞，而且無法停止。這個字也成了 Collins Dictionary 的年度代表字。

也可以說 doomsurf，字尾 surf (the net) 就是「上網」的意思。這個字其實在 2018 年就出現了，當時正值 social media 社群媒體如 instagram 與 twitter 盛行，許多人無法克制自己一直刷這些媒體的消息而產生焦慮的情緒。

covidiot

[n.] ☑ [v.] ☐ [adj.] ☐

是 COVID-19 + idiot「白痴」的混合字，這個俚語有歧視意味，用來指那些低估病毒威力，無視新冠肺炎安全規則的小白。

spendemic

[n.] ☑ [v.] ☐ [adj.] ☐

疫情大爆買

由 spend 加上 pandemic [pænˋdɛmɪk]「大流行病」而來，指疫情期間大家出於恐慌而上網大量購買囤積民生用品的行為，像是疫情剛開始時，大家爆買衛生紙導致一度缺貨的情形。

New Words

rona ☑[n.] ☐[v.] ☐[adj.]

是 coronavirus 新冠肺炎的非正式縮寫，常用 the rona 表示。

quaranteam ☑[n.] ☐[v.] ☐[adj.]

疫情社交圈

這個字是由 quarantine [ˈkwɔrən.tin]「隔離」加上 team 而來，指人們在疫情期間因限制外出令，無法想去哪就去哪，因而建立起的小小社交圈（social circle）。

coronasomnia ☑[n.] ☐[v.] ☐[ad...]

新冠失眠症

昨晚又失眠了嗎？還是一直刷疫情消息到凌晨四點才睡？記不起前一天晚上幾點才睡著？你並不孤單。

這個新字就是由 coronavirus 加上 insomnia [ɪnˈsɑmnɪə]「失眠症」而來，指因疫情爆發而導致的集體失眠現象。許多人在這段期間（尤其是國外的人）都因為擔心疫情而失眠。

walktail ☑[n.] ☐[v.] ☐[adj.]

外帶調酒

由 walk 加上 cocktail 而來，顧名思義，就是「帶著走的酒精飲料」。這個字之所以會出現是美國紐約的酒吧為了讓客人在疫情期間稍微放鬆，開始推出可以外帶的調酒。而在這之前，美國街上等公共場合其實是禁止邊走邊喝的。

在美國，飲料酒精濃度在 0.5% 以上就算是酒精飲料（alcohol），而美國有多達 43 州都有 open container law，也就是禁止民眾在街上、車上等公共場合公然飲酒，即使只是手拿酒精飲料沒有喝也算違法，所以去到美國，要注意不要把國內的習慣也帶過去了喔。

quarantini ☑[n.] ☐[v.] ☐[adj.]

疫情雞尾酒

由 quarantine 加上 martini [mɑrˈtinɪ]「馬丁尼」而來，一開始是指由維他命 C、柳橙汁和伏特加或琴酒調成的增強免疫力飲料，現在泛指隔離期間喝的任何調酒。

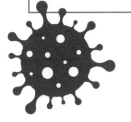

Science & Technology

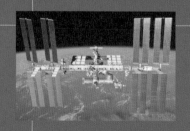

#NASA #Artemis #space travel
#moon #Mars

NASA©WikiCommons

時隔數十年，美國太空總署 NASA 發起 Artemis program，打算再次登月，這次要實現在
月球旅遊的夢想。

全文朗讀 🎵 055　　單字 🎵 056

NASA Shoots for The Moon Again
美國太空總署計畫再次登月，太空旅遊有望實現

🕐 **November 13, 2020**

Mankind has long dreamed of [1]**expanding** [2]**civilization**'s reach to the moon and beyond. The moon captured the world's attention during the **Space Race** of the 1950s and '60s, the competition between the U.S. and the Soviet Union that led to the [3]**technological** advances necessary for human spaceflight. With its **Artemis program**, **NASA** is now ⓟ**setting its sights** on Earth's largest natural [4]**satellite** once again, this time for an [5]**extended** stay.

人類長期以來一直夢想將文明範圍擴大到月球和更遠的地方。在 1950 和 60 年代的太空競賽期間，月球吸引了全世界的目光，太空競賽是美國和蘇聯之間的競爭，也促使了人類太空飛行所需的科技進步。太空總署現在透過阿提米絲計畫，再次將目光瞄準地球最大的天然衛星，這次打算延長停留時間。

The missions of the Artemis program will take [6]**astronauts** back to the [7]**lunar** surface for the first time since NASA's **Apollo program** ended in 1972. In the following decades, astronauts have only

Vocabulary

1. **expand** [ɪkˋspænd] (v.)
   擴大，擴展

2. **civilization** [ˌsɪvələˋzeʃən] (n.)
   文明，文化

3. **technological**
   [ˌtɛknəˋlɑdʒɪkəl] (a.) 科技的

4. **satellite** [ˋsætəˌlaɪt] (n.)
   衛星，人造衛星

5. **extended** [ɪkˋstɛndɪd] (a.) 延長的，動詞 **extend**

6. **astronaut** [ˋæstrəˌnɔt] (n.)
   太空人

Hasbul Aerial Stock ©Shutterstock

2019 年十月 SLS 火箭被移往位於 NASA 的 Kennedy Space Center。

[8]**ventured** to **low-Earth orbit** [9]**destinations** like the **International Space Station**, which lies 250 miles from the planet's surface. The moon is over 200,000 miles away. The Artemis crews, which will include the first woman to walk on the moon, are too young to have witnessed America's first moon landing.

阿提米絲計畫是太空總署自 1972 年阿波羅計畫結束以來，首次將太空人帶回月球表面的系列任務。隨後數十年中，太空人僅到過近地軌道的目的地，如國際太空站，其位置距離地球表面僅 250 英里；月球在逾 20 萬英里之外。阿提米絲計劃將包含史上首位女性登月漫步，該計畫成員尚年輕，沒有親眼目睹過美國的首次登月。

7. **lunar** [ˋlunə] (a.) 月球的

8. **venture** [ˋvɛntʃə] (v.) 冒險，探險

9. **destination** [ˌdɛstəˋneʃən] (n.) 目的地

10. **subsequent** [ˋsʌbsɪkwənt] (a.) 隨後的，後續的

11. **capsule** [ˋkæpsəl] (n.) 太空艙；膠囊

12. **voyage** [ˋvɔɪdʒ] (n.) 航行，太空旅行

13. **descend** [dɪˋsɛnd] (v.) 下降，下來（+ to）

14. **crater** [ˋkretə] (n.) 隕石、火山坑口

NASA plans to launch the *****unmanned** Artemis I mission in November 2021 to test the technology that will carry astronauts on [10]**subsequent** missions—the **Space Launch System** rocket and the **Orion** space [11]**capsule**. In 2023, Artemis II will carry four astronauts on a one-week trip around the moon. Like the first human [12]**voyage** to the moon in 1968 on **Apollo 8**, Artemis II will make no landing.

太空總署計畫於 2021 年 11 月發射阿提米絲 I 號無人太空任務，作為測試之後載人進入太空任務的科技—— SLS 火箭與獵戶座太空艙。2023 年，阿提米絲 II 號任務將載四名太空人繞月球飛行一週。正如 1968 年阿波羅 8 號人類首次航向月球之旅，阿提米絲 II 號也不會降落月球。

Artemis III, scheduled for launch in October 2024, is the mission that will make history with the first woman and next man on the moon. Four astronauts will leave earth on the Orion, which will dock with the **Gateway**, a small space station in lunar orbit. Two astronauts, a man and a woman, will then [13]**descend** to the surface in a lunar **lander** and use a **rover** to search for ice, which satellite images have shown to exist in [14]**craters** near the moon's south pole.

阿提米絲 III 號預定於 2024 年 10 月發射，將創下首位女性和下一位男性踏上月球的歷史。有四名太空人將搭乘獵戶座太空艙離開地球，並將獵戶座與月球軌道上的小型太空站「月球門戶」對接。然後一男一女兩名太空人將搭乘月球登陸器降落月球表面，並利用探測車尋找冰，衛星圖像已顯示月球南極附近的隕石坑中有冰存在。

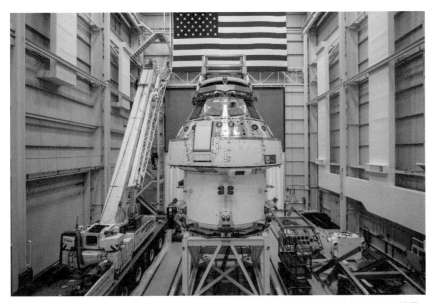

圖片中為 Artemis program 中的 Orion 獵戶座太空船。Artemis 取名自希臘神話中 Apollo 阿波羅的孿生姊姊名稱。

15. **vital** [ˋvaɪtəl] *(a.)*
不可缺少的，極為重要的

16. **establish** [ɪˋstæblɪʃ] *(v.)*
建立，建設

17. **permanent** [ˋpɝmənənt] *(a.)*
永久的，持久的

18. **exploration** [͵ɛkspləˋreʃən]
(n.) 探索，探測

進階字彙

＊unmanned [͵ʌnˋmænd] *(a.)*
無人的

A reliable supply of ice, which can provide water for drinking and oxygen for breathing, will be [15]**vital** for future Artemis missions to [16]**establish** a [17]**permanent** human base on the moon. NASA's long-term goal is to use the Artemis program to develop the scientific knowledge and technologies necessary for eventual human [18]**exploration** of Mars.

可靠的冰源供應可提供飲用水和供呼吸的氧氣，這對阿提米絲未來在月球上建立永久人類基地的任務至關重要。太空總署的長期目標是利用阿提米絲計畫開發人類最終探索火星所必需的科學知識和科技。

Grammar Master

too...to vs. enough to

本文「The Artemis crews... are too young to have witnessed America's first moon landing.」中用到 too... to 句型，指「太過於⋯以致於無法⋯」，這個句型可以用 enough to 改寫為：The Artemis crews... are not old **enough to** have witnessed America's first moon landing. 但因為 enough to 沒有帶有否定意味，因此要加上 not。

1. Space Race 太空競賽

1950-1960 年代蘇聯與美國展開科技競賽，兩國爭相發射人造衛星、火箭等作為展現國力的象徵，1969 年美國的 Apollo 11（阿波羅 11 號）首先完成登陸月球，完成人類史上首次登月，使太空競賽達到顛峰，1975 年美蘇兩國首度合作太空計劃 Apollo-Soyuz，為最後一波阿波羅任務，此後太空競賽趨於緩和。

▲ 美蘇最後以合作太空計劃 Apollo-Soyuz 任務，為兩國冷戰畫下休止符。

2. NASA 美國太空總署

全名為 National Aeronautics and Space Administration「美國國家航空暨太空總署」是全球太空機構的執牛耳，於 1958 年美國總統艾森豪任期創立，負責美國的各種太空探索，包含知名 Apollo program「阿波羅計畫」、Skylab「天空實驗室」與這次的 Artemis program「阿提米絲計畫」，也進行民用與軍用的航空太空研究。

3. `Phrase` set/have one's sights on 立志、決心要…

sight 在這裡指「槍的瞄準器」，當你瞄準某目標，也就是說要「立下志向」，後面接 on sth.，進一步說明抱負或志向為何。

例：Carl set his sights on attending law school. 卡羅的志向是進法學院。

4. Apollo program 阿波羅計畫

是 NASA 於 1961 年到 1972 年間從事的一系列載人登月任務，前後共派出了 20 座太空船（spacecraft，也稱「飛行器」），阿波羅 8 號完成太空飛行器首次環繞月球，阿波羅 11 號則是完成著名的阿姆斯壯（Armstrong）登月創舉。1990 年太空人登陸火星的想法被提出後，阿波羅計畫便轉向火星，然而因阿波羅 13 號發生氧氣罐爆炸使三名太空人喪生，引發人民關切。雖然阿波羅計畫一直安排到 20 號，不過實際上此計畫在 17 號畫上句點，主因是花費高昂，時值美國發生越戰，財務縮緊。

▲ 阿波羅計畫使得人類實現首次登陸月球。

5. low-Earth orbit 近地軌道

orbit [ˋɔrbɪt] 指天體運行軌道。low-Earth orbit 簡稱 LEO，指距離地表較近的軌道，高度約距離地表 300-2000 公里之間。絕大多數的太空站（space station）或衛星（satellite）都採用近地軌道繞行地球。

6. International Space Station 國際太空站

太空站（space station）是科學研究設施，設置於近地軌道上繞著地球運行，讓人類能在微重力環境下執行科學研究。International Space Station，簡稱 ISS 的「國際太空站」是地球上第九個載人的太空站，由美國、俄羅斯、日本、加拿大與歐洲太空總署（European Space Agency，ESA）合作經營。近期 NASA 計畫讓一般民眾也能上國際太空站，作為商務太空旅遊的第一步。

7. Space Launch System 太空發射系統

由 NASA 設計，簡稱「SLS 火箭」，是從太空梭（Space Shuttle）演變而來可載人載物的運載火箭，也是 Artemis 計畫中預計使用的太空載具之一。

8. Orion 獵戶座太空艙

是 NASA 研發的新一代載人飛行器，一架 Orion 可承載四名太空人，目標是再次將人類送往月球與其他太陽系星球如火星。此飛行器原名是 Crew Exploration Vehicle「載人探索飛行器」，但在發表前洩漏，最後改以「Orion」發表。

9. Lunar Gateway 月球門戶太空站

為 NASA 和 ESA 計劃建造的太空站，作為將太空人載往月球與火星的中繼站，此計畫預計以商業與國際合作方式運行。此計畫也是繼 Artemis program 之後，NASA 與 ESA 攜手合作的計畫；NASA 將提供歐洲太空人從地球飛往太空站的機會，而 ESA 則是在 Lunar Gateway 上打造居住艙、提供加油與電信服務。

10. lander & rover 登陸器與探測車

不同行星使用的 lander（登陸器）因重力不一樣各有不同。rover 又稱 planetary rover「探測車」，則是在其他行星表面上移動的車輛。

PERFORMANCE

gogoro.

#gogoro #Taiwan
#swappable battery
#electric scooter #green energy

StreetVJ©Shutterstock.com

Gogoro S2 ABS 系列發表會。Gogoro 為台灣電動機車製造商。

全文朗讀 ♫ 057　單字 ♫ 058

Gogoro Receives Global Company of the Year Award

台灣電動機車廠商 Gogoro 榮獲年度全球公司獎

🕐 December 16, 2020

Vocabulary

1. **consult** [kənˋsʌlt] (v.)
   諮商，**consulting firm**
   顧問公司

2. **manufacturer**
   [ˌmænjəˋfæktʃərə] (n.)
   製造商，製造廠。
   動詞 **manufacture**

3. **scooter** [ˋskutə] (n.)
   機車，**electric scooter** 電動
   機車，簡稱 **e-scooter**

4. **intelligent** [ɪnˋtɛlədʒənt] (a.)
   聰明的，智慧的。
   名詞 **intelligence**

Silicon Valley [1]**consulting** firm **Frost & Sullivan** has selected Taiwanese electric [2]**scooter** [3]**manufacturer** Gogoro as winner of the 2020 Global Company of the Year Award. Gogoro, the only company in Taiwan to ever receive the honor, was awarded based on the Mountain View, California consulting firm's recent analysis of the global **swappable battery** electric scooter market.

矽谷顧問公司弗若斯特沙利文評選台灣電動機車製造商 Gogoro 為 2020 年度全球最佳公司。Gogoro 是台灣有史以來唯一獲此殊榮的公司，該獎根據加州山景城顧問公司針對全球交換式電池電動機車市場的最新分析所頒發。

According to Frost & Sullivan, Gogoro was recognized because of the success of the company's Gogoro Network, which it called "an [4]**intelligent** energy platform that combines the power of ***connectivity**, [5]**artificial** intelligence, and **machine learning**." Launched in 2015 with 70 battery swapping stations, called GoStations, the Gogoro Network has grown to nearly 2,000

[6)]**locations** in Taiwan. "It has established [7)]**consumer** battery swapping on a mass scale, performing 265,000 battery swaps each day," said Frost & Sullivan. "It [8)]**demonstrates** that its business model is *viable and practical."

根據弗若斯特沙利文，Gogoro 之所以獲得認可，是因為其 Gogoro Network 智慧電池交換平台的成功，此平台被稱為「結合連通性、人工智慧與機器學習的智慧能源平台」。此平台於 2015 年推出時，有 70 座稱 GoStation 的電池交換站，現已經成長到將近有 2000 個交換站。弗若斯特沙利文表示：「該公司已大規模建立消費性電池交換站，每天有 26 萬 5000 次的電池交換次數，證明其商業模式是可行且實用的。」

YamiOdymel©WikiCommons

Gogoro places its GoStations at strategic locations like gas stations, convenience stores, malls and parking lots, making battery swapping fast and convenient for Gorogo riders. In Taiwan's six largest [9)]**metropolitan** areas, there are now more GoStations than gas stations, with a battery swapping station every 500 meters. When customers arrive at a GoStation and place their used batteries in empty slots, they receive two freshly-charged batteries back just six seconds later. During those six seconds, the GoStation *authenticates the owner and performs vehicle **diagnostics** to ensure safety.

Gogoro 將自家的 GoStation 設在加油站、便利商店、購物中心和停車場等策略性地點，讓 Gorogo 車主能快速方便地更換電池。目前在台灣的六大都會區中，GoStation 的數量已經超過加油站數量，每五百公尺就有一座電池交換站。顧客到 GoStation 將用過的電池放入空插槽中，只要六秒鐘就能收到兩顆新充滿電的電池。在這六秒鐘內，GoStation 會驗證車主身分，並執行車輛診斷以確保安全。

Gorogo was founded in 2011 by former HTC chief [10)]**innovation** officer Horace Luke, who was born in Hong Kong and raised in Seattle. The Taoyuan-based company launched its first electric scooter, and the Gogoro Network, in 2015, and while it now controls 90% of Taiwan's e-scooter market, it's been generous with its battery swapping technology. Under the Powered by Gogoro Network program, Gogoro has helped other manufacturers, including Yamaha, Suzuki, Aeon, PGO and CMC, design e-scooters

5. **artificial** [ˌɑrtəˋfɪʃəl] (a.)
   人工的，**artificial intelligence** 人工智慧，簡稱 **AI**

6. **location** [loˋkeʃən] (n.)
   地點，位置。動詞 **locate** [ˋloket]

7. **consumer** [kənˋsumə] (n.)
   消費者

8. **demonstrate** [ˋdɛməˌstret] (v.)
   展現，證明

9. **metropolitan** [ˌmɛtrəˋpɑlətən]
   (a.) 大都會的

10. **innovation** [ˌɪnəˋveʃən]
    革新，創新，**chief innovation officer** 創新長

Gogoro Smartscooter 電動機車的高度客製化，並針對各種客群量身打造的多種系列，使 Gogoro 在年輕族群中相當受到歡迎。

11. **large-scale** [ˋlardʒˌskel] (a.)
大規模的

12. **sustainable** [səˋstenəbəl] (a.)
永續的，持續的，**sustainable energy** 永續能源

進階字彙

* **connectivity** [kəˌnɛkˋtɪvəti] (n.)
連通性，指設備與軟體連結整合。

* **viable** [ˋvaɪəbəl] (a.) 可實行的

* **authenticate** [ɔˋθɛntɪˌket] (v.)
驗證身分

that use the same battery swapping system."Gogoro is steadily achieving its goal of enabling the [11]**large-scale** transition from **fossil fuels** to [12]**sustainable** energy," said Frost & Sullivan.

Gorogo 是由前宏達電創新長陸學森於 2011 年創辦，他於香港出生，在西雅圖長大。這家總部位於桃園的公司於 2015 年推出第一款電動機車和 Gogoro Network 智慧電池交換平台，雖然目前已掌控台灣九成電動機車市場，但從不吝分享自家的電池交換技術。在 Gogoro 智慧電池交換平台推動計畫中，Gogoro 已經幫助山葉、台鈴、宏佳騰、摩特動力和中華汽車等製造商設計使用相同電池交換系統的電動機車。弗若斯特沙利文表示：「Gogoro 正穩定實現從化石燃料大規模過渡到永續能源的目標。」

Grammar Master

include 各種「包含」用法

文中「Gogoro has helped other manufacturers, **including** Yamaha, Suzuki,... and CMC...」，including 意思為「包含」，也可改成以下寫法：

● **Ns, inclusive of N1, N2, and N3：**

manufacturers, **inclusive of** Yamaha, Suzuki, ... and CMC...

● **Ns, N1, N2, and N3 included：**

manufacturers, Yamaha, Suzuki, ... and CMC **included**

● **Ns, such as N1, N2, and N3：**

manufacturers, **such as** Yamaha, Suzuki, ... and CMC...

1. Silicon Valley 矽谷

是位於美國加州舊金山南端一條 1500 平方公里的狹長谷地 Santa Clara Valley 的別稱，早期當地多為製造高濃度 silicon 「矽」的半導體產業與電腦工業，因而有 Silicon Valley「矽谷」這個別稱。矽谷是 Apple、Google、HP 等科技企業與人才的發源地。總部位於此處的 Frost & Sullivan，是一家研究國際市場並提供各種產業企業顧問諮詢的公司。

achinthamb©Shutterstock

▲ Google 總部 Googleplex 就位於矽谷。

2. swappable battery 可更換電池

swap 當動詞，指「交換、更換」，加上形容詞字尾 -able「能夠、可以…的」形成 swappable，指「可更換的」。swappable battery 一詞專門指用在電動汽機車中的可更換電池，如果要說「更換電池」，可說 **battery swapping/switching**。這個電動車電池更換技術，可省去等待電池充電的時間，讓車主立刻拿到充滿電的電池。

◀ Gogoro 就是運用 swappable battery 技術作為機車動力。

3. Gogoro Network & GoStation

Gogoro Network「智慧電池交換平台」是由 Gogoro 自家研發、結合軟硬體的智慧型平台，除了有電池交換站 GoStation，也整合 Gogoro App、Gogoro 智慧電池、GoCharger 智慧電池快充座與 GoCharger Mobile 隨車電池充電器。此平台除了能更換電池，也應用 AI 搭配大數據，歸納車主使用習慣，調整最合適的充電模式。當車主到 GoStation 換電池時，電池會同步行車資料，檢查車況並提醒車主保養。

4. machine learning 機器學習

machine learning「機器學習」是 artificial intelligence「人工智慧」發展的一環，指的是讓機器能「自主學習」並「自主增強」的演算法（**algorithm**）。透過演算法分析，機器能從一堆數據中找出規律並做出預測，當輸入的數據越來越多，演算法也會持續調整，做出更精準的分析，拿文中所介紹的 GoStation 為例，當車主更換電池的次數越多，其 AI 就能根據車主行車里程數等行車數據做出更精準分析，以更有效的方式為電池充電。

5. vehicle diagnostics 車輛檢測

動詞 **diagnose** 原指「（醫療上的）診斷」，可延伸用於其他非醫療領域，形容詞為 **diagnostic**，本文中加上 s，形成 **diagnostics**，專指 IT 產業中對機器等的「一套診斷系統或方法」。

6. fossil fuels 化石燃料

fossil fuel「化石燃料」指如煤（**coal**）、石油（**fossil oil**）或天然氣（**natural gas**）等動力燃料，是幾世紀以來的主流燃料，然而其資源有限，加上燃燒後所產生的排放物（**emissions**）對環境造成污染，因此目前科技正轉向開發其他對環境友善的能源（**green energy**）或永續能源（**sustainable energy**）。

相對於文中介紹的 **electric scooter** 電動機車以電力為動力來源，傳統汽機車這類油車（**gasoline car**）則是以石油（**gasoline**）為動力來源，而介於其中的「油電車」則是使用電力與石油混和能源，稱 **hybrid**。

Environment

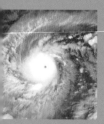

#Typhoon Goni #Typhoon Rolly
#the Philippines #tropical cyclone

Franco Amian©Shutterstock

在菲律賓稱 Rolly、國際上稱 Goni 的超級颱風對當地造成重創。

全文朗讀 🎵 059　單字 🎵 060

Typhoon Goni [1] Batters the Philippines
天鵝颱風重創菲律賓

⏱ **November 1, 2020**

Super Typhoon Goni struck the Philippines over the weekend, causing heavy damage to homes and agriculture and resulting in at least 25 deaths. With **sustained winds** of 140 mph and **gusts** of 174 mph, the storm—known in the Philippines as Super Typhoon Rolly—is the most powerful **tropical cyclone** of the year so far. Goni is also one of the largest typhoons to impact the Philippines since the ***devastating** Typhoon Haiyan, which [2] **claimed** [3] **approximately** 7,300 lives in 2013.

超級颱風天鵝週末重創菲律賓,嚴重破壞房屋和農業,並造成至少 25 人死亡。這場暴風雨在菲律賓被稱為超級颱風羅里,持續風速以每小時 140 英里行進,陣風為每小時 174 英里,是今年至目前為止最強大的熱帶氣旋。天鵝颱風也是繼 2013 年奪走約 7300 人性命的致命海燕颱風以來,橫掃菲律賓的最大颱風之一。

After forming as a **tropical depression** on October 26, the storm quickly [4] **intensified** and became a **Category 5** super typhoon on Friday. At dawn on Saturday, Goni **made landfall** on the

Vocabulary

1. **batter** [ˋbætɚ] (v.)
   猛擊,重創,造成衝擊

2. **claim** [klem] (v.) 奪走(性命)

3. **approximately** [əˋprɑsəmɪtli]
   (adv.) 大概,近乎

4. **intensify** [ɪnˋtɛnsəˏfaɪ] (v.) 增
   強,加劇。名詞 **intensity**
   [ɪnˋtɛnsəti] 強度,烈度

5. **province** [ˋprɑvɪns] (n.)
省，州

6. **residence** [ˋrɛzədəns] (n.)
住宅

7. **slam** [slæm] (v.) 猛撞，衝擊

8. **isolated** [ˋaɪsə͵letɪd] (a.)
被孤立的，隔絕的

9. **utility** [juˋtɪlətɪ] (n.) 公共事業，
如水電、瓦斯等，**utility pole**
電線桿

10. **complicate** [ˋkɑmplə͵ket] (v.)
使複雜化，使難對付

ymphotos©Shutterstock

2013 年超級颱風海燕重創菲律賓。

11. **evacuation** [ɪ͵vækjuˋeʃən] (n.)
撤離。動詞為 **evacuate**
[ɪˋvækju͵et]

12. **shelter** [ˋʃɛltɚ] (n.)
收容所，避難所

13. **potentially** [pəˋtɛnʃəlɪ] (adv.)
潛在地，可能地

14. **inspection** [ɪnˋspɛkʃən] (n.)
檢查，審視

15. **spare** [spɛr] (v.)
饒過，（使）免遭

16. **volcanic** [vɑlˋkænɪk] (a.)
火山的

17. **eruption** [ɪˋrʌpʃən] (n.)
（火山）爆發，動詞 **erupt**

18. **disaster** [dɪˋzæstɚ] (n.)
災難，禍害

19. **prone** [pron] (a.)
有⋯傾向的，易於⋯（+ to）

Philippine island [5]**province** of Catanduanes at peak intensity. Officials there estimated that 13,000 [6]**residences** were damaged or destroyed by the storm. Catanduanes was already ***reeling** from the effects of **Typhoon Molave**, which [7]**slammed** the island nation just a week previously, leaving many residents [8]**isolated**. According to Governor Joseph Cua, Goni caused **storm surges** as high as 16 feet, resulting in the loss of 80% of [9]**utility** poles. In the neighboring province of Albay, a landslide buried around 150 houses in a community in the town of Guinobatan.

這場暴風雨在 10 月 26 日形成熱帶低壓之後便迅速加劇，在週五成為五級超級颱風。週六黎明時分，天鵝以最高強度登陸菲律賓的島嶼省分卡坦端內斯。當地官員估計有 1 萬 3000 戶住宅遭暴風雨破壞或摧毀。卡坦端內斯原本因為莫拉菲颱風受創未平，那場颱風才剛在一週前重創這座島國，導致許多居民與外界隔絕。根據省長柯孫福表示，天鵝造成的風暴浪潮高達 16 英尺，導致八成電線桿損失。鄰近的阿爾拜省發生土石流，導致吉諾巴坦鎮一個社區約 150 棟房屋遭掩埋。

The coronavirus pandemic has [10]**complicated** [11]**evacuation** and **relief** efforts following Typhoon Goni. While cases have fallen since peaking in the summer months, bringing displaced residents together in temporary [12]**shelters** could [13]**potentially** cause new outbreaks. The army has been distributing food and water to affected residents and Philippine President Rodrigo Duterte made an ***aerial** [14]**inspection** of the devastated region.

新冠病毒疫情使天鵝颱風過後的撤離和救援工作變得更困難。儘管自夏季高峰期以來病例有所減少，但將流離失所的居民聚集在臨時避難所可能會引起新疫情爆發。軍隊一直在為受災居民發放食物和水，菲律賓總統杜特蒂也到災區上空視察災情。

Typhoon Goni weakened in intensity after making landfall and then changed direction, [15]**sparing** the capital city of Manila. The storm, which has now been **downgraded** to a tropical storm, is heading west over the South China Sea in the direction of Vietnam. The Philippines is hit by an average of 20 typhoons and tropical storms each year. It's also located in the **Ring of Fire**, where many earthquakes and [16]**volcanic** [17]**eruptions** occur, making it one of the world's most [18]**disaster**-[19]**prone** countries.

NASA©WikiCommons

為 Typhoon Goni 於 10 月 30 日的衛星雲圖，當時為其威力最大之時，暴風眼清晰可見。

天鵝颱風在登陸後強度減弱，隨後改變方向，讓首都馬尼拉躲過一劫。這場暴風雨現已降級為熱帶風暴，正朝西橫渡南海往越南的方向行進。菲律賓每年平均受到 20 次颱風和熱帶風暴襲擊，此地也位於環太平洋火山帶，經常發生地震和火山噴發，因此是世上最容易遭受天災的國家之一。

Grammar Master

表達「結果、後果」的句型

本新聞提到颱風造成許多災害，因此用到許多「導致」的句型，如「Goni caused storm surges as high as 16 feet, **resulting in** the loss of 80% of utility poles.」就用到 result in，後方接颱風導致的結果。這裡統一整理表示「導致，造成…的後果」所有片語：

● lead to：
例：Drunk driving often leads to fatal accidents. 酒駕常造成致命意外。

● bring about：
例：Financial reform brought about great changes in the economy. 財政改革導致經濟劇變。

● give rise to：
例：The Japanese manga's success has given rise to a number of movie adaptations. 這部日本漫畫的成功引起許多電影改編。

● result in：
例：Advances in technology have resulted in safer airplanes. 科技進步造就出更安全的航機。

● 反義則可以用 result from 表示，後面接「原因」：
例：Her obesity resulted from an unbalanced diet. 她的肥胖源於不均衡飲食。

1. sustained wind & gust 持續風速與最大瞬間陣風

sustained 指「持續性的」，因此 sustained wind 在颱風報導中就是指颱風的「持續風速」。而 gust 不同於 wind，指「一陣強風」，在颱風報導中就是指「最大瞬間陣風」。常聽到的颱風相關名詞還有：

- typhoon eye 颱風眼，暴風中心
- typhoon path 颱風路徑
- total rainfall 總降雨量

2. typhoon, storm, hurricane 颱風、暴風雨與颶風

不管是颱風（**typhoon**）、熱帶低氣壓（**tropical depression**）、或是熱帶風暴（**tropical storm**），其實都是屬於熱帶氣旋（**tropical cyclone**），只是根據其風速強弱不同而有不同稱呼。當熱帶氣旋生成於太平洋西北海域，且風速高達每小時 119 公里以上時，這些熱帶氣旋就被叫做 typhoon。

Arthur Villator©Shutterstock

而 **hurricane**「颶風」跟 typhoon 不同之處只有一個，就是生成地方不同；同樣條件的暴風雨如果在大西洋或太平洋東北海域生成，就叫 hurricane。

3. 颱風分級標準

不同國家對颱風分級標準各有不同，在台灣，颱風強度是依照「近中心最大平均風速」來做劃分。有時我們會聽到「超級颱風」「超級強烈颱風」，但其實這並不屬於台灣中央氣象局的分級標準，中央氣象局把颱風分成以下三級：**mild typhoon** 輕度颱風、**moderate typhoon** 中度颱風與 **severe typhoon** 強烈颱風。陣風規模（**Category scale**）其實是描述颶風等級的正式用語，不過偶而也會在報導颱風相關報導中使用；強烈颱風通常相當於 4-5 級陣風規模。

4. make landfall & downgrade 登陸與風速減弱

當颱風眼一登陸陸地，就可以說 make landfall「登陸」，更多颱風相關的動詞還有：

- strengthen 增強
- downgrade/weaken 減弱
- pick up speed 增強
- move north 往北移動

5. storm surge 暴潮

surge 指「暴升，短時間大量上升」之意，而 storm surge 便是指颱風或暴風帶來的自然災害現象。由於颱風往往夾帶大量水氣，在短短數小時內降下 300mm 以上雨量，這些水會快速聚集在低窪地帶的河域，引發河水暴漲，造成海平面暴升，加上潮汐影響，此時浪潮比潮汐水位還要高，這就稱為 storm surge「暴潮」。

Arthur Villator©Shutterstock

6. relief 救援

relief 常出現在災害相關文章中，指「救援（行動）」，如 **international relief operation**「國際救援行動」、**relief supplies**「救援物資」。

7. Ring of Fire 環太平洋（火山）帶

是一個太平洋沿岸地質活動頻繁的地區，這個火山帶上有一連串的海溝、火山帶與版塊活動。地球上約 90% 的地震都在這個地帶發生，菲律賓、台灣、印尼等就是位於此地帶上，因此地震頻仍。

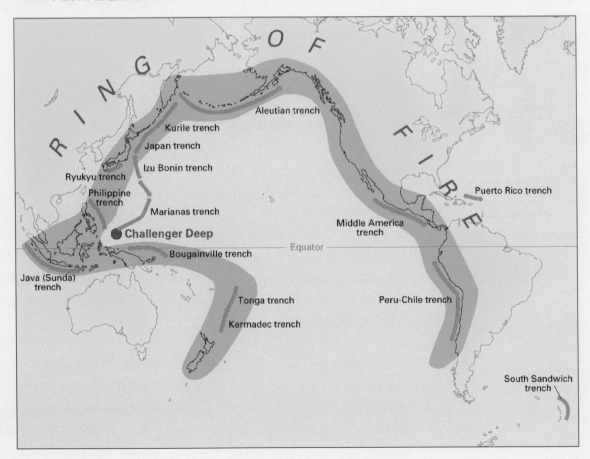

26

#California wildfire #drought
#heat wave
#climate change
#extreme weather #disaster

全文朗讀 ♫ 061　　單字 ♫ 062

California Is Burning
加州森林大火持續延燒

🕐 **September 3, 2020**

Vocabulary

1. **bless** [blɛs] (v.)
祝福，**be blessed with** 指「得力於（先天條件）」

2. **inland** [ˋɪnlənd] (a.) 內陸的

3. **rainfall** [ˋren͵fɔl] (n.)
降雨（量）

4. **acre** [ˋekɚ] (n.) 英畝 =
4,046.85642 平方公尺

California is ¹⁾**blessed** with a sunny **Mediterranean climate** that makes it one of the most desirable places to live in the country. But this climate, marked by warm, dry summers and cool, rainy winters also has a dark side. During the summer months, ²⁾**inland** areas of California can reach over 38 °C, and ³⁾**rainfall** is extremely scarce, making these areas prone to **wildfires.**

受惠於陽光明媚的地中海型氣候，使得加州成為全美最適合居住的地方之一。不過這個以夏季溫暖乾燥、冬季陰涼多雨為特徵的氣候型態也有其缺點。在夏季月份期間，加州內陸地區氣溫可高達攝氏 38 度，降雨量極為稀少，使這些地區容易發生野火。

In fact, wildfires are a natural part of California's ***ecosystem**, even a necessary one. The seeds of many coniferous trees actually require heat from fires for their seeds to ***germinate** properly. Scientists estimate that before 1850, over 4,000,000 ⁴⁾**acres** burned each year during the fire season, which lasts from July to October. In the old days, the native peoples of California used

controlled burns to protect the areas they lived in while at the same time maintaining the natural balance in the ecosystem.

事實上，野火算是加州生態系統的自然現象之一，甚至可以說是必備要素。許多針葉樹的種子需要火的熱度才能發芽。科學家估計，1850 年之前，每到六月到十月間的野火季節，就會有超過四百萬英畝的土地被野火燒盡。在過去，加州的原住民會使用「控管燒除」以保護自己所居住的地方，同時也維持整個生態系統的平衡。

In recent years, however, the authorities in California have ⁵⁾**aggressively** ⁶⁾**suppressed** wildfires, causing a ***buildup** of ⁷⁾**fuel**—fallen branches, dead leaves, etc.—which increases the risk of large, ⁸⁾**uncontrollable** fires. For this reason, along with a record-breaking heat wave, California's 2020 wildfire season has been the worst in recorded history. So far this season, a total of 7,718 fires have burned over 3.4 million acres, which is more than 3% of the state's land area. The fires have destroyed over 6,000 buildings and resulted in 29 deaths and billions in ⁹⁾**economic** damage.

5. **aggressively** [əˋɡrɛsɪvlɪ] *(adv.)* 積極地，攻擊性地。形容詞 **aggressive**

6. **suppress** [səˋprɛs] *(v.)* 壓制，鎮壓

7. **fuel** [ˋfjuəl] *(n.)* 燃料，易燃物

8. **uncontrollable** [͵ʌnkənˋtroləbəl] *(a.)* 無法控制的

9. **economic** [͵ɛkəˋnɑmɪk] *(a.)* 經濟的

進階字彙

* **ecosystem** [ˋiko͵sɪstəm] *(n.)* 生態系

* **germinate** [ˋdʒɝmə͵net] *(v.)* 發芽，萌芽

* **buildup** [ˋbɪld͵ʌp] *(n.)* 大量堆積

加州消防員進行預防性的控管燒除作業。

由於森林野火發生時範圍遍佈過於廣大，當發生野火時，當地並不會採取積極滅火，因為效率太差。而是以先保護尚未受波及的地區，先砍伐距離野火較近的易燃樹木，並疏散周圍民眾。

然而，近年加州政府當局對野火進行過度壓制，導致燃料——即掉落的枯枝樹葉等——過度堆積，反而大大增加無法控制的大型野火發生機率。正因如此，加上破紀錄的熱浪來襲，今年的野火季節是加州歷年來最嚴重的。至今為止，已經有七千七百一十八件野火發生，共燒毀超過三百四十萬英畝的林地，占了全加州土地面積超過百分之三。今年的加州野火已經燒毀超過六千棟建築，造成 29 人死亡，以及數十億美元經濟損失。

Grammar Master

use to 用法整理

文中「the native peoples of California **used** controlled burns **to** protect the areas...」的 used to 意思為「過去使用某物用來」，英文中其他易混淆用法：

● **used to + 原形動詞，表達「過去經常做某事」：**

例：I used to drink a lot of soda before I lost weight. 我減肥之前經常喝汽水。

例：I didn't use to watch cartoons when I was a kid. 我小時候不常看卡通。

● **be used to + 原形動詞，表達「被用來作…」，為文中句子的被動語態：**

例：The app is used to track the location of people in quarantine. 此應用程式被用來追蹤隔離者的位置。

● **be used to + Ving/ n.，表達「習慣做某事；對某物習慣」：**

例：Mexican people are used to eating spicy food. 墨西哥人習慣吃辣的食物。

例：Growing up in a tropical country, he is not used to the cold weather in Russia. 從小在熱帶國家長大，他不適應俄羅斯的寒冷氣候。

1. Mediterranean climate 地中海型氣候

與 weather「短期天氣狀態」不同，climate 指「長期的氣候變化」。Mediterranean Climate 指「地中海型氣候」，夏季乾熱且日照充足，冬季則溫和多雨，這類氣溫分布於地中海沿岸、美國西岸沿海、南美洲智利中部、非洲南端的好望角地區與澳洲南部。由於這類氣候區的夏天剛好符合野火必備的「高溫乾燥」條件，因此野火好發。

▶ 地中海型氣候相當適合人類居住。

2. wildfire 野火

野火的發生需具備兩個條件，一個是高溫，高溫使得枯枝落葉容易自燃，第二個條件是乾燥，乾燥的枯枝落葉便是最佳燃料。因此位於熱帶地區的熱帶草原氣候，由於其乾雨季分明，便常在乾季時發生草原野火。

Anna LoFi©Shutterstock

▲ 2019 年澳洲也發生規模龐大的野火。

3. coniferous tree 針葉樹

常見的針葉林有松樹（pine）、柏樹（cypress）與杉樹（cedar），這些樹木共同特徵就是長得像針的細長型樹葉，這是為了在降雨稀少的氣候下減少水份蒸發而演變來的，其樹幹較為厚實，也是為了減少水份流失，濡樹木更為耐寒，因此，針葉林比闊葉樹（broad-leaved tree）更適合在寒帶生長。

4. controlled burn 控管燒除

又稱 **prescribed turn**，是一種預防性保護環境行為。指在受控的範圍下人為引發小型野火，以避免日後發生大型不受控的野火，也能達到森林生態平衡。

#ecosystem
#murder hornet #invasive species

全文朗讀 ♫ 063　單字 ♫ 064

Invasion of the Murder Hornets
殺人蜂亞洲大黃蜂入侵美國

🕐 **November 12, 2020**

Vocabulary

1. **organism** [ˈɔrgəˌnɪzəm] (n.)
生物，有機體

2. **prompt** [prɑmpt] (v.)
引發，促使

3. **gear** [gɪr] (n.) 器材，用具

4. **specialized** [ˈspɛʃəˌlaɪzd] (a.)
專業的，專門的

5. **intruder** [ɪnˈtrudə] (n.)
侵入者，闖入者

6. **pierce** [pɪrs] (v.) 刺穿，刺破

Dangerous alien ¹⁾**organisms** have invaded the **Pacific Northwest**, ²⁾**prompting** local authorities to ℗**raise the alarm**. First spotted on Vancouver Island in August, 2019, the **invasive species** soon crossed the Canadian border into Washington State. Whenever a sighting is made, teams of scientists wearing protective ³⁾**gear** use ⁴⁾**specialized** weapons to *****eradicate** the threat. But these fierce ⁵⁾**intruders** didn't come from outer space. They are thought to have arrived in North America aboard cargo ships. They are **Asian giant hornets**.

危險的外來生物入侵太平洋西北地區，促使地方當局拉起警戒線。入侵物種是在 2019 年 8 月首次在溫哥華島上發現，隨後便越過加拿大邊界進入美國華盛頓州。每當發現此物種時，科學家小組便穿戴防護裝備並以專用武器來消除威脅。但這些兇猛的入侵物種不是來自外太空，牠們被認為是搭上貨船抵達北美，稱為亞洲大黃蜂。

Named "murder hornets" by the media due to their large size—up to three inches—and aggressive behavior, Asian giant hornets can easily ⁶⁾**pierce beekeeping suits** with their long ⁷⁾**stingers**. Their ***venomous** stings can be extremely painful, and though a handful of people are killed by them each year in East and Southeast Asia, their greatest danger isn't to humans. The hornets ⁸⁾**prey** on native ***wasps**, ***disrupting** the ecosystem, and also attack the honeybees that play a vital role in ***pollinating** food crops. A ⁹⁾**swarm** of Asian giant hornets can destroy a hive of bees in mere hours.

▲ 穿著防護衣的人員正試圖拔除蜂巢。

由於牠們的大小可達 3 英寸，加上攻擊性強，因此被媒體稱為「殺人黃蜂」，亞洲大黃蜂（台灣稱為大虎頭蜂）可以輕易用牠們長長的針刺穿防蜂衣。被牠們有毒的針螫到會十分痛苦，儘管東亞和東南亞每年都有少數人被牠們螫死，但牠們最大的危害對象不是人類。大黃蜂會捕食美國本土黃蜂，破壞生態系統，還會攻擊蜜蜂，而蜜蜂在替農作物授粉時扮演重要角色。一群亞洲大黃蜂可以在短短幾小時內摧毀蜜蜂的蜂巢。

When the first murder hornet sightings where reported in Blaine, Washington—just across the border from Vancouver—in late 2019, scientists at the Washington State Department of Agriculture (WSDA) ᴾ**went on high alert**. On October 20 of this year, they successfully trapped several of the hornets and ¹⁰⁾**attached** radio ***transmitters** to them. Three days later, the scientists tracked the hornets back to their nest in a tree east of Blaine—the first found in the U.S. After pumping the nest with ***carbon dioxide** and sealing it with ¹¹⁾**foam**, the scientists sawed off the section of the tree containing the nest and took it back to their laboratory at Washington State University.

2019 年底首次在與溫哥華接壤的華盛頓州布蘭接獲報告發現大黃蜂時，華盛頓州農業局的科學家們便提高警覺。今年 10 月 20 日，他們成功捕獲幾隻大黃蜂，並在牠們身上安裝無線發射器。三天後科學家藉由大黃蜂追蹤到布蘭以東一棵樹上的蜂巢，這是在美國首次發現。科學家將二氧化碳灌入蜂巢並用泡棉封住後，將帶有蜂巢的樹枝鋸下，並帶回華盛頓州立大學的實驗室。

After careful ¹²⁾**analysis**, the nest was found to contain around 500 live ¹³⁾**specimens**, including **larvae**, **pupae** and adults. Worryingly, nearly 200 of these specimens were queens, which have the potential to mate and start their own **colonies**. "It really seems like

7. **stinger** [ˋstɪŋɚ] (n.)
（昆蟲的）螫針

8. **prey on** (phr.)
補食，劫掠。名詞 **prey** 獵物

9. **swarm** [swɔrm] (n./v.)
（昆蟲）群；群集，蜂擁

10. **attach (to)** [əˋtætʃ] (v.)
裝上，貼上

11. **foam** [fom] (n.) 泡棉，泡沫

12. **analysis** [əˋnæləsɪs] (n.)
分析，複數為 **analyses**
[əˋnæləˏsiz]

13. **specimen** [ˋspɛsəmən] (n.)
標本，樣本

* **eradicate** [ɪ`rædɪˌket] (v.)
  根絕，消滅

* **stinger** [`stɪŋɚ] (n.)
  （昆蟲的）螫針

* **venomous** [`vɛnəməs] (a.)
  有毒的，分泌毒液的

* **wasp** [wɑsp] (n.) 黃蜂

* **disrupt** [dɪs`rʌpt] (v.)
  使混亂，使中斷

* **pollinate** [`pɑləˌnet] (v.)
  授花粉

* **transmitter** [`trænsˌmɪtɚ] (n.)
  發射器，傳輸器

* **carbon dioxide** [`kɑrbən
  daɪ`ɑksaɪd] (phr.)
  二氧化碳

* **entomologist** [ˌɛntə`mɑlədʒɪst]
  (n.) 昆蟲學家

示意圖，拔除後的亞洲大黃蜂蜂巢內還有許多活體樣本。

we got there just **ⓟin the nick of time**," said WSDA ***entomologist** Sven Spichiger at a press conference on Tuesday. "Even though we're fighting this fight in Washington right now, it literally is for the rest of the country."

經過仔細分析，發現蜂巢內含有約 500 個活體樣本，包括幼蟲、蛹和成蟲。令人擔憂的是，這些樣本中有近 200 隻是蜂后，都有交配和建立新蜂群的潛力。華盛頓州農業局昆蟲學家斯芬史皮奇格週二在新聞記者會上說：「看來我們真是在千鈞一髮之際趕到。即使我們是在華盛頓州努力奮戰，其實也是在為全美其他地區奮戰。」

Grammar Master

whenever 無論何時

whenever 當副詞連接詞等於 no matter when「無論何時」，因此本句「**Whenever** a sighting is made, teams of scientists wearing protective gear use specialized weapons to eradicate the threat.」 也可改寫為：「**No matter when** a sighting is made, teams of scientists wearing protective gear use specialized weapons to eradicate the threat.」注意，使用 whenever 連接兩個子句時，與主要子句之間要有逗點隔開。

● 相似用法還有 whatever (= no matter what) 與 wherever (= no matter where)：
例：Whatever happens, you know you can count on me. 不管發生合適，你知道有我讓你依靠。

● whenever、whatever 與 wherever 等也可以當「複合關係代名詞」，等同 anytime/anything/anywhere (that)「所有的…時間／東西／地點」，此時與主要子句之間就不需用逗點：
例：Whatever he says is not true. = Anything that he says is not true. 他說的話都不是真的。

1. Pacific Northwest 太平洋西北地區

為美國西北部地區和加拿大的西南部地區，又稱 Cascadia（得名自北美洲的 Cascade Range 喀斯開山脈）。包含美國阿拉斯加東南部、華盛頓州、奧勒岡州、愛達荷州、加州北部、蒙大拿州西部、內華達州北部，以及加拿大卑詩省。此區降雨量充沛、夏季氣候舒適，擁有北美洲最廣闊的森林。

2. `Phrase` **raise the alarm 發出警報，拉警報**

警告他人危險即將發生的意思，也可說 **sound the alarm**，sound 在這裡當動詞，指「發出聲響」。

例 A doctor at a local hospital was the first to raise the alarm about the new virus.
一名當地醫院的醫生首先發現新病毒並提出警告。

3. invasive species 入侵物種

species 為「物種」，invasive [ɪn`vesɪv] species 指被人為引進原本不存在於該生態地區的物種，引入之後於當地快速繁衍，而威脅到當地物種，並且對生態系統（ecosystem）造成莫大傷害，如原生於南美洲亞馬遜河流域的福壽螺，便是在台灣造成農害且生態失衡的入侵物種。本新聞提到的 Asian giant hornet「大虎頭蜂」分布於亞洲，在台灣有「殺人大黃蜂」之稱，體型巨大，具有強烈腐蝕性劇毒。

4. beekeeping suit 養蜂裝

beekeeping 的 keep 指「養育」，如 **keep a pet**（養寵物），因此 **beekeeping** 就是指「養蜂」一職，為了不在養蜂過程中被蜂螫，養蜂人 **beekeeper** 都要穿戴防針螫的防護衣與防護罩，整套裝備就稱 beekeeping suit。

5. `Phrase` **go/be on high alert 進入高度警戒狀態**

alert 指「警報」，後面接介系詞 for，be on high alert for sth.，就是對後面所接的事物提高警覺。也可將 high alert 改為 **red alert**。

例 The airport was placed on high alert following a bomb threat.
發生爆炸威脅之後，機場便進入高度警戒狀態。

6. larva & pupa 幼蟲與蛹

生物學與植物學有許多字都是源自於拉丁文和希臘文，這兩個字就是來自拉丁文。larva [`lɑrvə] 來自於拉丁文的 larva（有「幽靈」、「假面」的意思），指昆蟲幼蟲，指牠們孵化之後但尚未發育完全的狀態，複數為 larvae。而 pupa [`pjupə]（拉丁文的 pupa 指「木偶」，有未開發完成的意思），複數寫作 pupae，指昆蟲如蝴蝶、蛾等要變形前會先形成的「蛹」。英文的 pupil「學徒」就是來自拉丁文 pupa。

7. colony 群落

在生物學上，colony 則是指動植物、昆蟲或細菌的群落，如 **a colony of ants**「蟻群」。

8. `Phrase` **in the nick of time 千鈞一髮之際，緊要關頭**

nick 指木頭上的刻痕，以前人在計時的時候會在木頭上刻痕，尤其比賽時這個刻痕就是指最後一刻，因此 in the nick of time 就是指最後一刻，延伸有「在緊要關頭」、「及時」。

A: Did the house burn down? 房子被燒光了嗎？
B: No, a fire engine arrived just in the nick of time. 沒，消防隊及時趕到。

Business & Economy

財經

28

#Korea #Samsung
#Galaxy Note

Republic of Korea©WikiCommons

2013 年三星集團李健熙（左一）與南韓官員的早餐會面。李健熙於 2020 年 10 月 25 日因心機梗塞病逝，享年 78 歲。

全文朗讀 ♫ 065　　單字 ♫ 066

Chairman's Death Marks End of Era for Samsung

🕐 October 26, 2020

三星集團會長李健熙病逝

The [1]**reign** of a business titan has ended. Lee Kun-hee, chairman of Samsung Group and South Korea's richest citizen, died yesterday. The 78-year-old was surrounded by his family in his final moments. Lee was ***instrumental** in the [2]**transformation** of the Korean *chaebol*, or conglomerate, into one of the world's largest business [3]**empires**. The company has become such a powerful economic, and even political force in South Korea that the nation is sometimes called the "Republic of Samsung."

商業巨頭的統治已經結束。三星集團會長和南韓首富李健熙昨日去世。78 歲的李健熙在家人陪伴下走完最後一程。李健熙在這家韓國財閥（或稱企業集團）轉變成世界最大的商業帝國過程中，擔任關鍵角色。該公司在南韓已經是強大的經濟甚至政治力量，以至於該國有時被稱為「三星共和國」。

Vocabulary

1. **reign** [ren] (n.) 統治，稱霸

2. **transformation** [ˌtrænsfɚˋmeʃən] (n.) 變化，轉變，變形

3. **empire** [ˋɛmpaɪr] (n.) 帝國

1930 年代的三星。三星於 1987 年被韓國官方正式定義為大型公司集團。

4. **retail** [ˋritel] *(n./a.)*
   零售（業）；零售的

5. **electronics** [ɪlɛkˋtrɑnɪks] *(n.)*
   電子科技，電子學，電器用品

6. **invest** [ɪnˋvɛst] *(v.)* 投資，入股。名詞 **investment** 投資（額、標的）

7. **navigate** [ˋnævɪˏget] *(v.)*
   導航；度過難關

8. **brink** [brɪnk] *(n.)*
   （懸崖、危險、絕種等）邊緣

9. **bankruptcy** [ˋbæŋkrʌptsɪ] *(n.)*
   倒閉，破產

10. **emerge (from)** [ɪˋmɝdʒ] *(v.)*
    走出，浮現

11. **devote (to)** [dɪˋvot] *(v.)*
    將…奉獻給，致力於（+ Ving/N）

12. **controversial** [ˏkɑntrəˋvɝʃəl] *(a.)* 有爭議的

13. **bid** [bɪd] *(n.)*
    申請（比賽等的）主辦權，投標

Samsung was founded by Lee's father, Lee Byung-chul, as a trading company in 1938. Over the years, the elder Lee grew Samsung into a conglomerate with businesses in food processing, insurance and 4)**retail**, and later construction and 5)**electronics**. When the younger Lee took over from his father in 1987, he saw the growing demand for consumer electronics, and began 6)**investing** heavily in areas like televisions, memory chips and *semiconductors. Lee's shrewd business sense helped Samsung successfully 7)**navigate** both the 1997 Asian financial crisis—of the Four Asian Tigers, South Korea was hit the hardest—and the burst of the dot-com bubble, which brought many companies to the 8)**brink** of 9)**bankruptcy**.

三星是由李健熙的父親李秉喆於 1938 年以貿易公司的形式創辦。多年來李秉喆將三星發展成橫跨食品加工業、保險業和零售業的企業集團，後來又加入建築業和電子產品業。李健熙在 1987 年從父親手中接管企業時，看到消費電子產品的需求不斷增長，於是開始大量投資電視、記憶體晶片和半導體等領域。李健熙敏銳的商業頭腦幫助三星成功渡過 1997 年的亞洲金融風暴（在四小龍中，南韓遭到最嚴重打擊）和網路泡沫化衝擊，後者使許多公司瀕臨破產。

10)**Emerging** from those challenging years, Lee 11)**devoted** his efforts **to** developing the product that would turn Samsung into a global consumer brand: the Galaxy smartphone. Samsung Electronics, which is just one of Samsung Group's many companies, is worth $350 billion today, and is the world's largest maker of consumer electronics.

從那充滿挑戰的年代之後，李健熙便致力於開發使三星成為全球消費品牌的產品：Galaxy 智慧型手機。三星電子只是三星集團旗下的眾多公司之一，如今市值達 3500 億元，也是全球最大的消費電子產品製造商。

But Lee was also a 12)**controversial** figure. In the late 2000s, he was convicted of *bribery and tax evasion. He was later pardoned, in part so he could help South Korea win its 13)**bid** for the 2018 Winter Olympics. Lee beat lung cancer in the late 1990s, but after a heart attack in 2014 he remained 14)**hospitalized** for six years

Karlis Dambrans©Shutterstock

14. **hospitalize** [ˋhɑspɪtḷˌaɪz] *(v.)*
讓人住院接受治療

15. **successor** [səkˋsɛsə] *(n.)*
接班人，繼承人

進階字彙

* **instrumental** [ˌɪnstrəˋmɛntəl] *(a.)*
發揮關鍵作用的

* **semiconductor**
[ˌsɛmɪkənˋdʌktə] *(n.)* 半導體

* **bribery** [ˋbraɪbərɪ] *(n.)*
收賄；行賄。動詞 **bribe**「賄賂，
收買，行賄物」

圖片為三星於 2020 年出的 Galaxy Note 系列最新手機，此系列是三星最知名的電子產品，特色是旁邊的 S Pen。

until his death on October 25. He leaves behind a wife and four children, as well as a $20 billion fortune. Lee's son, Lee Jae-yong, who has been running Samsung since his father's heart attack, is set to become his [15]**successor**.

但李健熙也是具有爭議的人物。2000 年末，他因賄賂和逃稅被定罪。他後來被赦免，部分原因是為了讓他幫助南韓贏得 2018 年冬季奧運會的申辦權。李健熙在 1990 年代後期戰勝肺癌，但在 2014 年心臟病發作後，住院治療了六年，直到 10 月 25 日去世。他身後留下妻子和四名子女，以及 200 億元的財富。李健熙的兒子李在鎔自父親心臟病發後一直管理三星，準備好成為他的接班人。

Grammar Master

devote (efforts, oneself) to「投身、致力於」

本句「Lee **devoted** his efforts **to** developing in the product...」中的 devote... to 指「致力於、投身於…」，這裡的 to 為介系詞，後方接名詞，如果要接動詞，需改為 Ving 動名詞形式。

● 表達相同意思的片語還有 commit to + Ving：

例：Mother Teresa committed her life to helping the poor. 德蕾莎修女奉獻一生幫助窮人。

● 此類片語也常以被動式表現：sb. + be devoted to...，意同 be committed to、be dedicated to：

例：The charity is dedicated to the prevention of cruelty to animals. 該慈善機構致力於預防動物虐待。

1. titan 巨頭

titan [`taɪtən] 為希臘文,「巨大」之意,Titan 指希臘神話中曾統治宇宙的古老巨神族,由天神 Uranus 烏拉諾斯和大地女神 Gaia 蓋亞所生,曾統治世界,後被宙斯推翻取代。現在這個字可指任何領域的「巨頭,泰斗」,也可用 giant 一字表達。titan 也可指最大的東西,如土星的最大衛星就名為 Titan。

2. chaebol, conglomerate 韓國財閥

chaebol,念作 [`tʃebl],專指南韓大型商業集團,又稱 **conglomerate** [kən`glɑmmərɪt]。稱財閥是因為這些企業多半是家族企業,與政府關係密切,經濟實力強大到能左右韓國經濟。家族控制和多角化經營是最主要特徵。知名韓國財閥除了三星,還有現代、LG、SK 集團等。

Arcansel©Shutterstock

▲ Hyundai 現代汽車 Logo。

3. 1997 Asian financial crisis 1997 年亞洲金融風暴

crisis 指危機,複數寫作 crises。1980 年代末,全球預期亞洲許多發展中國家會快速發展,大量資金便湧向亞洲,讓泰國、馬來西亞、印尼、新加坡、韓國等東南亞國家資產上漲。傳統產業為擴大規模向銀行貸款,或要求外國投資客將外匯流入金融市場中,此時政府為了固定匯率便動用外匯儲備。換言之,這場「亞洲經濟奇蹟」其實是因資金增加而出現的榮景假像,國家本身的經濟實力並沒有提升,一當體質較差的國家無法負荷,便造成經濟泡沫化。其中以韓國與多數東南亞國家受創最甚。

1000 Words©Shutterstock

economic collapse.

4. Four Asian Tigers 亞洲四小龍

大家熟知的「亞洲四小龍」the Four Asian Dragons 在國外更常稱 the Four Asian Tigers「亞洲四虎」，指 1960 年代末至 1990 年代亞洲四個發展迅速的經濟體：韓國、台灣、香港及新加坡。1997 年發生亞洲金融風暴，韓國成為四小龍中受創最嚴重的國家。

另有「亞洲四小虎」Tiger Cub Economies，則指印尼、泰國、馬來西亞和菲律賓，這四個東南亞國家在 1990 年代就像 1980 年代的亞洲四小龍一樣突飛猛進，因而得名。然而受到 1997 年亞洲金融風暴衝擊，四小虎未能像四小龍一樣打穩經濟基礎，經濟受到重創。

5. dot-com bubble 2000 年美國網路泡沫

美國網路泡沫，稱 dot-com bubble 或 **Internet bubble**，是 1997 到 2000 年的金融泡沫。1995 年網際網路的發明，讓大家看好網路新創事業，只要名字加上 .com 的公司幾乎就能吸引大筆高額投資。2000 年 3 月 10 日，以科技股為主的 NASDAQ 指數升至歷史新高 5132.52 點後突然重挫近百點，引發股災，1 個月後總體市值蒸發 1 兆美元。不少企業如 Pet.com 關門大吉，Cisco 股價跌 8 成。

6. tax evasion 逃稅

evasion 念作 [ɪˋveʃən]，有「逃避，避開」的意思，tax evasion 就是「逃稅」，為非法行為。合法稱「避稅」，英文稱 **tax avoidance**。

7. 2018 winter Olympics 2018 冬季奧運

2018 年第 23 屆冬季奧運於韓國平昌舉辦，為韓國第一次主辦冬季奧運。

railway fx©Shutterstock

#Tesla #automobile
#S&P500 #stock market
#electric car #green energy

Zigres©Shutterstock

Tesla Motors 為電動車（electric car）巨頭，連續幾季銷量成長使該公司獲得入 S&P 資格。

全文朗讀 ♫ 067　　單字 ♫ 068

Tesla to Join S&P 500 Index
特斯拉入標普 500 指數，馬斯克身價飆漲

⏱ **November 6, 2020**

Vocabulary

1. **inclusion** [ɪnˋkluʒən] (n.)
   納入，包含，動詞 include

2. **surge** [sɝdʒ] (v./n.) 激增，暴漲

3. **prestige** [prɛˋstiʒ] (n.)
   聲望，威望

4. **soar** [sor] (v.) 激增，飛漲

Tesla will be added to the **S&P 500** at the start of trading on December 21. [1]**Inclusion** in the widely followed **stock market index** is expected to cause investor enthusiasm for Tesla to [2]**surge**. With its addition to the S&P, the Silicon Valley maker of electric vehicles will gain a mark of [3]**prestige** held by other tech titans like Microsoft, Apple, and Netflix. Monday's announcement caused Tesla stocks to [4]**soar** 13.7% in **after-market trading**. If Tesla were to join the S&P 500 on Tuesday, it would be the ninth largest company on the index by **market capitalization**, based on its current **market cap** of $420 billion.

特斯拉將在 12 月 21 日開盤交易時納入標準普爾 500 指數。特斯拉被納入廣受關注股市指數的消息，預計將引發一波特斯拉投資潮。這家位於矽谷的電動汽車製造商加入標準普爾一事，意味著它將獲得與微軟、蘋果和 Netflix 等科技巨頭已享有的威望。週一消息才宣布，就導致特斯拉股票在盤後交易飆升 13.7％。特斯拉倘若在週二納入標準普爾 500 指數，根據目前的 4200 億美元市值，屆時將成為市值第九大的公司。

Elon Musk, Tesla's controversial CEO, believes the company's electric cars are an important step away from [5]**dependence** on fossil fuels toward the [6]**solar** electric economy of the future. Such a statement may have made investors [7]**cautious** when Musk first made it in 2006, but Tesla's remarkable success has turned [7]**caution** into confidence. Tesla's [8]**shares** have risen around 450% in 2020, causing the company to replace Toyota as the most valuable automaker in the world.

特斯拉具爭議性的執行長伊隆馬斯克認為，該公司的電動車是擺脫依賴化石燃料並邁向未來太陽能發電經濟的重要一步。馬斯克於 2006 年發表這種聲明時，可能讓投資人抱持謹慎態度，但特斯拉的傑出成就將這種謹慎轉變成信心。特斯拉的股價在 2020 年上漲約 450%，使該公司取代豐田，成為世上身價最高的汽車製造商。

Tesla became [9]**eligible** to join the S&P 500 after posting its fourth ***consecutive** profit in the second quarter of this year. However, the company was not selected for inclusion by the index committee at **S&P Dow Jones Indices** at that time due to concerns about the ***sustainability** of its growth. After reporting its fifth consecutive quarter of profit, Tesla finally made the cut. When it joins the S&P 500 in December, it will be one of the largest companies ever added to the **benchmark** index.

5. **dependence** [dɪˋpɛndəns] (n.)
   依賴

6. **solar** [ˋsolɚ] (a.)
   利用太陽光的，太陽的

7. **cautious** [ˋkɔʃəs] (a.)
   小心的。
   caution [ˋkɔʃən] (n.) 謹慎

8. **share** [ʃɛr] (n.) 股份，股票

9. **eligible** [ˋɛlɪdʒəbl] (a.)
   合乎資格的

Sundry Photography©Shutterstock

圖片大樓為 Tesla 位於 Silicon Valley 的總部。

dennizn©Shutterstock

標準普爾 500 指數為美國股市三大指數之一，能入標普 500 的都是體質優良的大型上市公司。

特斯拉到今年第二季度已連續四季獲利，因此獲得納入標準普爾 500 指數的資格，但當時標普道瓊指數的指數委員會擔心該公司的成長永續性，因此選擇未將其納入。特斯拉在第五個季度連續獲利後終於晉級。該公司在 12 月納入標準普爾 500 指數時，將成為有史以來加入此標竿指數中最大的公司之一。

Because of Tesla's large market cap, S&P DJI is considering adding its shares to the index in two **tranches** to make it easier for investment funds to [10]**digest**. Its addition means funds that track the S&P 500 will have to sell about $50 billion worth of shares of companies already in the S&P 500 and use that money to buy Tesla shares so that their **portfolios** correctly reflect the index. When this process is complete, Tesla will make up about 1% of the index.

由於特斯拉的鉅額市值，標普道瓊指數公司正考慮將其股票分兩階段納入指數，好讓投資基金更容易消化。股票的納入表示，追蹤標準普爾 500 指數的基金必須先出售約 500 億元的標準普爾 500 家公司股票，並用這些資金購買特斯拉股票，好讓他們的投資組合能正確反映該指數。待完成此過程後，特斯拉將佔該指數約 1%。

10. **digest** [daɪˋdʒɛst / ˋdɪdʒɛstʃ]
(v./n.) 消化

進階字彙

* **consecutive** [kənˋsɛkjʊtɪv] (a.)
連續的

* **sustainability** [sə.stenəˋbɪlɪti]
(n.) 永續性

Grammar Master

表達「原因」的句型整理

because of 指「由於，因為」，後面只能接名詞或名詞片語，英文中表達「因為」的用法有很多，以下整理用法：

● **because of + N.，相同用法還有 due to，on account of：**
例：The accident was due to poor visibility. 這起意外肇因於視線不良。

● **because + 子句，可放句中或句首，相同用法還有 since，as：**
例：Since she loves music so much, Carrie has decided to become a musician. 因為凱莉熱愛音樂，所以她決定要當個音樂家。

例：We decided to head home as it was getting late. 因為時間已晚，我們決定回家。

● **for 也可以當「因為」，不可放在句首，只能放在句中，後面接子句：**
例：Jake told the truth for he had nothing to lose. 傑克說了實話，因為他已經豁出去了。

1. Tesla & Elon Musk 特斯拉與伊隆馬斯克

從早期創立網路軟體公司、投資太空計劃到涉足電動車產業，伊隆馬斯克可說是引領科技的先鋒，據說電影《鋼鐵人》（*Iron Man*）中 Tony Stark 的角色就是根據馬斯克的形象所創造。現在大家說到 Tesla 就會想到他，但實際上馬斯克是在 Tesla 創立後 9 個月才加入，成為 Tesla 的董事長兼公共形象代言人。

vasilis asvestas©Shutterstock

2. stock market index 股價指數
S&P 500 標普 500 指數

stock market index，或作 **stock index**，是反映股票價值的指數。S&P 500「標準普爾 500 指數」、Dow Jones Industrial Average Index「道瓊工業平均指數」與 NASDAQ Composite Index「那斯達克指數」並列美國股市三大指數。S&P 500 全名為 Standard & Poor's 500 index，包含科技、金融、資訊等產業更為豐富的 500 家美國大型上市公司。能被歸為標普 500 指數，都是體質優良、財務狀況健康的企業，目前有 Facebook、Google、微軟、Amazon 等。

3. after-market trading 盤後交易

股市交易所的營業時間為美東時間早上 9 點半到下午 4 點，這段時間之後所進行的股市交易就是盤後交易，又稱 **after-hours trading**。

4. market capitalization 市值

capitalization 指「資本額」，可簡寫為 **cap**，因此 market capitalization 可簡稱 **market cap**，指一間公司在市場上流通股票的總價值。

5. benchmark index 標竿指數

benchmark [ˋbɛntʃˏmɑrk] 是「基準點」的意思，**benchmark index** 就是指投資人用來衡量其投資績效的比較標準，通常會拿該市場最具代表性的指數來看，如文中提到的 S&P 500 就是看美國股市的一個 benchmark index。

6. tranche（金額、股份、資金等的）一部分

當名詞，只用在金錢相關方面，這個字是從法文字 trancher 而來，意思是 to cut「切分」，簡單來說，a tranche 就是某金額的一部分。如：The loan will be repaid in three tranches.（負債將分成三階段償清。）

7. portfolio 投資組合

指一個投資者的全部資金所擁有的各項資產。比如他的投資組合可以是現金、股票、基金加上債券。

#Korean Air #Asiana
#aviation #acquisition

Nataliya Hora©Shutterstock

全文朗讀 🎵 069　　單字 🎵 070

Korean Air to Acquire Asiana Airlines
大韓航空將收購韓亞航空，躋身全球十大航空

🕐 **November 16, 2020**

Korean Air has announced that it will buy its former [1]**competitor**, Asiana Airlines. The **acquisition** comes with price tag of $1.6 billion. The combined airline will be among the 10 largest in the world. South Korea's **Hanjin Group**, which owns Korean Air, says that the main goal of the plan is "to [2]**stabilize** the Korean [3]**aviation** industry." Asiana proved unable to [4]**weather** the [5]**decrease** in [6]**revenue** resulting from the coronavirus pandemic.

大韓航空已宣布將收購前競爭公司韓亞航空。此次收購價格為 16 億美元。兩家航空公司合併後將躋身世界十大航空公司之列。擁有大韓航空的南韓韓進集團表示，這項計畫的主要目標是「穩定韓國航空業」。韓亞航空已證實無法承受因新冠疫情而造成的虧損。

South Korea's [7]**Deputy** Minister for Civil Aviation at the [8]**Ministry** of Land, *****Infrastructure**, and Transport said the **merger** was an " [9]**inevitable**" decision designed to [10]**minimize** losses at both airlines during a time of reduced travel. According to Hanjin, having two major airlines in competition is unusual for a country the size of South Korea. This has left South Korea at a [11]**disadvantage** compared to countries like France, Germany and Singapore, which all have one major carrier. Hanjin says its goal is to continue providing quality service to passengers without relying on a public **bailout**.

Carlos Yudica©Shutterstock

Asiana Airlines 原為南韓第二大航空公司，僅次於大韓航空。

南韓國土交通部民航局副局長表示，為了減少兩家航空公司在旅行量減少期間所造成的損失，此次合併是「無可避免的」決定。根據韓進集團說法，以南韓這樣的國家大小，有兩家主要航空公司互相競爭是罕見的。相比之下，法國、德國和新加坡等國家都只有一家主要航空公司，這使南韓處於劣勢。韓進表示，它的目標是在不依靠政府紓困的情況下，繼續為乘客提供優質服務。

To finance the deal, Korean Air plans to sell up to $2.25 billion in shares early next year. Hanjin will also [12]**contribute** around $720 million **to** the deal, a portion of which is a [13]**loan** from the state-run Korea Development Bank, which has long been Asiana's main *****creditor**. The deal [14]**awaits** approval from South Korea's **anti-trust *regulators**.

為替這筆交易融資，大韓航空預計在明年初出售最多 22 億 5000 萬元的股份。韓進也將為這筆交易提供約 7 億 2000 萬元，其中部分是由國營的韓國產業銀行提供的貸款，該銀行長久以來一直是韓亞航空的主要債權人。這筆交易正等待南韓反壟斷監管機構批准。

Hanjin plans to keep the Korean Air and Asiana brands separate for now. However, the [15]**low-cost carriers** attached to each brand—Korean Air's Jin Air and Asiana's Air Busan and Air Seoul—will be combined to form a single low-cost entity. Hanjin pledges to do everything it can to minimize **layoffs**.

韓進計畫暫時將大韓航空和韓亞航空的品牌分開。但各品牌所擁有的廉價航空公司——大韓航空的真航空與韓亞航空的釜山航空和首爾航空——將合併為單一廉價航空。韓進承諾盡力減少裁員。

7. **deputy** [ˋdɛpjətɪ] (a./n.)
副的，代理的；副手，代理人

8. **ministry** [ˋmɪnɪstrɪ]（政府的）部，如 **Foreign Ministry** 外交部、**Health Ministry** 衛福部

9. **inevitable** [ɪnˋɛvətəbl] (a.) 不可避免的，必然發生的

10. **minimize** [ˋmɪnəmaɪz] (v.) 減至最小。**maximize** 最大化

11. **disadvantage** [͵dɪsəˋvæntɪdʒ] (n.) 壞處，劣勢

12. **contribute** (v.) 為…貢獻，提供…給…（+ to V）

13. **loan** [lon] (n./v.) 貸款；借出

14. **await** [əˋwet] (v.) 即將降臨，等待

15. **carrier** [ˋkærɪə] (n.) 運輸業者，航空業者，如 **low-cost carrier** 廉價航空、**major carrier** 主要航空

16. **cooperate** [ko`ɑpə͵ret] (v.)
合作，配合

17. **transfer** [`trænsfɝ] (n./v.)
轉乘（飛機、車等）

進階字彙

* **infrastructure** [`ɪnfrə͵strʌktʃə]
(n.) 基礎建設

* **creditor** [`krɛdɪtə] (n.)
借款人，貸方

* **regulator** [`rɛgjə͵letə]
法規者，監督單位

ricochet64©Shutterstock

Star Alliance 為全球最大航空聯盟之一，算是台灣知名度最高的聯盟，包含了長榮航空、全日空、泰國航空與聯合航空等。

Asiana Airlines will likely become part of the **SkyTeam** alliance following the merger. **Airline alliances** are agreements between major carriers to [16)]**cooperate** and share resources, which can provide travelers with benefits like lower prices, more efficient [17)]**transfers** and better **frequent flyer programs**. Asiana would be leaving **Star Alliance**—the world's largest airline alliance—to join SkyTeam, which includes Korean Air and American aviation giant Delta.

合併後韓亞航空可能加入天合聯盟。航空聯盟是各大主要航空公司之間進行合作和共享資源的協議，可提供旅客優惠價格、更有效的轉機和更好的飛行常客獎勵計畫等好處。韓亞航空將離開全球最大的航空聯盟星空聯盟，並加入天合聯盟，該聯盟包括大韓航空和美國航空業巨頭達美航空

Grammar Master

proved + to V「結果是…，竟然是…」

● prove 可做及物動詞，表示「證明」：

例：The investigation proved his guilt. = The investigation proved him guilty. 調查證明他有罪。

● prove 也做不及物動詞，像本句一樣，此時意思是「結果顯示…，結果是…」：

例：The dispute over the house proved impossible to resolve. 結果是，房屋的爭執根本無法解決。

例：The new treatment has proved to be efficient. 新療法結果是有效的。

1. acquisition, merger, takeover 各種「收購」說法

公司之間「合併」的動作稱 **merge** [mɜdʒ]，名詞是 **merger**。大公司「收購」小公司的行為稱 acquisition。企業間的合併與收購經常一起發生，稱 **mergers and acquisitions**，常縮寫成 **M&A**。

另一個常聽到的名詞 takeover「收購」，由動詞片語 take over「掌管，接收」而來，商場上的 take over 偏向「惡意收購」，即未經對方同意就逕行收購股權、成為大股東的行為。

2. bailout 紓困

由 bail「舀水用的桶子」和 out 組成，bailout 原本指在航海中，將船身進水往外舀出的行為，延伸有「幫助…擺脫困境」之意，經濟上指出面拯救一個企業或國家免於破產。這個詞在 2008 年金融海嘯時流行起來，還成為 Merriam Webster Dictionary 當年風雲字。

3. anti-trust 反托拉斯

也可寫成一個字 antitrust。trust 這裡是指「信託」，antitrust 最初意思是反壟斷（**antimonopoly**），1882 年美國石油大王 John D. Rockefeller 聯合了 40 家相關企業，集體信託給標準石油信託 Standard Oil Trust 來管理業務，透過聯合管理達成壟斷石油價格，引起其他業界仿效，美國政府為正此歪風，於 1890 年通過 Sherman Act「休爾曼法」起訴這些信託企業。如今 antitrust 泛指各種跟反壟斷有關的法規，禁止操控價格、濫用獨佔地位等不當商業行為，以達到公平交易，維持市場健康競爭。

Eric Broder Van Dyke©Shutterstock

▲ 科技巨頭如 Google、Facebook 與 Amazon，近日受歐盟指控其違反了反托拉斯法。

4. airline alliance 航空聯盟

就是航空公司之間的聯盟概念，兩間以上的航空公司達成合作協議，以達到更多的資源共享與資源利用，如代碼共享、維修機組共享等。旅客也能在同一航空聯盟的航空公司之間享有更多的優惠服務，如里程數（**mileage**）共用、轉機更方便等。全球前三大航空聯盟分別是：Star Alliance 星空聯盟、One World 寰宇一家以及 Sky Team 天合聯盟。

Sorawit Pootonglor©Shutterstock

▲ 中華航空 China Airlines 為 Sky Team 天合聯盟，圖片是 Sky Team 所塗裝的中華航空波音 747 客機。

5. frequent flyer program 飛行常客獎勵計畫

航空公司針對常客所推出的優惠方案，常搭乘飛機的旅客，可搭配有累積里程數的信用卡，透過累積點數換取免費機票，有些信用卡的累積里程數也能換取優惠價格入住合作飯店。

Consumer 消費

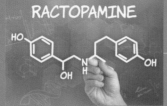

**#chess #grandmaster
#streaming service #Netflix
#Anya Taylor-Joy**

示意圖。《后翼棄兵》找來了《羅根 Logan》導演 Scott Frank 改編劇本，角色的深刻刻劃與棋局的真實呈現，使此劇盤踞多週 Netflix 冠軍。

全文朗讀 ♫ 071   單字 ♫ 072

The Queen's Gambit Sparks Chess Boom

🕐 **December 21, 2020**

《后翼棄兵》激起西洋棋熱潮

Thanks to Netflix **miniseries** *The Queen's Gambit*, the ancient game of chess is enjoying **unprecedented* [1]**popularity**. The show, which reached no. 1 on the **streaming service** in 63 countries, follows a young orphan who discovers she has an **innate* talent for the game. The [2]**fictional** Beth Harmon (played by rising star **Anya Taylor-Joy**) has the remarkable ability to [3]**visualize** entire chess games on the ceiling, allowing her to anticipate her opponents' moves. With her talent and [4]**determination**, the young **prodigy* overcomes addiction to [5]**alcohol** and drugs to win major international tournaments. She also **defies* the **sexism** of the chess world that causes many to [6]**underestimate** her.

多虧了 Netflix 的迷你劇集《后翼棄兵》，把歷史悠久的西洋棋前推向前所未有的流行風潮。這齣美劇在 63 個國家的串流媒體登上榜首，是一部敘述一名年幼孤兒發現自己有下棋天賦的故事。虛構女主角貝絲哈蒙（由新星安雅泰勒喬伊

Vocabulary

1. **popularity** [ˌpɑpjə`lærəti] (n.)
   流行，廣受歡迎

2. **fictional** [`fɪkʃənəl] (a.)
   虛構的，小說的

3. **visualize** [`vɪʒuəˌlaɪz] (v.)
   想像，設想，視覺化

4. **determination**
   [dɪˌtɜmə`neʃən] (n.)
   堅毅，決心

5. **alcohol** [`ælkəˌhɔl] (n.)
   酒，酒精

©WikiCommons

個性派女星 Anya Taylor-Joy 在《后翼棄兵》的傑出表現，讓她一炮而紅。

飾演）具有非凡能力，能將每盤西洋棋局顯化在天花板上，預測對手步數。這位神童憑藉才華和決心，克服酒癮和毒癮，贏得數場重大國際比賽。西洋棋界因性別歧視，使得許多人低估她的能力，她也起身反抗之。

In addition to winning over audiences, *The Queen's Gambit* has earned [7]**credibility** in the chess community for its authentic [8]**depiction** of the game—something often [9]**neglected** in other shows and movies about chess. The show has also won praise for its [10]**representation** of women in professional chess, a world traditionally dominated by men. By taking both chess and women seriously, *The Queen's Gambit* has created an explosion of new interest in the game.

除了贏得觀眾青睞外，《后翼棄兵》也因真實描繪西洋棋賽而贏得西洋棋界的讚譽，其他西洋影集與電影往往會忽略這一點。本劇也因為在職業棋賽上出現女棋手身影而獲得讚揚，因為傳統上西洋棋界一直是以男性為主。由於認真刻畫西洋棋賽和女性棋手，《后翼棄兵》激起大眾探索西洋棋的一波新熱潮。

6. **underestimate**
[ˌʌndəˈɛstəˌmet] (v.)
低估。**estimate** 預估；
overestimate 高估

7. **credibility** [ˌkrɛdəˈbɪlətɪ] (n.)
可信度，信譽

8. **depiction** [dɪˈpɪkʃən] (n.)
描寫，敘述

9. **neglect** [nɪgˈlɛkt] (v./n.)
忽視，不注重

10. **representation**
[ˌrɛprɪzɛnˈteʃən] (n.) 代表，表現

World-famous chess masters **Garry Kasparov** and **Judit Polgár** have expressed their hope that the show will lead to a more inclusive chess community. Polgár, who became a **grandmaster** at age 15 and is widely considered the greatest female chess player of all time, hopes more girls [11]**embrace** chess and that their skills are [12]**nurtured** by parents and schools. "I think it's very important for everybody to see talented girls get the same encouragement that boys do," says Polgár.

世界知名西洋棋大師蓋瑞卡斯帕洛夫和朱迪波爾加表示，希望這齣劇能讓西洋棋界更具包容性。波爾加在 15 歲時已經是特級大師，是史上公認最偉大的女棋手，她希望能有更多女性接觸西洋棋，並希望她們的才華能獲得家長與學校的栽培。波爾加說：「讓世人看到有才華的女孩能獲得跟男孩一樣的鼓勵，我認為這點是非常重要的。」

Chess was already growing in popularity this year as people sought [13]**recreation** during the pandemic, but *The Queen's Gambit* has **sparked** a chess [14]**boom**. Since the show's release in October, Google searches about chess have [15]**tripled**, and sales of **chess sets** and books have increased dramatically. And **Chess.com**, a website that allows users to play live games against other users or **chess engines**, has gained over five million members

被認為史上最強的女棋士 Judit Polgár，於 15 歲就成為 Grandmaster，可說是真人版的 Beth。

during the same period. Whether or not this trend continues, 2020 has been a historic year for the ancient **game of kings**.

由於人們在疫情期間尋找消遣，西洋棋在今年人氣本來就有攀升之勢，不過《后翼棄兵》的上映，更是激發西洋棋熱潮。自十月上映以來，谷歌上有關西洋棋的搜索量就增加三倍，西洋棋組和相關書籍的銷量也急劇增加。能讓用戶即時對奕或與西洋棋引擎對奕的西洋棋網站 Chess.com 也在同期增加了超過五百萬名會員。無論這股熱潮是否會持續，2020 年對這古老的王者遊戲來說，是別具歷史意義的一年。

11. **embrace** [ɪmˋbres] (v.)
擁抱，欣然接受

12. **nurture** [ˋnɝtʃɚ] (v./n.)
培養，栽培

13. **recreation** [ˌrɛkrɪˋeʃən] (n.)
娛樂，消遣

14. **boom** [bum] (n./v.)
熱潮，繁榮；快速發展

15. **triple** [ˋtrɪpəl] (v./a.)
增至三倍。**double** 兩倍；
quadruple 四倍

進階字彙

* **unprecedented**
[ənˋprɛsəˌdɛntɪd] (a.) 史無前例的

* **innate** [ɪˋnet] (a.) 與生俱來的

* **prodigy** [ˋprɑdədʒɪ] (n.)
天才、神童

* **defy** [dɪˋfaɪ] (v.) 反抗，挑戰

* **sexism** [ˋsɛksɪsm] (n.)
性別歧視

Grammar Master

be considered「被認為…」

文中「Polgár, who became a grandmaster at age 15 **is** widely **considered** the greatest female chess player of all time.」的 consider 意思為「認為」，這裡以被動語態呈現，指「被視為」，英文中也有其他用法可替換：

● **be considered/thought (to be) + N**：注意，這裡的用法不需加 as。
例：Martin Luther King Jr. is considered the leader of U.S. civil rights movement. 金恩博士被視為美國民權運動的領袖。

● **be referred to/regarded/viewed/looked upon + as + N**：
例：Blackpink is regarded as one of the most iconic K-pop acts. Blackpink 被視為韓國流行音樂最代表的團體之一。

1. miniseries 迷你影集

或寫成 mini-series，在英國又稱作 serial。迷你影集與一般影集最大的不同是其集數已預先設定，在有限集數內講述一個故事，且播出日期通常不會延續超過一年，如本新聞所介紹的《后翼棄兵 *The Queen's Gambit*》共七集。其他 Netflix 製作的知名迷你劇還有《黑鏡 *The Black Mirror*》。

2. *The Queen's Gambit* 《后翼棄兵》

The Queen's Gambit《后翼棄兵》是由 Netflix 所於 2020 年 10 月推出的劇情迷你劇，改編自美國小說家 Walter Tevis 於 1983 年出版的同名小說。由知名導演 Scott Frank 和 Allen Scott 改編。劇名中的 gambit [ˋgæm.bɪt]，指的是西洋棋技巧中的「開局讓棋法」，指開局時以刻意犧牲一兵（pawn）的方式取得更大優勢，延伸指「精心策劃的險招（通常帶有風險）」，如：Her clever opening gambit gave her an early advantage.（她精采的開棋讓她在一開始就佔了優勢。）

3. streaming service 串流服務

指將多媒體資料壓縮後，經過網路分段傳送資料，即時傳輸影音以供觀賞的平台，此技術使得資料封包得以像流水一樣傳送，如果不使用此技術，就必須在使用前下載整個媒體檔案。常見的影音串流媒體有 Netflix（網飛）、Apple TV+（蘋果公司）、Spotify、YouTube Music 等。這個技術也使得觀眾能在觀看影片時能即時與直播主（**livestreamer**）互動，因此這個技術的出現，也使得直播互動變得相當興盛。

4. Anya Taylor-Joy 安雅泰勒喬伊

為美國、阿根廷和英國混血的女演員與模特兒。2015 年在電影《女巫 *The Witch*》中飾演主角 Thomasin 成名。其他代表作品包含《巴瑞精神 *Barry*》、《分裂 *Split*》等。2017 年曾獲英國電影學院獎（British Academy Film Award, BAFTA）、新星獎（Rising Star Award）提名。

5. grandmaster 西洋棋特級大師

縮寫為 GM，是世界西洋棋聯合會（FIDE，為法語 Fédération Internationale des Échecs 縮寫）授予的棋手頭銜。除了在世界西洋棋錦標賽中勝出的世界冠軍稱號，特級大師便是棋手目前可以獲得的最高頭銜，為終身頭銜，FIDE 至今共授予約二千個該頭銜。

Garry Kasparov 加里卡斯帕洛夫為俄羅斯籍 GM，1985 年至 2006 年間曾 23 次獲得世界排名第一。退出棋壇後積極參與政治，成為俄羅斯反對派的領袖。Judit Polgár 朱迪波爾加為匈牙利籍 GM，被認為是歷史上最強的女西洋棋士。在 1991 年 12 月年僅 15 歲的朱迪波爾加便成為西洋棋特級大師。

6. chess set 西洋棋組

西洋棋的棋盤由 64 個黑白相間的八乘八網格組成，分為 1 至 8 行及 A 至 H 列。每位玩家開局時各有 16

個棋子：一國王（king）、一皇后（queen）、兩城堡（rook）、兩騎士（knight）、兩主教（bishop）和八兵（pawn），各具不同功能與走法。棋手行棋目標是殺掉對方的國王，因此文中將西洋棋又稱為「game of kings」。遊戲過程分三個階段：開局 opening、中局 middlegame、殘局 endgame，共有 10^{43} 種棋局變化。

7. Chess.com & chess engine 西洋棋引擎

2007 年創立於美國的全球網路西洋棋論壇兼遊戲平台，提供會員免費與付費訂閱的西洋棋遊戲、教學資源分享等服務。會員可在該網站與其他玩家競賽，或與 AI 系統分析之西洋棋引擎（chess engine）進行訓練。至今已有 4 千萬註冊會員。

萊豬害台灣

#ractopamine #US pork import
#Taiwan pork label
#food safety

美國萊克多巴胺豬肉自 2021 年進口台灣，引起上千人上街抗議，也有人擔心政府是否有完整配套保障人民健康。

全文朗讀 ♪ 073　　單字 ♪ 074

Taiwan Allows U.S. Pork Imports
2021 年 1 月 1 日起，台灣開放進口美國豬肉

🕐 October 30, 2020

Vocabulary

1. **consume** [kən`sum] (v.)
   吃喝，消費。名詞 **consumer**
   [kən`sumə] 消費者

2. **livestock** [`laɪv͵stɑk] (n.)
   （總稱）家畜

3. **lean** [lin] (a.)
   低脂的，精瘦的

4. **anxiety** [æŋ`zaɪəti] (n.)
   焦慮，不安。**anxious** [`æŋkʃəs]
   (a.) 對…感到焦慮的

5. **pulse** [pʌls] (n.) 脈搏，心跳

On January 1, 2021, Taiwan will begin importing U.S. pork from pigs that have been fed **ractopamine**, along with U.S. beef from cattle over 30 months old. The decision comes after fierce debate, with many worried about [1]**consuming** pork from ractopamine-fed pigs.

自 2021 年 1 月 1 日起，台灣將開始進口餵食過萊克多巴胺的美國豬肉，以及 30 個月齡以上的美國牛肉。該決定是經過激烈辯論後做出，許多人對於吃餵食萊克多巴胺的豬肉感到擔憂。

Ractopamine, a type of drug called a **beta-agonist**, is used as a [2]**livestock** feed *additive to promote growth while keeping animals [3]**lean**. Because other beta-agonists can cause [4]**anxiety** and increased [5]**pulse** in humans, many believe that eating meat containing ractopamine may [6]**endanger** human health. Others, however, argue that ractopamine does not cause the same reactions as other beta-agonists and that there is no risk in consuming it at low levels. As debate over ractopamine continues, new labels will help Taiwan's [1)] **consumers** decide which meat products to [7)] **purchase**.

萊克多巴胺是一種稱為 β2 促效劑的藥物，用於家畜的飼料添加劑以促進生長，同時保持動物的瘦肉。由於其他 β2 促效劑可對人造成焦慮和心悸，因此許多人認為食用含有萊克多巴胺的肉類可能危害人體健康。不過另有人認為萊克多巴胺不會引起與其他 β2 促效劑相同的反應，且低劑量食用不會有風險。隨著萊克多巴胺的持續延燒，新標章將有助於台灣消費者決定購買哪種肉品。

美國豬肉進口開放引起朝野間爭議。

In 2012, the United Nations set international [8)] **guidelines** for the [9)] **maximum** acceptable levels of ractopamine in livestock: 10 **micrograms** per kilogram of pig or cattle muscle, 40 micrograms per kilogram in liver, and 90 micrograms per kilogram in kidneys. The feed additive is currently banned in over 150 countries. Taiwan's Ministry of Health and [10)] **Welfare** has pointed out that all meat imported from the United States will also need to meet Taiwan's safety and [11)] **hygiene** standards. Pork that contains more than a [12)] **trace** amount of ractopamine will either be returned to the [13)] **supplier** or destroyed.

2012 年，聯合國為家畜中的萊克多巴胺最高可接受劑量制訂國際規範：每公斤豬或牛肉可含 10 毫克，肝臟每公斤 40 毫克，腎臟每公斤 90 毫克。目前 150 多個國家禁止使用這種飼料添加劑。台灣的衛生福利部已指出，從美國進口的所有肉品也需符合台灣的食安和衛生標準。豬肉中所含的萊克多巴胺含量稍微超過，便將退還給供應商或銷毀。

Ahead of the easing of import [14)] **restrictions**, the Ministry of Health and Welfare [15)] **declared** that all products containing pork must be labeled with the pork's **place of origin**. [16)] **Retail** stores, restaurants and snack [17)] **stalls** must all comply with the new labeling requirements, which apply to both raw pork and **processed foods** containing pork. Other government policies to [18)] **safeguard** consumers include inspections of U.S. farms and checks to ensure that businesses accurately label their products.

在鬆綁進口限制前，衛福部已宣布所有含豬肉的產品必須標示豬肉原產地。零售店、餐廳和小吃攤都必須遵守新的標示規定，該規定適用於生豬肉和含豬肉的加工食品。其他保護消費者的政策包括視察美國農場，並抽查商家以確保商品標示精確。

6. **endanger** [ɪnˋdendʒɚ] (v.)
   危害，危及。**endangered**
   [ɪnˋdendʒɚd] (a.) 瀕臨絕種的

7. **purchase** [ˋpɝtʃəs] (v./ n.)
   購買；購買（品）

8. **guideline** [ˋgaɪ͵laɪn] (n.)
   （常用複數）指導方針

9. **maximum** [ˋmæksəməm]
   (n.) 最大值 (a.) 最大量的。
   minimum (n.) 最小值

10. **welfare** [ˋwɛl͵fɛr] (n.) 福利

11. **hygiene** [ˋhaɪdʒin] (n.)
    衛生，保健

12. **trace** [tres] (n.)
    微量，痕跡，如 **trace
    element** 微量元素

13. **supplier** [sə`plaɪɚ] (n.)
供應者，供應商，廠商

14. **restriction** [rɪ`strɪkʃən] (n.)
限制。**restricted** [rɪ`strɪktɪd]
(a.) 受…限制的

15. **declare** [dɪ`klɛr] (v.)
宣告，宣布；申報（關稅）

16. **retail** [`ritel] (n./a./v.)
零售；**retailer** 指「零售業者」

17. **stall** [stɔl] (n.) 攤販，貨攤

18. **safeguard** [`sef.gɑrd] (v.)
保護，維護

19. **equip (+ with)** [ɪ`kwɪp]
(v.) 提供；使有能力，訓練；
equipped (+ with) (a.)
附有…配備的

20. **undermine** [.ʌndɚ`maɪn] (v.)
損害，削弱

進階字彙

* **additive** [`ædətɪv] (n.)
添加劑

* **hog** [hɑg] (n.)
豬；（口）貪吃的人

豬肉為台灣飲食習慣中主要之蛋白質來源，食品安全議題也因此再度受到關注。

Some have claimed that importing U.S. pork will [19]**undermine** Taiwan's local *****hog** producers. Consumers who want to support local farmers and avoid ractopamine can look for pork that bears the newly introduced "Taiwan Pork" label. Labeling the place of origin on pork products [20]**equips** consumers with more information, helping them to decide whether to buy the U.S. meat soon to hit the shelves in Taiwan.

有些人聲稱進口美國豬肉將對台灣本地豬農造成衝擊。想支持本地豬農並避免吃到萊克多巴胺的消費者可尋找貼有新推出「台灣豬」標章的豬肉。在豬肉產品上標示原產地可為消費者提供更多資訊，有助於他們決定是否購買即將在台灣上架的美國肉品。

Grammar Master

shelf 用法

文中「...decide whether to buy the U.S. meat soon to hit the shelves...」的 hit (the) shelves 意思為「商品上架」。shelf 指「架子」，複數寫成 shelves。以下整理跟 shelf 相關的片語：

● **remove from (the) shelves 商品下架**

例：Several rice-based baby foods have been removed from the shelves, after being found containing heavy metals. 被檢測含有重金屬後，數個嬰兒米製品已被下架。

● **on the shelf** 為「被忽視，不使用，擱置」，不是上架的意思！英式英語中 **on the shelf** 也可以說一個人滯銷，單身很久，找不到對象。

例：We have left the project on the shelf for six months. 我們已讓計畫停滯半年。

● **off the shelf**「（商品）現成的，不需訂製的」，也不是下架的意思！

例：It is cheaper to buy a suit off the shelf. 買現成的西裝比較便宜。

1. ractopamine 萊克多巴胺，瘦肉精

念作 [rɛkˋtopəmɪn]，是一種 β2 促效劑（β-agonist），最常見於瘦肉精，用來增長牲畜瘦肉，並降低脂肪。美國稱在測定的容許殘留量下合法使用，並不會對人類造成中毒或短期危害。然而目前的實驗數據無法確定其是否會對人體產生其他副作用。部分臨床受試者易表現心跳過速，面頸、四肢肌肉顫抖，頭暈、頭疼、噁心、嘔吐，特別是患有高血壓、心臟病的病人，可能會加重病情。另外，瘦肉精相關成份多為禁藥組成，故國際體育賽事上是禁用的。除美國外有 116 個國家禁用，世界上核准於豬牛飼料中添加萊克多巴胺的國家有 27 國，包括加拿大、墨西哥、印尼等。

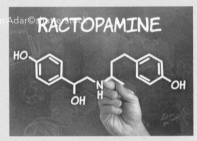
▲ 萊克多巴胺化學分子式

2. beta-agonist β2 腎上腺素受體促效劑

全名為 β2-adrenergic receptor agonists，簡稱 β2 促效劑，能與 β2 腎上腺素受體結合，並形成刺激效應的藥物。可用於鬆弛肺部肌肉、擴張呼吸道與支氣管。常見的副作用是肌肉震顫、心悸，以老年人多見。文中的瘦肉精萊克多巴胺即是 β2 促效劑。

3. microgram 微克（質量單位）

毫克符號為 μg 或 mcg。1,000 微克等於 1 毫克；1,000,000 微克等於 1 公克。公克的英文為 gram，符號為 g。毫克為 milligram，符號為 mg。

4. place of origin 產地

食品追溯（food traceability）指追蹤完整的食品供應鏈，包含原物料、加工、包裝到運送等完整過程。在台灣，「產銷履歷」能有效控管食品，釐清責任歸咎，進而提高產品辨識性，培養消費者品牌認同。針對美國豬進口，政府鼓勵使用 2016 年啟動的「國產生鮮豬肉追溯系統」，在購買豬肉時，消費者只要依標示掃描 QR Code，就能搜尋到國產豬的產地。

▲ 翻攝農委會臉書。

5. "Taiwan Pork" label 「台灣豬」標示

2020 年 11 月 26 日衛福部公布兩種豬肉標示，分別是圓形綠底金字的「台灣豬標示」，與三角形粉底藍字的「進口豬標示」貼紙無需申請，廠商可自行於經濟部官網下載使用。另一方面，農委會公布的「台灣豬證明標章」則需要申請，待中央檢驗核可後才可使用。

© 衛福部、© 農委會
▲ 左一為衛福部的「台灣豬貼紙」，店家可自行下載印製。左二為農委會的「台灣豬證明標章」，則需要認證。三角形為各國「進口豬標示」。

#Sale #shopping spreed
#Black Friday #Cyber Monday
#Thanksgiving

Nelson Antoine©Shutterstock

示意圖。黑五第一天，民眾將賣場擠得水洩不通，搶購電器產品。

全文朗讀 ♫ 075　單字 ♫ 076

Black Friday Kicks Off at Costco
好市多黑五折扣開打

🕐 **November 21, 2020**

Vocabulary

1. **exception** [ɪkˋsɛpʃən] (n.)
   例外，除外

2. **bulk** [bʌlk] (a.)
   大量的，大批的

3. **household** [ˋhaʊs.hold] (a./n.)
   家庭的，家用的；家庭，戶

4. **exclusive** [ɪkˋsklusɪv] (a.)
   獨家的，限定資格的

5. **wholesale** [ˋhol.sel] (a./n.)
   批發的，成批售出的；批發

6. **post-** [post] (prefix)
   …後的，晚於…的

Although **Black Friday**—the day after Thanksgiving that marks the kick-off of the Christmas shopping season—doesn't officially start until the early morning hours of November 27, many **big box stores** are offering deals throughout the month this year. Major retailers like **Best Buy**, **Walmart** and **Target** have launched their Black Friday sales early, and Costco is no [1]**exception**.

感恩節隔天的黑色星期五，象徵聖誕節購物季的開始，儘管今年要到 11 月 27 日清晨才正式展開，但許多大賣場早在 11 月初就開始提供優惠。大型賣場如 Best Buy，Walmart 與 Target 早早就推出各自的黑五優惠，當然，好市多也不例外。

Costco memberships come with ⓟ**their fair share** of *perks—everyday low prices on [2]**bulk** groceries and [3]**household** items, and of course all those free samples—but one of the best parts of having a Gold Star card is all the [4]**exclusive** deals available during their Black Friday sale. Like most other stores, the [5]**wholesale** club is doing things a bit differently this year. Rather than hosting one large [6]**post**-Thanksgiving sales event, Costco is [7]**slashing** prices all through the month of November.

好市多的會員當然有不少好康可拿（大宗食品雜貨與家用品每日促銷，不免俗地有一堆免費試用品可拿），但擁有金星卡的最大好處之一，就是在黑五享有專屬優惠。今年這家會員制批發大賣場跟其他多數賣場一樣，促銷手法稍有不同。好市多不舉辦大規模的單一感恩節後促銷活動，而是在整個 11 月推出極低優惠價。

The first ***markdowns** began on November 5, and deals will be released in waves through **Cyber Monday** on November 30. These deals, which will be available both online and in Costco warehouse [8]**outlets**, Ⓟ**run the gamut** from ***apparel** and consumer electronics to furniture, groceries, toys and much more.

首波降價促銷從 11 月 5 日開始，更多優惠活動會持續推出，直到 11 月 30 日網路星期一為止。促銷活動於好市多的線上商店與實體賣場同步展開，優惠遍及服裝、電子產品、家具、食品雜貨到玩具等。

To access all these [9]**bargains**, you'll need to [10]**register** for Costco's Gold Star membership, which costs $60 per year and can be automatically renewed on an [11]**annual** basis. Bargain hunters can also opt for the Gold Star Executive membership, which costs $120 a year but provides greater benefits, rewards and savings on Costco purchases and services. All new Gold Star Members receive a $10 Costco Shop Card—Gold Star Executive members receive a $20 Shop Card—which can be applied toward any purchase. Membership cards can be used at any Costco warehouse or gas station, and online at Costco.com.

要獲得這些優惠，首先要註冊成為好市多的金星會員。會員年費 60 美元，資格每年更新一次。精打細算的買家還可以選擇金星進階會員資格，年費雖然是 120 美元，但能享有更棒的福利與回饋，與更多好市多購物折扣以及服務。所有新辦金星卡的卡友將獲得額度 10 美元的好市多購物卡（金星進階會員卡新辦卡友則能獲得額度 20 美元的購物卡），不限購物品項。會員卡可以在好市多旗下的賣場或加油站使用，也可以在好市多線上商店使用。

What kinds of Black Friday bargains can you look forward to? For under $100, how about a Fitbit Charge 4 fitness tracker for

7. **slash** [slæʃ] (v.)
砍，大幅減低或降低

8. **outlet** [ˋaʊtlɛt] (n.)
暢貨中心，門市

9. **bargain** [ˋbɑrgɪn] (n./v.)
划算價格，特價品；討價還價

10. **register** [ˋrɛgɪstə] (v.)
登記，註冊

11. **annual** [ˋænjʊəl] (a.)
全年的，一年一次的

進階字彙

*perk [pɜk] (n.)
額外的津貼、福利，即 **perquisite** 的縮寫

*markdown [ˋmɑrk͵daʊn] (n.)
減價，削價，動詞 **mark down**

*apparel [əˋpærəl] (n.)（不可數）
服飾

$89.99? Or for under $250, you can get a pair of Sony WH-1000XM3 wireless noise canceling headphones for $229.99 (originally $299.99). And for under $500, you can't go wrong with an LG 65-inch UN7300 **4K LCD** TV.

你正在觀望哪些黑五優惠呢？低於 100 美金的商品，建議可以看看售價 89.99 元的健身手環 Fithit Charge 4。預算低於 250 美元的話，可以考慮用 229.99 元（原價 299.99 元）的價格購買 Sony 無線降噪耳機 WH-1000XM3。預算有到 500 美金的，絕對不要錯過 LG 的 65 吋 4K 液晶電視 UN7300。

Grammar Master

to 當介系詞的片語

本文出現片語 look forward to，這裡的 to 為介系詞，後面需加上名詞或是動名詞 Ving，以下整理常見的 to 當介系詞的片語：

● **confess to sth. 坦承犯錯或犯罪：**
例：He has confessed to the murder. 他供認犯下謀殺罪行。

● **adjust to sth. 適應某事：**
例：Sue's mother hasn't adjusted 的 to the life in the big city. 蘇的母親不適應大城市的生活。

● **object to sth. 反對、不贊成某事：**
例：She objected to my proposal. 她拒絕我的求婚。

● **dedicate/devote sth. to sth. 全心投入做某事：**
例：Mother Teresa devoted her life to helping the poor. 德雷莎修女一生投入於幫助窮人。

● **when it comes to sth. 一當提及某事：**
例：When it comes to Christmas, kids are excited. 一提到聖誕節，孩子都很興奮。

● **be committed to sth. 致力於某事物：**
例：The government is committed to improving the economy. 政府致力於改善經濟。

● **be addicted to sth. 對某事上癮：**
例：I am addicted to watching dramas on Netflix. 我沉迷於看 Netflix 影集。

● **be used to sth. 習慣於某事物：**
例：Jim is not used to driving on the left. 吉姆不習慣左駕。

● **be opposed to sth. 阻止某事物：**
例：I am opposed to the tax increase. 我反對增稅。

1. Black Friday & Cyber Monday 黑五與網路星期一購物節

每年 11 月第四個禮拜四是 Thanksgiving，而隔天美國人習慣稱為 Black Friday「黑色星期五」，象徵美國購物季的開始，規模或折扣下殺堪稱年度最優。百貨大賣場會在這天展開特賣，持續到聖誕節前一天達到銷量高潮。

之所以用 black 形容，是因為在會計本上，獲利通常用黑字記錄，而支出則用紅字。黑五期間許多商家會推出 **deal/ bargain**「低價熱門商品」，想搶購的民眾會提早甚至在前一天就去排隊搶買（Early birds get the worms.）。

黑五的下個禮拜一就是 Cyber Monday，這個新興購物節是從 2005 年開始，當時網購正蓬勃發展，商家便趁勢推出 Cyber Monday，現今的海外年終優惠通常都是結合黑五跟網路星期一。

2. Phrase (one's) fair share (of sth.) 應得的（量），不少

fair 指「合理或充分的」，而 fair share 可指「數量上不少」的。

A: Are you and Elizabeth still together? 你跟伊莉莎白還在一起嗎？
B: Yes. We've had our fair share of problems, but we're still together.
　是啊，我們是有過不少問題，但我們還是在一起。

3. big box store 大型（連鎖）賣場

國外如 Walmart、Best Buy、Target 就是屬於這類大型批發商場。之所以叫做 big box store，是因為這類賣場外型都蓋得像個巨大盒子，也稱 **superstore** 或 **megastore**，歐洲則稱 **hypermart**。

4. Phrase run the gamut 五花八門

gamut [ˋgæmət] 指一件事物的全部範圍、所有特質或內涵，所以 run the gamut of sth. 指「囊括該事情的所有種類」。

A: Does that winery have a good selection of wines? 那間酒莊有不錯的紅酒嗎？
B: Yes. Their wines run the gamut from dry to sweet. 有啊，他們家的紅酒五花八門，從烈的到甜的都有。

5. 4K resolution 4K 解析度

4K（K 是畫素單位）正式名稱為 Ultra HD，簡稱 UHD，解析度是 3840×2160，畫素可達到 829 萬，解析度為 Full HD 的四倍。由於畫素數量相比 FHD 多了四倍，4K 的清晰度也大幅提高。要觀賞 4K 的影片，不僅要有 4K 電視，所播放的影片也要是 4K 內容才行。如果用 4K 電視播放 FHD 畫質影片，只會呈現 FHD 的畫質。

6. LCD 液晶螢幕

為 Liquid Crystal Display 縮寫，是平面薄型的顯示裝置，早期的 smartphone 智慧型手機大多採用 LCD 螢幕作為顯示器，近年由於 OLED 或 AMOLED 具備更好顯色力、低延遲（高閃頻）、省電、輕薄、可摺疊的優勢，越來越少手機使用 LCD 螢幕。不過 LCD 有其不閃頻的優勢，較不傷眼，也不容易產生螢幕烙印，更為耐用。

NOTE

NOTE

新聞英文年度關鍵字：EZ TALK 總編嚴選特刊 = 2020
News words/EZ TALK 編輯群 , Judd Plggott 作 . -- 初
版 . -- 臺北市：日月文化出版股份有限公司 , 2021.02
　面；　公分 . -- (EZ 叢書館；38)

ISBN 978-986-248-941-3 (平裝)

1. 新聞英文 2. 讀本
805.18　　　　　　　　　　　　　110000053

EZ 叢書館 38

新聞英文年度關鍵字
EZ TALK 總編嚴選特刊

總　編　審：Judd Piggott
作　　　者：EZ TALK編輯群，Judd Piggott，Luke Farkas
　　　　　　Jacob Roth，Sandi Ward
企 劃 責 編：鄭莉璇
翻　　　譯：黃書英、鄭莉璇
補充資料撰寫：鄭莉璇
校　　　對：鄭莉璇、許宇昇
封　面　與
版 型 設 計：謝志誠
內 頁 排 版：簡單瑛設
行 銷 企 劃：陳品萱

發　行　人：洪祺祥
副 總 經 理：洪偉傑
副 總 編 輯：曹仲堯
法 律 顧 問：建大法律事務所
財 務 顧 問：高威會計師事務所

出　　　版：日月文化出版股份有限公司
製　　　作：EZ 叢書館
地　　　址：臺北市信義路三段151號8樓
電　　　話：(02)2708-5509
傳　　　真：(02)2708-6157
客 服 信 箱：service@heliopolis.com.tw
網　　　址：www.heliopolis.com.tw
郵 撥 帳 號：19716071日月文化出版股份有限公司

總 經 銷：聯合發行股份有限公司
電　　　話：(02)2917-8022
傳　　　真：(02)2915-7212
印　　　刷：中原造像股份有限公司
初 版 一 刷：2021 年 2 月
定　　　價：420 元
I　S　B　N：978-986-248-941-3

日月文化集團 HELIOPOLIS CULTURE GROUP

客服專線 02-2708-5509
客服傳真 02-2708-6157
客服信箱 service@heliopolis.com.tw

日月文化集團 讀者服務部 收

10658 台北市信義路三段151號8樓

對折黏貼後，即可直接郵寄

日月文化網址：**www.heliopolis.com.tw**

最新消息、活動，請參考 FB 粉絲團

大量訂購，另有折扣優惠，請洽客服中心（詳見本頁上方所示連絡方式）。

日月文化

EZ TALK

EZ Japan

EZ Korea

大好書屋・寶鼎出版・山岳文化・洪圖出版　EZ叢書館　EZ Korea　EZ TALK　EZ Japan

日月文化集團
HELIOPOLIS
CULTURE GROUP

感謝您購買 新聞英文年度關鍵字

為提供完整服務與快速資訊，請詳細填寫以下資料，傳真至02 2708-6157或免貼郵票寄回，我們將不定期提供您最新資訊及最新優惠。

1. 姓名：＿＿＿＿＿＿＿＿＿＿＿＿ 性別：□男 □女

2. 生日：＿＿＿年＿＿＿月＿＿＿日 職業：＿＿＿＿＿

3. 電話：（請務必填寫一種聯絡方式）

 （日）＿＿＿＿＿＿（夜）＿＿＿＿＿＿（手機）＿＿＿＿＿＿

4. 地址：□□□＿＿＿＿＿＿＿＿＿＿＿＿

5. 電子信箱：＿＿＿＿＿＿＿＿＿＿＿＿

6. 您從何處購買此書？□＿＿＿＿＿縣/市＿＿＿＿＿書店/量販超商

 □＿＿＿＿＿網路書店 □書展 □郵購 □其他

7. 您何時購買此書？ 年 月 日

8. 您購買此書的原因：（可複選）

 □對書的主題有興趣 □作者 □出版社 □工作所需 □生活所需

 □資訊豐富 □價格合理（若不合理，您覺得合理價格應為＿＿＿＿）

 □封面/版面編排 □其他＿＿＿＿＿＿＿＿＿＿

9. 您從何處得知這本書的消息： □書店 □網路／電子報 □量販超商 □報紙

 □雜誌 □廣播 □電視 □他人推薦 □其他

10. 您對本書的評價：（1.非常滿意 2.滿意 3.普通 4.不滿意 5.非常不滿意）

 書名＿＿＿內容＿＿＿封面設計＿＿＿版面編排＿＿＿文/譯筆

11. 您通常以何種方式購書？□書店 □網路 □傳真訂購 □郵政劃撥 □其他

12. 您最喜歡在何處買書？

 □＿＿＿＿．縣/市＿＿＿＿＿書店/量販超商 □網路書店

13. 您希望我們未來出版何種主題的書？

14. 您認為本書還須改進的地方？提供我們的建議？

＿＿＿＿＿＿＿＿＿＿＿＿＿＿＿＿＿＿

＿＿＿＿＿＿＿＿＿＿＿＿＿＿＿＿＿＿

＿＿＿＿＿＿＿＿＿＿＿＿＿＿＿＿＿＿

＿＿＿＿＿＿＿＿＿＿＿＿＿＿＿＿＿＿